Zara S ... ...hor of *The Wedding Date*.

She lives in a Cheshire village with her family, a lively cockapoo called Harry, and a very bossy (and slightly evil) cat called Saffron.

Zara's bestselling novels include *The First Date, Four Christmases and a Secret, No One Cancels Christmas, The Wedding Date, The Holiday Swap, Summer with the Country Village Vet* and the popular Tippermere series.

www.zarastoneley.com

twitter.com/ZaraStoneley
facebook.com/ZaraStoneley
instagram.com/zarastoneley

Also by Zara Stoneley

Standalones

Summer of Surrender

Love is a 4 Letter Word

The Holiday Swap

The Wedding Date

No One Cancels Christmas

Bridesmaids

Four Christmases and a Secret

The First Date

The Dog Sitter

Hot Desk

The Tippermere Series

Stable Mates

Country Affairs

Country Rivals

The Little Village on the Green Series

Summer with the Country Village Vet

Blackberry Picking at Jasmine Cottage

MEET ME ON PLATFORM 3

ZARA STONELEY

One More Chapter
a division of HarperCollins*Publishers*
1 London Bridge Street
London SE1 9GF
www.harpercollins.co.uk
HarperCollins*Publishers*
1st Floor, Watermarque Building, Ringsend Road
Dublin 4, Ireland

This paperback edition 2022
1
First published in Great Britain in ebook format
by HarperCollins*Publishers* 2022

A catalogue record of this book is available from the British Library

ISBN: 978-0-00-853566-7

This novel is entirely a work of fiction. The names, characters and
incidents portrayed in it are the work of the author's imagination. Any
resemblance to actual persons, living or dead, events or localities is
entirely coincidental.

Printed and bound in the UK using 100% Renewable Electricity
by CPI Group (UK) Ltd

For Harry and Tilly.
Without you I would write books faster, and be richer, but my life
would be immeasurably poorer.

Chapter One

MILLIE

Thursday 3rd March

'You're on your way home now? But it's only Thursday!'

'I know it's Thursday, Mum, but…' Oh, shit. The HUGE clock above the entrance to King's Cross station catches my eye.

Bugger, bugger, bugger. I try and ignore the flutter of panic in my chest. If I miss my train there is another one, but today of all days I need to get there at a reasonable time.

I love this country, I love London, but oh my God this place is a total pain in the neck if the rain is teeming down and I'm in a hurry.

If I hadn't hung around for a reply to my email, I might have set off ten minutes earlier. But then I'd have been worrying that Carla hated what I'd written, and I wouldn't have been able to check until I was on the train, and I wouldn't have been able to stop thinking about what she *might* have said and if I was about to be demoted to some third-assistant-twice-removed position that she'd just invented specially for me.

I don't think I'm any more insecure than the next person, but I'm just very aware (as one should be) that speed bumps seem to have been inserted into my smooth career trajectory, and if I'm not careful I will sustain irreparable damage. Like my car suspension did after I weirdly found it impossible to avoid potholes.

When you grew up with the wild Northumberland national park as your playground, not the city, went to the local state not some posh private (and very expensive) school, don't have an English Lit or Media or journalism degree from Oxbridge, but went to Liverpool Uni and have the hybrid accent to match all of the above, then it can make you hyper-aware of how easily what you've worked for can be taken away. You can feel the odds are stacked against you.

I'd always dreamed of escaping the countryside and having a job like mine in the big city. I'd told everybody I was going to do it, and it made me even more determined when my English teacher gently told me not to get my hopes too high and to have an option B, and my boyfriend laughed and told me that 'people like us don't do that'.

I worked bloody hard, and I made it. I got here, but just looking at my boss (who has the right accent, the right clothes and the right education) makes me acutely aware that she might have thought I was an intern worth keeping,

2

but I have high expectations to live up to. And I'm partly here because it proves she is 'woke'. And she's keeping note of every cock-up I make and can drop me as quickly as she picked me up. There are plenty more desperate, quota-filling individuals in the sea. I was one, after a brief stint on a local rag in Yorkshire which shed all its staff and closed down six months after I joined. Which meant literally no redundancy, no notice period and no experience to add to my C.V.

Looking on the bright side though, it was good for me in a bigger-picture sense. Which is how I sold the disaster to friends, family and doubters. Yorkshire had always been my second choice; my first had been a job in London. Losing my job made me go after what I really wanted. The real dream. Even if 'it' was initially working as an unpaid intern. A bloody hardworking one.

When Carla announced that she thought I might have potential and was willing to take a chance on me and offer me a proper *paid* contract I was excited, proud, a nervous wreck and terrified in turn. In my heart I knew I could do it, but my head kept telling me I had to work harder than ever to prove that I deserve this. No slip-ups. No letting Carla down. No letting myself down.

I can't fail. I can't go back and admit that everybody else was right. They're not. I've earned this, and I fully intend to keep it.

So anyway, prioritising my career meant that I left *just in time* to catch the train. Providing there were no hold-ups.

Then it bloody well started to rain.

The umbrellas came out, normally sane people who marched at high speed in a predictable fashion with a destination in mind started to duck and dive to avoid raindrops and puddles, the traffic went on a go-slow and I got splashed, jostled, stopped and sodden.

I am wet, hot and flustered. And late. Very late. I really, really want to barge through and shove everybody out of my way, but of course I don't. I can't, can I? I must be frightfully British and dance about trying to get past people without being rude.

'Millie?'

'Yes, Mum.' I must also not sigh or be impatient with my mother when I am talking to her on the phone. I love her and I really am trying my best to carve out more time to be with her. But there just aren't enough hours in the week. I can at least be positive and upbeat when we do chat. She needs my support, not my bad mood. 'We talked about this! I said I wou—' My mobile phone nearly shoots out of my hand as I hit the brakes and swerve to avoid slamming into the back of some dork who has stopped abruptly in front of me, just inside the entrance to the station.

I tighten my grip round my phone, trying not to swear.

Then I get a face full of freezing water.

I stare up open-mouthed at the umbrella that has snapped closed inches from my nose. Droplets of water settle on my eyelashes, teeter on the tip of my nose. I'm about to sneeze, I need to sneeze.

Then, 'Bloody hell!', he gives his umbrella a couple of violent shakes and I'm showered again, this time with a fine spray that splatters the bits of my face he missed first time as he whacks it open again.

Oh my God. I cannot believe this! The yell bursts out through my gritted teeth before I can stop myself. 'Oi!' I doubt the sound has even got through his thick skull, but I needed to do it. I'm soaked and I've got to sit on a train for hours. How can this be happening to me?

'Millie!' Mum doesn't like me shouting, or swearing. 'Millie, what's happening?'

'Hang on. I'll call you back…' I'm about to say, *when I've finished glaring at this arse*, but then the 'arse' spins round, snapping his umbrella shut and sending a final splash my way. Straight into my eye.

'What the—' I flinch, reaching up automatically to wipe the water away.

'Oh shit. Oh hell, I am so sorry. I didn't realise anybody was behind me.'

'You didn't look!'

'You were pretty close.' I swear there's laughter in those eyes. If his mouth as much as twitches he is so dead.

I glare.

The umbrella drops to his side, he leans forward to dab at the drips and something weird happens. Call me shallow but the words die in my throat. This man is beautiful. He has the most direct gaze, the most gorgeous eyes. If I was after a romantic hero, he totally matches the blueprint. Spot on. But I'm not. I've got work 24/7 and Mum. But there's no rule that says I can't stare at a hunk of gorgeousness when it's shoved in my face, is there?

He is just the right amount tanned. His dark hair short on the sides, slightly longer and slicked back on the top. But sun-kissed in that slightly metro but still totally all-man way. I want to run my fingers through it as I snog him.

Snog him? Where did that come from? The closest I've got to a snog recently is blotting my lipstick on a tissue.

I do not have room in my life for snogging. Because that leads to drinks, and meals and nights out, and nights in. And sex. I definitely don't have time for sex.

Or extra washing of sheets, and towels on the bathroom floor, and having my books moved to make way for his guitar.

'Are you okay?' He is staring at me. One eyebrow is slightly lifted. The corner of his mouth quirked as though he is really tempted to laugh at this.

'Yes, sure, yes. In shock.' Or going a bit crazy. How can the thought of a snog leave me thinking about my shelving arrangements? I'm losing the plot. And, okay, I admit it, a part of me does wish I was here for snogging. He's seriously hot. Just a snog though.

No crumpled sheets or fabulous sex.

'Sure?' That single word is making me feel a bit gooey inside. How ridiculous. But I can't seem to drag myself away from those eyes.

'Millie!'

I blink. Spell broken. Okay it wasn't that hard after all. 'Sorry Mum, I'll call you in a bit,' I whisper and automatically press the end call button with my thumb, but the rest of me is paralysed. Even if my vision and vocal cords aren't. I can't move.

Oh my God, talk about 'across a crowded room', or in this case the crowded entrance to a railway station. It's weird, I feel like I know him, I need to know him. That I can't breathe properly because it's too important a moment to waste to do anything but stare.

The world fades into the background, there is just the two of us. Those intent dark eyes were always supposed to be looking straight into mine.

'No way!' There's a bellow inches from my ear as a noisy group push through the small gap between us forcing me away from him. 'She didn't? You have to be kidding, mate!'

'Bloody hell, you're soaked. I'm so sorry.' His gaze travels over my body as he closes the gap between us. He's not smiling now; he's just looking straight at me. Serious. Sexy. Making me hotter and more bothered than I was before.

His eyes are actually not dark, they're blue-grey. Intent. But still slightly twinkly.

'I'm such a jerk.'

I shake my head, because I can't get my words out. Oh my. This guy is the complete package. Even his voice is knee-tremblingly good. And his eyes are definitely twinkling.

'I'd offer my handkerchief for you to wipe your face with, if I was the type of guy who had one.'

I can't help myself; I grin. Swallow. Manage to find my voice. 'Which you're not.'

''Fraid not.' The corner of his mouth twitches. This guy really is dying to laugh. 'Best I can offer is…' He holds up the end of his red scarf.

Something flutters deep inside me. 'Oh, don't worry, it's fine. I was already wet. Sky, rain, you know. Not *all* your fault.' I wave a hand above my head and shrug, but I want to smile; I want to laugh with him.

'But I didn't help! Seriously though, I didn't catch you with the umbrella? I know I'm a big, clumsy, oaf…' His hand lightly brushes my upper arm and a shiver rockets through my body. Bloody hell. 'Sorry.' He backs off and looks worried. I'm not surprised, because I am staring at him, in a daze and acting like he's just given me an electric shock.

This kind of thing never happens to me though.

Bumping into gorgeous guys. Guys who send a sizzle straight to my erogenous zones.

We could go off and do some baby-making practice while I'm in the mood. I've not felt in the mood like *this* for, like, well, for ever. I shouldn't waste it. I might never feel it again. I get it now, why people do stupid, impulsive things.

Oh my God, what am I thinking? He's a stranger. With a life. He could be anybody.

And we're standing in the entrance of King's Cross bloody train station!

And sheets, mess, arguments, must concentrate on the yukky side of relationships and how I'm such a disaster at them.

'I'm fine. Right as rain.' Did I really say that? 'Ha ha.'

He chuckles. 'Wet as...'

I grin back.

Is it really so long since I had a proper boyfriend and actually shagged, that one touch from a man and I turn into a wanton hussy?

I need to get a life, or at least get back on the dating scene.

No, I don't. No, no, no.

My life is complicated enough, relationships take up time, energy. Men don't like you working overtime, weekends. Well, the last guy didn't. They don't want you to spend time with your mother.

I decided a long time ago that I would concentrate on my career.

When I was younger, I was naïve. I did think I could have it all. The fab job, the friends, the wonderful man and maybe even the family. But being given an 'it's the job or me' type ultimatum the day you apply for your dream job in the city, being dumped by text by the boyfriend you'd thought you'd be with for ever as you walk up the office steps for your interview, well, that's one helluva reality check. His parting line had been that 'I'd never find a guy who'd put up with me'. That's one challenge I refuse to rise to. I mean, what if he's right?

So, one thing at a time. Being heartbroken wrecks your concentration, as well as your make-up. Now is not the time to be thinking about men, seriously dating. Sex.

He shakes his head, smiles ruefully as he smooths his hair back out of his eyes as somebody pushes past, jostling his elbow. Oh my God, that hair is made for the tousled look. For fingers. 'We-ll—' it's long and drawn out, he's probably worried about my mental state '—I guess we should move, we're a bit in the way.' He hesitates, but I know that any second now he's going to go, leave my life. For ever. I need a few more minutes. Another touch would be nice.

I don't care if I'm now the obstacle in everybody else's way. I've done enough dodging about today to earn this.

I also can't blame him for wanting to get away. I'm standing here looking like a drowned rat. I wasn't looking that good before he gave me an extra shower. Now I'm pretty sure my hair is actually dripping. Why do I never meet hot men when I'm looking good? Or even halfway normal.

My timing is so crap.

'Guess so." I manage to force out, against my will. "I've got a train to catch.'

'Sure. Great. Me too, funnily enough!' He grins properly this time, dimples at the sides of his mouth, a fan of wrinkles by his eyes. 'We've got something in common!' He reaches out again as though he's as reluctant as me to break this up, touches my elbow ever so lightly, and it sends another shiver through my body. His gaze never leaves mine. 'Right, better not hold you up. And I'd better go and sort my ticket. I need to change it and... Too much info, I know!' He shrugs slightly self-consciously. It makes him even cuter.

'No, not too much! Sure. Sure, you should...' I must not

blurt out something regrettable, like 'Fancy a shag?' I'm not that girl, honestly. I do not ask random men if they'd like to see my knickers.

I don't even ask not-random men. I'm not very good at the transition from kissing to bonking. So awkward. So likely to ruin everything.

He raises a hand in a half wave, hesitating, then a gaggle of giggling teenage girls swarm round us, and before I know it, he's been swept away.

Who is he? Where he's going? Will I ever see him again?

My mobile phone rings and as I look down a droplet of water drips from my hair onto my forehead and trickles down my nose, and this time I do sneeze. So loudly, several people turn round. Which kind of brings me back out of my daze.

As Thursdays go, it had not been the best so far. Until now.

This tiny bit of the day has been the froth on the cappuccino.

Apart from the fact that I'm distinctly soggy and I've got to sit on a train for four hours. My froth has fizzled away and all I'm left with is the hint of sweet chocolate on my upper lip.

'Mum?'

'You said you'd call back.'

'When I was on the train. I was a bit held up.'

'You sound stressed, darling.'

Oh wow, that isn't stress. That is something I really can't talk to her about. 'I'm fine. I'm just out of breath.' Tot-all-y breath-less. I should have taken a photo of him, stuck it up on my wall, for when I needed cheering up. Or is that a bit too weird? 'Honestly, it's just busy, and raining. The station is packed, and I don't want to miss the train,' I say, trying to sound normal, and realising that there's also more steam coming off me than a greasy kebab.

Attractive. One way to bring me back down to earth.

My mother sighs. Gently. 'You don't have to come home today, Millie.'

I slow my pace. The distant chatter of Radio Four in my ear as neither of us speaks for a moment.

Mum always has the radio on in the background these days, for company.

'I know how busy you are, and it's such a long way when there's no need.'

This time the heavy silence lingers. The unspoken words. She's never accused me of being too busy to spend time with her, she wouldn't. She isn't like that; she's always been keen on me being independent. But it is there. I can feel it, *I* know it.

I step out of the fast, teeming, lane of people rushing. Into the slow lane. Blink away the sudden heat in my eyes, blaming the rain that is running off my hair into my eyes. Stinging. I come to a halt and take a deep breath. 'I do have to; you know I do.'

'I can cope, Millie. I'm fine.' Her soft, gentle tone makes me feel worse.

I swallow the lump in my throat. 'I know you are.' Though I suspect she's not really. 'I want to come home,

Mum. For me.' It's the second anniversary of Dad's death. The first one was horrible. It had hit me then, properly, that he'd really gone. He wasn't here. He'd never be here again.

I'd had work to bury myself in during those first twelve months, so on normal days I'd hidden, buried my head in the sand, tried to pretend it hadn't happened. He hadn't actually gone. For ever.

But each milestone that passed, each birthday, event, when he should have been there but wasn't, had hurt like hell.

It was almost like the protective layer I'd built during those first few months was being scraped off, bit by bit painful bit, exposing more and more of the rawness that was still there underneath.

One of the worst days was when I'd nearly broken down and sobbed in Marks and Spencer. It was their Christmas display of handkerchiefs and socks. I always bought them for him, it was one of our little in-jokes.

I'd dropped my shopping and fought my way through the happy shoppers, choking, needing the icy cold air of the December evening on my cheeks, in my lungs, to chase the heat away.

How can the sight of festive socks smash your heart into smithereens?

And, oh my, musical ties. I've nobody to buy a musical tie for.

Just the thought brings a lump to my throat.

What do they say? It doesn't go away; you just find a way to handle it.

It has taken me to the grand old age of twenty-nine to discover that time doesn't heal, it just fuzzes things over so that the pain isn't quite as harsh.

I think my wound has reached the itchy, scabby stage. Ugly, impossible to ignore, drawing my attention back at times when I least expect it, when it snags on something. Rips it open a tiny bit.

I need to be with my mum today. For her, for me. For him. Well, yes, most of all for him. I'd promised him I'd look after her, and I've failed. I'm a crap daughter. I'm never there. I spend all my time running round like a blue-arsed fly trying to prove to Carla that I'm indispensable, and Mum has definitely taken a back seat. Because it's easy to take your family for granted, isn't it?

'But can they manage without you at work, love? It's a whole day off and you're so busy.'

See? She thinks I'm so busy, I can't take a day off for her. I can't prioritise her. How bad is that? 'I've already booked the day off, though I can work from home tomorrow if I need to, Mum. Modern technology and all that!' I fall back on breezy, light sarcasm, my go-to protective blanket.

Dad always said that sarcasm was the lowest form of wit.

Oh, Dad.

The lump forms in my throat.

'I'd better go, Mum.' I croak the words out, trying to be cheery and normal, and failing. 'Don't want to miss my train. Be with you soon.'

'Okay darling. Love you.'

'Love you t—'

The train shortly departing platform three is the…

The loud announcement stops me dead. Oh shit. That's my train!

'Gotta go, Mum.' I'm going to miss it, there won't be another one for ages. Bugger, bugger, bugger. I sprint towards the steps, shoving the phone in my pocket, dodging totally inconsiderate, slow people, clutching the strap of my bag.

The guard hesitates as he reaches out to slam the nearest train door shut, and I fling myself past him and stagger my way towards a seat. Then casually wipe the misted-up window with the side of my hand. Stare over to the other platform to see if *he's* there. The guy with the umbrella. There's no sign. He's gone for ever.

Train-guy.

I should have said yes to his offer of the scarf to wipe my face. Unhygienic, and possibly not an actual genuine offer. But then I could have offered to take it home, wash it, post it back to him.

Sniff it. Before washing it of course. Hand-deliver it back to him.

See him again.

Not fast thinking enough, Mills, not fast thinking enough.

I start up my phone – there's a WhatsApp message from Mum. *'Pizza night? X'*

I send back a thumbs-up and sink into the seat. And glance out of the window one last time. And he's there!

Actually there. On the other side of the tracks. Staring my way. Except it doesn't feel like it is my way. It feels like I've missed my chance. Lost him.

My phone rudely pings again and brings me back to reality. It's an email from my boss, Carla.

Sugar. Emails from her at this time on a Thursday are bad news.

I look up one more time, before opening it, just in case, but he's gone. Disappeared.

As promised, stats for your latest.

I'm, for want of a better description, a confessional journalist. I write about life, people, things I see, things I overhear. Funny snippets of my life, your life, or the life you'd quite like to have. Or not. And my column comes out on a Thursday morning. At one time, by Thursday lunch it was red hot. Smokin', as my workmate Zoe would say.

People were waiting impatiently for it to appear and reading, sharing and tweeting the moment it did. Now it appears it's got double pneumonia.

It's more than a gradual decline now, you've fallen off a cliff edge.

My stomach lurches and I can feel myself shrinking into my seat as though everybody around me knows and will think I'm rubbish.

I can't afford to fall off anything, I'm supposed to be peaking, approaching my prime. If I can't achieve something by the time that I'm thirty, I might as well just admit I couldn't cut it in the city. They were all right after all.

The pointed switch from 'we' to 'you' is a worse sign than any statistic.

We need to talk. Confessions of a Commuter *isn't cutting the mustard. Regards, Carla.*

The 'regards' is part of her signature; she wouldn't have signed off at all if she had a choice. My boss is not happy.

I shut down my phone and close my eyes.

I'm grateful for Carla for giving me this job, for singling out a girl who had none of the 'right connections' and giving her an opportunity. But one day I dream of moving onwards and upwards. To a job where I don't owe my boss anything but hard graft. But I so need her onside now – if there's one thing I do know, it's that you look for your next job when you're on the up. Not when you're sliding.

It might sound paranoid, but I'm sure Carla likes to work with people she can bully. She likes to have the upper hand.

One day she won't. One day *I'll* be in the driving seat.

But, shit. Not only am I letting my mum down, but I have also let my boss down.

Or as one very annoying, preachy schoolteacher used to say. 'You've not let me down, you've let yourself down, Amelia.'

Chapter Two

MILLIE

Thursday

'Oh, it is good to see you.' Mum wraps me in the kind of hug she's been inflicting on me since I was two years old. I wriggle; it's been obligatory to object since I reached the age when I was embarrassed to admit I liked public displays of affection. It would be cool to say that was around the time of my third birthday, but that would be a lie. I didn't actually stop wanting to hold her hand until I was around ten years old. I'm not cool at all.

I give her a squeeze back before I reluctantly free myself, because I do need this hug. I need my mum. Like I always have done when I've had a bit of a shit day or, well, a shit week.

Carla's latest email is the most pointed yet. I'll be demoted if I don't find a way of spicing things up. I need to prove I'm not a one-trick pony. That I have ideas, I'm motivated, I can inspire!

The problem is, I don't feel inspirational. I feel bloody knackered at times. My life is not exciting or funny enough to meet the current demand for over-the-top emotional outbursts, or scandalous behaviour. It doesn't help that Dale, my closest male friend, and the guy who has (figuratively) held my hand since I converted from country bumpkin to city girl, has been a bit of a prick. I'm not a particularly huggy type of person, but there are days when I'd like the comforting touch of another human being. Plus, some reassurance. Not his analytical summing up of the current market trends, and why I'm not matching them.

When I moved down to London, the first flat I went to see belonged to Dale. He flung the door open, smiled at me and just like that all my big-city dreams materialised. It was all happening! And then he opened his mouth and I almost keeled over. His smooth, posh, almost aristocratic voice brought me out in goosebumps. The excited type, not the sexy type (that should have told me something). I practically begged him to let me have the place, before I'd even checked for damp, funny smells and dodgy electrics like Dad would have told me to.

Luckily, I fell on my feet and the flat is perfect. No mould or short-circuits. And so is Dale (or so I thought, ha ha). He was supportive, generous and quite attractive in a metro-man kind of way – more friend than landlord from day one.

He lives next door and was always at hand to help out at

first. He knew the places to go, the people to see. In short, Dale was the type of man I thought I *should* know, the type I should aspire to, that would become significant in my future.

He is dynamic, enthusiastic (to the point of manic) about work and politics.

In sharp contrast to the tractor-driving, big-jumper-wearing, country-odour-smelling guy who was my last boyfriend. Not that I've got anything against any of those attributes, I just felt my future would be brighter, shinier. Cleaner. Without smelly feet. And a swigging milk then wiping his palm over the top of the bottle habit.

With somebody who was supportive of my life choices.

Anyway, Dale is not becoming significant, he's turning into a bit of an arse. I'm all for constructive criticism, but he's just being fucking destructive, and smug with it. Not at all supportive, or anything else.

If Dad had been here, he'd have been on the phone telling me to believe in myself.

Except he's not here, is he? In his place there's this massive chasm. A hole that has got deeper and darker over the last two years. At first, I felt I could still talk to him, that he could hear, and it helped. Now he's drifting out of reach.

For ages he felt tangible, but the link has weakened, it's like he's fading away. A wispy cloud that I can't quite grasp like I could before.

So I need this hug from Mum. And I need to be here. Home. With her.

She loosens her grip so that we're at arm's length and we look at each other for a moment.

If I feel this bad and lonely, if I'm missing Dad this much – how does she feel?

I should be here more often, not just paying flying visits. With my mind half on work.

'I'm fine, Millie,' she says, her fingers touching my cheek briefly, as though she knows what's going through my head. Questions about what I should do. Thoughts about how guilty I feel. About how out of touch with how she feels I am, even though I've been coming home for the weekend at least once a month since Dad died.

I feel a sudden need to grab her hand, hold her there, ask her to hold me and stroke my hair like she used to. But I don't because I'm a strong, independent woman. And it's me that should be supporting her.

'It is lovely to have you home though.'

Home. Funny, isn't it, how I still think of my parents' house, the family house, as home? Home is not my place in London. That's 'my apartment'. But Hexham is home.

'I love having both of you back. It's a shame Lou is so far away.'

I bite my tongue. Lou, my sister, lives in Edinburgh. Which isn't that far away. In an uncharitable moment, after we'd had an argument about spending more time with Mum, I actually worked it out. Whether you look at driving time, road distance or journey time on public transport, Google reliably tells me that Lou is closer than I am.

By the time I'd checked it out, I'd cooled down. It

seemed petty to actually use this information. She also has a demanding family, and a demanding camping business ('*glamping, Millie, it's glamping,*' she'd enunciated carefully when I made the mistake of calling it this) which does tie her down a bit. But I do get tired of the way she assumes that my single status and slightly more portable (have laptop will travel) career means I can take on all family responsibility.

'She finds it difficult,' Mum adds. My feelings must be showing on my face again. I'd never make a poker player. Or professional fibber, if there is such a thing.

'She's never been very good at knowing how to handle her emotions.' She squeezes my shoulder.

Mum is right. As she always is. She looks beyond our spats and excuses. Lou is practical, and sensitive. She doesn't express things, she does things. When Dad died, she did come home for a while, but struggled once all the practical side had been handled and she couldn't hide behind tidying up and managing things any longer. She fled back to Edinburgh.

I guess we all have our different ways of handling things, and I know I have to respect our differences.

But at times it's difficult. It's not just the tetchy tone on the phone, or the bossiness. It's the absences. We used to get together for all the celebrations – Christmas, Easter, birthdays, anniversaries – but she skips most of them now. Comes up with excuses.

Dad dying hasn't made us closer, because Lou can't cope

with the empty space at the table, the fact he's not here with us.

I know she tries to do her bit by calling Mum several times a week, but we never see her.

'I miss her.' I finally admit.

'She'll come round. She just needs some more time.'

I nod. It's easier to resent her staying away and expecting me to fill the gaps, than it is to empathise – especially when she's in a scratchy mood.

'So, how's work?' Mum moves the conversation on. She knows that Dad not being here still hurts, knows that deep down I feel like I've lost Lou as well.

'Good.' I shrug. 'You know, the normal.' I'd gone to the big city with a head full of images of the bright lights, an extrovert amazing boyfriend, money, success. I'd have the fabulous career, and the glossy lifestyle. I'd have it all. But nobody has it *all*, do they?

I do love working in the media, I do love my colleagues, I do love the buzz. Hell yeah, I can't imagine life without those highs when something has worked out just right.

When people get it.

But I seem to have got myself an 'all about the career' lifestyle and I don't know how to step off the treadmill. Especially now I've hit a bump in the popularity stakes and feel like I need to run faster than ever to make it right again.

I mean, I can't stop now, can I? That would be admitting I'm a failure. And I'm not.

And the nearest I've got to a boyfriend is Dale, who is

not amazing, and definitely not my boyfriend, though he is extrovert.

I did flirt briefly with the idea of us moving from friends to lovers. Because, hell, that would have been romantic, wouldn't it? I could have put that in my column! No, I couldn't. I wouldn't. Can you imagine if it all went tits up and I had to admit to the whole world why it went wrong?

Anyway, I only flirted with the *idea*, and not with him.

OMG I am so glad I never actually tried it on with him.

I mean, can you imagine the shame of it? How stupid I'd be feeling right now if I found out he was a self-righteous jerk with zero empathy when we were mid-shag?

Is it a sign of total desperation when you start wondering if maybe somebody you've lived next door to for ages, and get on with, could be the perfect boyfriend? I mean, I knew the first time I saw him that the tremors were excitement, not lust – so why didn't I remember that?

But I've cottoned on recently. Dale is all about Dale, he doesn't have room for an 'us' in his life, or in his vocabulary. I'm not a gusher, but he is so totally emotionally unavailable, it's like I've skipped into the future and am socialising with a man-bot. One that has been programmed by somebody with narcissistic tendencies and a zero rating on the sexually adventurous scale. I imagine.

I mainly imagine this because he is so well-groomed, he'd probably be affronted if somebody ruffled up his hair when they were in the throes of passion.

Or made him break out in a sweat.

Can you imagine the convo? 'Excuse me, darling, can

you stop kissing me there? You're leaving a trail.' Or 'Sorry? Orgasm? You wanted an orgasm as well? Well, you'll have to work out how to get one quicker. Drop me a message when you do. I'll get B.O. or streaks in my tan if I have to keep going any longer.'

I'm sure this is the reason why I have never heard any kind of floorboard-creaking, orgasm-squeaking or headboard-banging through our adjoining wall.

Anyway, more to the point (and less cringeworthy), I'm neglecting Mum.

Right now, my life is one massive compromise and I'm not doing anything quite right.

'But you are still enjoying it?' There's a hint of concern colouring her tone, her expression.

Luckily, she cannot see in my head. While I'm thinking about sex with a man-bot, or Dale, Mum is still talking about work. I nod vigorously. I do enjoy my job. I love it. I can't imagine doing anything else. Even if I have hit a blip. I need to work out how to fix that, I really do. Maybe a long walk on the moors will clear my head.

'Good! Dad was so proud of you. He always said you should follow your dreams, and you have. Now come on, come in, the pizza will be getting cold, you can tell me all about what you're working on.'

The smell of cheese and tomato suddenly hits me, and I realise I'm starving. I normally grab a wrap or something to eat on the train but running late and bumping into train-guy disrupted my routine.

Shit, train-guy. I'd almost forgotten about him while I'd

ZARA STONELEY

been sitting on the train worrying about Mum and my job in turn.

Wow, maybe it really was meant to be. Not in a potential hot-sex way, but in a solution to my work problem way. I could write about him? Or at least the possibility of people like him. The meet-cute that never actually comes to anything but might do. That's what we all want, isn't it? The *thought* that it could happen. That we could fall in love or lust or just get a bit steamed up as we do ordinary stuff in ordinary places.

Confessions of a brief-encounters addict?

Maybe not. I deflate. It would be knackering trying to 'bump into' a hot guy every time I went into a train station. Not practical. I haven't even got time to shave my armpits these days, so how am I going to fit in something like that?

'And I've got something exciting of my own to tell you!' Mum carries on talking as I dump my bag and follow her through to the kitchen. She glances over her shoulder to check I'm listening, and she has a massive smile on her face.

'What?' I'm listening. It's totally ludicrous thinking I can save my career by writing about an unexpected clinch at King's Cross. Although that does have a Carla sort of ring about it.

'I'll tell you when I've put the food out.' She is practically *skipping*. This is not how I thought she'd be at all, today of all days, and all of a sudden I feel lighter. Ten times better. My work life might be shit, but Mum seems okay.

I can't help it; I smile back at her. The heavy feeling of responsibility lifts slightly, I don't feel quite as guilty.

I can sort this. I can get at least this part of my life right.

She clatters about with plates, waves a hand in the general direction of a bottle of wine and glasses, but is so obviously buzzing, I can't wait.

'Well? Come on, Mum, tell!'

'Patience!'

I pour the wine. Speculate on whether she's won big on the premium bonds, decided to get a new puppy, or booked a cruise for the two of us.

The food is finally on the table, and she sits down, then leans forward.

'Sam said I could get £500,000, or more!'

I look at her blankly. 'What?' Who is Sam?

'Half a million!' She declares.

'I know what £500,000 is. I mean, for what?' I am confused. Who hands out that kind of money? Has she been taking something stronger than wine? Should I be *really* worried? Oh my God, my mother is being scammed by a man called Sam.

Would that make a catchy title for my column? No, Millie. No, no, no. What is wrong with me?

'I could buy two apartments for that! Maybe three!'

'What? But you don't want two apartments.' I frown. What is she talking about? Scam-y Sam apart, why would she even think she wants one apartment, let alone three? My own excitement has fizzled away, and my stomach feels hollow.

'I know I don't want two,' she says a bit testily. Mum is good at testy these days.

'And who is Sam?'

'Sam is from Riding & Riding.'

It's like being smacked hard on the forehead. I get it and I have suddenly lost all appetite. This is worse than the threat of being scammed.

She's had the house, our home, valued by an estate agent. I gulp the angry retort down.

'I know I don't actually want two apartments,' she says conversationally, but all I can think of is that she is selling up, selling out. Leaving my childhood, leaving my dad, behind. 'But I could afford them if I sold this place. I'm just illustrating.'

Illustrating? I hate Sam. Sam is worse than a scammer, Sam is turning my mother's head. She's churning out estate-agent lingo.

'You don't need *any* apartments, Mum,' I say firmly, even though inside I'm wobbling like an angry jelly and have the quaver in my voice to match. 'You've got our home, you live here.'

'It's just a thought. Didn't I mention it before, darling? Last time we chatted?' She takes a sip of wine. I can't believe she's even thinking about selling our – her – lovely home.

She knows she didn't mention it before.

Okay, I need to at least try to be reasonable here. 'But do you really want to…?' I can't say the words 'sell' or 'move'.

'Not really, dear.' She busies herself with pouring more wine, even though the glasses don't need a top up. Avoiding looking at me. 'But it's sensible.'

Mum is always sensible. I am too, I get it from her. There was a brief time, just after Dad died, when she found it hard to concentrate, or think logically at all. But recently she's been more her old self again.

'The garden is getting too much for me.' She puts her fork down slowly, the effort of admitting she can't cope seeping into her hands. Failure is not an option my mother has ever allowed in; she's brought me up to believe I can achieve anything. She can.

It's a glorious garden. It was Mum and Dad's pride and joy. He kept the lawn like a bowling green, she looked after the rose beds, deadheaded flowers, trimmed the shrubs to within an inch of their lives. I grew up watching my parents potter in their beautiful garden.

Together.

Now, I look out of the window and try and see it through her eyes. It is big, massive. I find it hard enough to keep on top of a few houseplants, a sprig of parsley and some pots on the balcony.

There's a clatter as Mum's hand trembles slightly as she puts her glass down, knocking it against the bottle, and I feel totally shit for deflating her. Chasing her excitement away.

She meets my gaze then, and I can see the doubt in her eyes. It hits me hard, brings a lump to my throat. Mum is getting older. I've never thought of her as old until now, she's just Mum. She's my parent, has always looked after me.

No, Mum is not old, she's definitely not old, but I was a

late addition to the family. She was a 'mature' mother, of 'advanced maternal age'. I never got how you class a mother as 'geriatric' if she is over thirty-five years old. It's ridiculous.

As ridiculous as the term 'old-age pensioner'. Age is just a number. These days being in your mid-sixties and retired like Mum doesn't mean you're old, it means you've got lots of free time to enjoy life.

I glance back out of the window, not wanting to think about the fact that if I'm nearly thirty it means she's sixty-five. Not wanting to notice the start of liver spots and wrinkles on the back of her hands, the way she pours more slowly, more carefully now.

But it's still there in my peripheral vision, in my head.

And now I can also see the weeds in the border, the stray shoots at the top of the euonymus that she's not had time to snip off, the slightly too long grass.

'Can't the gardener do more?' She'd been reluctant to employ anybody to help; a mix of pride and wanting to keep control. But then I'd found Ed, a retiree who loved gardens and was happy to work alongside her. Do things her way. Dad's way.

'Well, he could, but he's not getting any younger either, you know. He's been ill, and I don't like to ask.' Mum never likes to ask. That's half the problem. My parents were fiercely independent. How can I expect her to change the habits of a lifetime now? 'And I would have more freedom to enjoy the time I've got left if I didn't have so much to think about here.'

I cut a piece from my pizza so that I don't have to look at her. 'Don't say it like that, you're not going to die for years.'

Bloody hell, how did I not *realise*?

'Probably not, but you never know, do you? I know you love this place, Mill.' She sighs. 'I do too, and it's strange because over the past six months I've had it in my head that if I leave here then I'm leaving your dad. We made this home together. But I think he'd want the best for me, don't you?'

I nod. He would. He always wanted the best for her.

'And I'll be taking our things, our memories, with me. I'm not abandoning him. He'll always be in my head, my heart. He's always with me, Millie.'

'I know.' I say softly. Except she'll be taking it all away from me, but I can't say that, can I? This isn't about me. 'If it was the other way round, he'd move if he was struggling.'

'There's no hurry though,' she says, picking up her fork again. 'It was just a thought. And it might be easier for Lou. She might come and see us more often if it was a new place.'

We eat in silence, each thinking our own thoughts.

'I should stay at home, here, with you more.' The words pop out of my mouth, even though I know I've not thought this through yet. 'I could help.'

'Oh love, don't be silly. That's not what you want, you haven't got time to worry about me and the garden. You always wanted to escape to the city, right from when you were little! They always say that you've done a good job as a parent when your kids are confident and ready enough to go off on their own. Build their own lives. So you've proved we did something right!' She winks and gives my hand a quick squeeze.

'But…'

She stands up. 'But nothing. Forget about me, I'm absolutely fine. You love your life, don't you? It's what you want, isn't it? You're happy?'

'Yes.' I nod. I watch the familiar movements that I've grown up with, as she bustles around, putting the plates on the side, pouring more wine. Looking after me.

Am I happy? Happy isn't something I've really been looking for. I mean, content is for old people, isn't it? My job, my life, is what I want. What I've always wanted.

I have built my own life. I have made my parents proud. But am I *happy*? Have I got everything I wanted, or is there a bit missing?

I sip my wine, the acid tang mingling with the questions I didn't know I had, bringing a lump to my throat. I miss all of this so much. I miss the house, the countryside. I miss Dad. I miss Mum. If I spend more time here with her, I could help her – but maybe it would be good for me too.

But could I still keep my job? Have I got the guts to risk losing what I've worked for and thought I wanted? Dad always said he loved his work, but he loved his home life as well, and he might never have had it in him to take the risks and be a self-made millionaire, but he was happy. He was content with his choices. He worked to live, not lived to work. Dad knew all about living an authentic life, about being genuine, before saying it was the 'in' thing to do.

Oh hell, I miss him so much. I wish he was here right now.

'You'll work it out, darling,' Mum says, without turning round. 'It takes time and a bit of growing up before we can work out what we really want from life, but you're smart enough to come up with the right answer. Now, how about a nice slice of parkin? It's still warm!'

The answer to that question is easy – but trying to work out the answer to what I really want from life could give me brainache.

Chapter Three

JOE

Sunday 6th March

'Calling Planet Joe! Anybody in there?'

Sophie taps the side of my head, and I bat her hand away gently as it dawns on me that the car has stopped. She's pulled up at the train station.

Which is a bit of a surprise, I haven't noticed any part of the journey at all – I've been miles away, thinking about the girl at the station. About how I could have done things differently. How I could have actually *talked* to her.

I drag myself back to the present and turn to look at my little sister, putting on an exaggerated sigh to try and distract her. 'You do realise you're still as annoying as you were when you were ten years old?' She might be all grown up now – married, and positively blooming in the early stages of motherhood – but her eyes still sparkle with mischief, her curls are as untamed as ever and her dimples haven't changed one iota.

'You were cheeky then, and you're bloody cheeky now!'

'And you do realise you're still as weird, big bro?' She grins at me, so I ruffle up her hair. She hates it, but I know she likes it really. 'What's going on in there, Joe-bro?' She's still smiling, but she's waiting. She's always wanted to know what I'm thinking. Age has just made her more persistent.

'Nothing is going on!'

'What are you thinking about?'

'Nothing.'

'You can't be thinking about nothing, it's impossible, people are always thinking about something.'

I shake my head and try not to smile. That's always been one of her go-to's, that you can't be thinking nothing. 'I was thinking about the price of eggs and whether Mum needs more chickens!'

She laughs, thumps me on the arm. 'No, you weren't, you little liar!'

'I might have been. Anyway I don't have to share everything with you.'

'Who else will you talk to?' She grins at me. 'Now you've not got Lisa.'

Lisa was my last girlfriend. It ended quite abruptly when she realised that I wasn't joking about London, that it wasn't something I just needed to get out of my system for twelve months. I genuinely love working there. Being there.

It wasn't that I wasn't upfront with her, more that deep

down I guess she'd thought it wouldn't actually happen. That all she had to do was go along with it, pretend she was excited for me. Proud that I'd got my degree, that I'd been offered my dream job.

She expected I'd come home, buy a house in the village, we'd get married and have kids. She didn't want to go beyond the boundaries of the life she had.

We'd both been too young to see clearly. I hadn't recognised that her sense of adventure was just teenage high spirits and wanting to challenge the world. That inside she was a home bird who would always want to return to the same place. The same people.

At the end of the day though, abandoning my dreams wouldn't only have been wrong for me – but I'd have been letting my family down. They've made massive sacrifices to give me the education I've had, to support me through uni, but more than that they are so proud I've succeeded at what I want to do. Mum was the happiest I'd ever seen her when they came to my graduation ceremony; in the photos she looks so young, so happy. And Dad actually hugged me! A proper man hug, not just a gruff 'well done' and pat on the back.

It might be daft, but I still get a bit choked up when Mum gets those photos out.

They are happy for me. For my future. They'd support me in whatever I want – even if it means moving away, despite us being so close-knit.

Lisa wasn't proud. She just wanted her happy ever after. Which is fine. I got that. It just took time for both of us to recognise, admit, that our ever afters were in very different places.

Soph knows as well as I do, though, that I've always talked to her more than I have to any girlfriend. As a family we're pretty close. I've got mates, I've always had one or two really good mates that I've known since school, but the friends I've made at work, in London, aren't people I really *talk* to. They're great, but they're workmates. Not people I'd share my innermost thoughts with.

I've always felt close to my little sister – is that odd? As a kid she was a pest at times, but our differences kind of drew us together. She was bubbly, noisy, naughty – but a safe kind of rebellion because she was ours.

I guess I've shared a lot with Sophie over the years, but not the really personal stuff. That would be weird. We're a get-on-with-it type of family, not a sit-down-and-share-our-feelings type. Dad would go into shock if either of us poured our hearts out over the roast beef and two veg. Which I guess is why Lisa and I trundled on for so long, without really knowing we had different futures in mind. We didn't talk. We weren't open with each other – not because we were hiding stuff, just because we aren't the oversharing types.

'I don't have to talk the whole time!'

Sophie is the chatterbox. Mum said she was born asking questions. Dad says the milkman has a lot to answer for. It's a running joke that she's either an alien or was found on the doorstep because personality wise she is nothing like the rest of us.

Strong, silent type – that's Dad in a nutshell. Mild, unassuming and uncomplaining – that's Mum.

I just get on with stuff, I guess.

'Go on, tell, you know you want to!' Sophie grins, 'and Mum's not here to tell me to leave you alone!'

I do want to spill. But I don't. What's in my head is too private to talk about. 'There's nothing to tell.' Oversharing, opening up, just doesn't come naturally to me. It drives Sophie mad. But what if I say it out loud, then it all goes wrong?

And this is big. I guess what I really want is for somebody to tell me I'm not going batshit crazy. Which means telling somebody.

Is it really smart to tell anybody though, especially my sister, that I feel like I've met 'the one'? That is just too weird. I have always thought people were talking bollocks when they said they saw a girl and decided she was the one they were going to marry.

I mean, what the hell is that about?

But I haven't been able to get the girl I saw at the station on Thursday out of my mind, and it's been driving me crazy all weekend. Though to be honest, it was a good thing when I somehow got roped into milking the cows and mucking out after them on Saturday morning. Much as I love my family, I haven't missed the 5 a.m. alarm call and l'odeur-de-cowshit at all since I moved to London.

The girl was a welcome distraction. But I don't even know her name.

I only saw her for a moment.

We only swapped a few words.

But all I know was we had an instant connection, or at least there was on my side. There was just something about the way she looked at me, her smile, the way she joked back at me that made me want to talk more. Find out what she is really like. Who she is.

As far as she's concerned though, I'm probably just some clumsy jerk who soaked her to the skin, then almost took her eye out.

I don't normally even use an umbrella. What the hell was I thinking? Sophie would have hysterics about that one. She'd tell everybody her I'd turned into a city slicker afraid of the weather.

'Yeah, yeah, course there isn't!' Sophie is studying me. 'No reason at all for you walking round all weekend in a world of your own.'

Nope, no way can I tell her. She'll either feel sorry for me or think it's hilarious.

'I've got stuff on my mind, work! Or maybe I was just trying to block you out!' We share a grin. She knows I love her really.

'I better go, or I'll miss the train. Thanks for the lift, Soph.'

'You're welcome.' She watches me intently as I get out of the car, then reach into the back for my rucksack. Then she smiles, her full-force broad smile. 'I'll get it out of you next weekend, loser!'

Oh God, if only she knew! I am a total loser. I've lost my head to a girl I'll never see again.

Chapter Four

MILLIE

Monday 7th March

Confessions of... when I fell for a guy

I have a confession to make. On Thursday evening I fell for a guy, and lost him, all within the space of five minutes. This is a record, even for me.

I probably should be clear here, when I say I fell for, it would be more accurate to say I fell on, and I should also say that this is not a return to my 'Confessions of a Single Girl Out on the Town' column, this is a single stone-cold-sober me heading back to the city after a weekend with my mother.

Forget Friday night on the town, or Saturday night at the movies – I'm telling you Thursday night on platform 3 at King's Cross is the hottest gig in town. Okay, maybe I should have kept that a secret, but you know how I like to share the good bits as well as the bad.

Anyway, I was not actually on the platform when our gazes

met, I was suspended several inches above it, caught by his warm hands, crushed to his manly chest.

I'd got off the train and was heading down the escalator, checking my Insta so that I could get back in my city headspace, and was bashed in the back by an oversize tote (come on, girls, think before you swing, please). I lurched forward, my heel snagged and before I knew it, I was hurtling down headfirst panicking about the embarrassment of being face planted into the platform.

My face did not hit the floor, but neither did my feet. Instead, I was left dangling, my boobs were crushed against a broad chest, and my nose was squished into a fluffy red scarf (I'm still finding bits up my left nostril). I peeled my face off the fabric and squinted up, and KAPOW, just like that, I realised I had landed in the arms of the dreamiest guy I have evah seen. Dreamy as in hot. I swear, my heart literally skipped a beat. Although whether this was because of his sexiness, or being crushed, I'm not one hundred per cent sure.

Anyway, for a moment I was dangling, and then he lowered me down until my feet touched the ground, and I wobbled. Really wobbled – with jelly legs! I think it was shock, I don't believe girls (well, I) actually swoon. So, he kept his large, warm, steadying hands on my arms, and we stared at each other.

Nobody has ever, in my entire life, looked at me like that. I couldn't tell you what colour his eyes were, only that they were caring, kind and my insides fluttered, and my outsides went all goosebumpy. This could have been indigestion and shock, but I was also seeing stars and hearing romantic music, and I couldn't have torn myself away from him if I'd wanted to. And honestly, I really didn't want to at all.

He tucked a loose tendril of hair behind my ear, and it was better than any foreplay I've ever had (see, I told you my experiences have not been super good). Shockwaves ran through my body as his hands drifted down over my forearms, brushing the goosebumps away.

He told me I needed to sit down, and gently led me towards a seat. There was a hint of humour in his eyes that made me want to smile back at him. And then, oh my God, he bent down and rubbed my ankle, my actual ankle! He picked up the shoe I'd lost, pressed it gently on my foot then his gaze met mine again. Gulp!

It was weird, I felt like I knew him, and this moment was meant to be. Romance with a capital R, and there I was with lippy that hadn't been touched up since I left the house and my hair was frizz-city.

What's it about, was I in shock?

Now, I'm not saying get your high heels on and hurtle down the escalator here. That's kind of death-wish territory and I don't want to get sued if you break an arm, leg or your neck. But OMG it was the best thing that has happened to me in ages. I'd say every girl needs to experience this feeling at least once in her life.

I'm hooked. I want to do it again. But I will probably never see him again. I was so shell-shocked I didn't get his number; I didn't even get his name.

Have I met my perfect match on Platform 3? I am in a quandary here. I didn't think there were heroes anymore, I certainly didn't think there was one strong enough to break my fall without breaking some part of his anatomy. So, do I need to *head back there and stake it out? Do I need to find out if he is 'the one', or just some poor guy who now has a hernia?'*

———————

'I like this. I like it a lot.'

Oh my God. My fingers freeze on the keyboard, and my entire body trembles as the relief floods through me. I'd thought this was good, and Carla has just confirmed it! I'm not finished, I've not lost my touch. Gloom and doom Dale can take a hike.

It's Monday and I'm back in the big city, back at my desk, back at work.

Hexham feels like it's in another world. A world that offered me acres and acres of unspoiled land to walk across and think. Properly think. Sometimes London is just too fast, too frenzied, too *busy* for thinking. Too busy for reading, too busy for daydreaming, too busy for living.

Sometimes I need that other world. I need a vast landscape and a proper full-blown gale to blow the negativity (and my very expensive haircut) away and inspire me. It seems like it has done its magic.

I look up. Carla, my boss, is nodding her head. She leans forward, narrows her eyes and stares at her screen intently. She taps. 'This!' As though I might not know what she is talking about. 'This is what I've been talking about, it's tons better than that crap—' I try not to flinch; say it like it is, Carla '—you've been churning out lately about the fucking tedious London Underground.'

Uh-oh, maybe I shouldn't mention my other brief-encounters-addict idea, can't be 'fucking tedious' can we?

She purses her lips; it is her thinking face (otherwise known to me and the rest of the office as her resting bitch face – because something totally negative usually comes out of her mouth two seconds later). 'Love, life and laughter on the lines.' She waves her hands about as though that will help me appreciate the bigger picture, and her brilliance. 'No, no. All aboard the love train! Or, confessions of a love train...' She pauses.

'Loser?' Zoe, who sits opposite me, chirps up unhelpfully. We both glare at her.

I am thinking straight again though. But right now, I am also thinking 'what the hell is she talking about?'

'Love train? But I didn't fall in love with him.' I state the obvious flaw before she gets too carried away. I mean, I wouldn't *totally* discount the idea of getting to know him – the way he looked, and the fact that we did seem to click in some weird way has stuck in my head. But love? Woah there! 'I don't even know him, and I am definitely not climbing aboard!'

Zoe sniggers.

Like I said, I write a 'confessions' column (but not *that* kind of confession), and I decided that using train-guy as inspiration is my only option. It seemed like a good idea when I was out in the wilds. Now I wonder if I might have lost the plot.

I was a bit desperate to try and come up with something before Carla 'called me in' for a chat, and to explain that I'd been demoted to office junior. And as my train-guy was all I could actually think about when I was on the train heading back, I thought, why the hell not?

I've been wobbling lately (along with my reader ratings) and starting to wonder if everybody else is right, if I have bitten off more than I can chew. The people (Dale and Carla) who've supported me, helped me, have started to make the same 'not good enough' type remarks that I got before I came to London, and for the first time in ages I've been doubting myself.

It's hard not to when things start going wrong, isn't it?

But over the weekend Mum reminded me how proud she is, how proud Dad was, how they hoped they'd brought me up feeling I could do anything, be anything I wanted if I worked at it.

If Mum is strong enough to cope on her own, then I should be able to cope with writing a bloody weekly column, shouldn't I?

And my long walk reminded me of the resolve I had inside me when I applied to uni, when I applied to work here.

I can do this. I will. I will be the best I can. But right now, I also know that if I lose this job nobody will take me on, yet. The timing isn't right. I still need to prove myself. Carla might be hard work at times, but she knows how it works, she's got a brilliant feel for what is good, what is marketable. So I need to take some of the shit, keep in her good books. It will be worth it.

And I have to ignore doubting Dale, because to be quite

honest I think he's all front and no substance, and I was so smitten, so wanting to be bowled over, that I let myself believe he was more than he was.

I realised while I was out walking, when my eyes were burning from the cold wind and my ears felt like they were about to drop off, that I have stopped going with my gut feeling. I have been too keen to please people, try and second guess what they want – and deliver it. That is why things have started to go a bit off track.

Anyway, let's face it, train-guy was a hunk so why wouldn't people want to read about him? He was kind (with gorgeous eyes, even if I can't quite picture them), which is I guess why I went all light-headed and why, when I got into work this morning, I *still* thought it was a good idea to write about him.

Well, not exactly him. I used him as inspiration. I used a bit of artistic licence. And used my trademark 'take the piss out of myself' angle.

My gut told me I had to.

I decided to play it for laughs. I mean, you can only eke out an umbrella shake and a sexy gaze so far, can't you? Unless you add in some lip action, which I am not going to do. It doesn't seem right. Sacrilege. If I don't know what the feel of his firm lips is like, then I'm not going to make it up for anybody else's sake.

Anyway, he was taking up all my headspace when the train pulled into King's Cross last night, and I dawdled through half-hoping I'd bump into him again.

As if!

I've never seen him before, I have never ever seen him on a Sunday, so why would it happen now? Anyway, the long and short of it was that I was so busy daydreaming about him, I wasn't concentrating. I was looking over heads, and under armpits, not in front of me and I caught my heel on the step and nearly took some middle-aged guy out.

Boy, was he livid. All red cheeks and spitty. I guess he was pissed off at having to leave his lovely family, gorgeous home, two spaniels and smog-free skies, and head back to the city (I like to give my fellow commuters a backstory) and the last thing he was expecting was for some female to split his lip and send his specs flying. It was probably the lip that made him angry, not the family bit. Anyway, once I'd clambered off him and he'd cooled down, he was fine. Honest. He said he wasn't going to sue me or call the police or the local press, so no GBH record for me. We even had a little joke, and he said his wife would never believe him if he told the truth, he'd have to elaborate, nudge, nudge, wink, wink. At which point it got a little uncomfortable if I'm honest.

Anyway, it gave me the idea for the post.

And it gave me a get-out clause. Because my stomach was doing little nervous flips every time I thought about writing about him. Train-guy, that is. I didn't feel I could, I didn't feel it was right. Don't ask me why.

I did want to write about him, but I didn't.

He feels a bit like a guilty secret that I'm not ready to share with anybody, let alone thousands of strangers who might have the kind of imaginations that will turn our magical moment into something far more sordid. And drop croissant flakes and jam on us – reading as they eat their breakfast.

I feel like I want to keep him to myself.

So, anyhow, I thought, why not do a bit of a mash-up? I could write that he (young, sexy, friendly train-guy, not nasty florid-faced middle-aged misery guts with sex-pest potential) caught me in his strong arms after I'd gone flying down, past the patient commuters, jumping the queue and jumped on the man.

To be honest, if I'd been pressed to his manly chest IRL I would probably have had a full-blown coronary given that when he'd brushed my arm, I'd got the tremors, but WTF this is faction. Mash-up faction. We all embroider life a bit, don't we? Especially if we are trying to write a post that will get hits. And followers. And job security.

And possibly a pay rise.

And yeah, okay, falling down an escalator is not that original.

But the sensation wasn't made up. It was SO real. The bit about the warmth and kindness in his eyes was real, and okay, in reality he only brushed my arm with the tips of his fingers for a nanosecond, but the feeling was real.

If I close my eyes he's there, and I get a shiver down my spine.

And I did want to smile at him. And it was pretty impossible to tear my gaze away until he backed off saying he had to go, and practically bolted for freedom. So the feelings are from my heart, even if my head has provided the scenario.

I might have got a bit carried away with the foot fondling and shoe bit though. I might have a fetish I didn't know about.

Oh my God, I've just realised I've given us a 'Cinderella' vibe. How corny is that? Shit, I have actually told a story about a shoe and a pumpkin (okay, train) and Carla is swallowing it whole. One of us is losing the plot here.

Are we all so desperate for love, sex or just something plain good in life that the retelling of a fairy tale sounds cool?

I do know train-guy won't actually be like a modern-day prince in real life; I've got this heroic view of him that isn't real. But hey, a girl can dream. We all need a hero at some time, don't we? And why not a big, strong, sexy one.

'What do you mean, you don't know him?' Carla isn't giving in. 'Of course you don't, that's the bloody point! You get to know him, or somebody else, anybody.' If she rolls her eyes back any further, she'll lose them underneath her black fringe.

I change tack slightly. 'He didn't even get on my train!' I have no idea where he went, where he was going. He ran off, never to be seen again. Well, not by me.

'Well, find somebody who does get on your train –' her tone has gone all spiky '– or find out which train he's normally on and catch that instead. It can't be that fucking difficult.'

'Catch that instead?' Is she mad? He could be travelling anywhere! 'Why would I get on the wrong train?'

She ignores me. 'I want romance, I want hope, not some sweaty ten-minute encounter on the tube, or some boring observation about mansplaining or manspreading as your bus goes over bloody London Bridge. That is so last decade.'

'I have never—' I object hotly, my cheeks burning. I have not actually included those in my commuter confessions. Yet. I might have to scrub them off my ideas list.

Carla doesn't pause for breath, she carries on, talking over the top of me.

'I want long distance, I want a modern-day *Brief Encounter*, a different guy each week if you like.'

Ha ha! Brief encounters, I might not discard that idea after all. Except I was thinking more along the idea of a meet-cute followed by a departure, with not a lot in between. Apart from hope.

I think she is over-estimating my attractiveness to the opposite sex. Seriously. She is also mad. 'Very modern day,' I say drolly, shuddering inwardly at the thought of prostituting myself for the sake of a column where I will probably take the piss out of myself, and him. Whoever 'him' turns out to be. 'Have you any idea of the state of most of the commuters on that train, Carla?' Probably not. Carla lives in a posh city centre penthouse, courtesy of daddy. She's probably never been on a train. Well, maybe the Orient Express, but that doesn't count.

'Whatever.'

'And I thought I was supposed to do "Confessions of"?'

'I suppose it could be "Confession of a Long-distance Commuter", but "Love Train" is sexier, and "all aboard" suggests...' She's almost forgotten me as she doodles ideas on a sheet of paper.

'Sex?' I am not climbing all over a man I don't know just to improve her bloody stats. Or my job prospects.

She ignores me, again, but dials up the sarcasm, so I know she heard. 'Try. Even you should be able to flirt. Your column has got a bit boring. Okay, if you want me to be honest –' I don't '– it's bloody pedestrian. Nobody wants to hear about your cat.'

'I do not write about my cat!' I splutter. 'I haven't even got a—' I swear, I have never ever written about a cat, real or invented. I am not a crazy cat lady. Just a bit crazy.

'Oh whatever.' She waves a dismissive hand. 'Never let the truth get in the way of a good story' could be her motto. 'You know what I mean. People want hope –' at least we are on the same page there '– love, happiness, not office gossip shit and the same old boring tat. Give them some *sex*, Millie –' different page '– or at least the possibility of it! Right, I've got a meeting, tighten up this piece and we'll put it out on Thursday as normal and see how it performs. Are you sure you can't track this guy down?'

I glare.

'Please yourself, I'm sure there are loads of hot guys on your way to Blackpool or Leeds or wherever it is you come from.' To Carla, it doesn't matter if it's Lancashire, Yorkshire or flaming Scotland. It's just 'north'. You'd think that actually having the north in 'Northumberland' would make it easier, wouldn't you?

I'm also not sure if she's being sarcastic or has this movie-style fantasy image of handsome surgeons and actors travelling the tracks. Huh.

'Hexham.'

'Fine. I suppose there must be rugby players? Or hunky farming types? But not Jeremy Clarkson or that Cable, Karl, tractor-boy one, whatever he's called.'

'Caleb,' cuts in Zoe.

'He's in the Cotswolds,' I say.

'Thank fuck for small mercies.'

I decide not to get into that. 'Could I have a private chat, Carla?' Now could be the perfect time to grab the opportunity to broach the subject of altering my lifestyle. Of spending a little bit more time with my mother. In whichever county Carla would like to place her. 'When he, er, caught me, I kind of wasn't concentrating because I'd just come back from Mum's and I was thinking about my moth—'

She rolls her eyes. 'You really do fuck up a lot, don't you?'

I don't. Not really, no more than the average person (I don't think), but for the sake of work I do. It's how I make my living. Maybe Carla thinks the 'me' I write about is more real than the 'me' she sees in the office each day. She's not at all bothered about employing the real me.

Okay, please don't judge me. But I do make a living out

of other people's cock-ups, as well as my own, of course. I'm not nasty, just observational.

People want to see that others make a mess of stuff, that their lives aren't perfect, don't they? And I do it quite a bit. Cock up. Which is why when I first started working for bitchy boss Carla, she suggested I turn my 'mishaps' into a weekly column alongside a blog. Well, what she actually did was stare at me for ages then say, 'You are actually quite funny in a fuck-up kind of way, aren't you?' She'd tapped her teeth with her pen, then pronounced, 'I want a kind of slummy mummy without the kids. Liz Jones without the angst, but with more booze –' she paused '– and food.'

At that time, I was newly appointed and keen to make the right impression (i.e. desperate) so jumped on this with total enthusiasm. I can do food; I can do booze. I was convinced it couldn't be that difficult.

It can be tough to be intentionally hilarious all the time though. I mean, it's just not normal to keep a diary of fuck-ups so you don't accidentally re-use them, is it? My notebook reads like this:

- *Skirt in knickers at awards ceremony,*
- *Top on back to front when interviewing famous rock star that I accidentally bumped into in wine bar while both of us very pissed, he insisted on taking it off just so I wouldn't be embarrassed. Though he did forget to put it back on the right way round*
- *Driving wrong way up motorway for lots of miles on*

way to wedding, where I was supposed to be bridesmaid. I mean, how was I supposed to know that when she said St Ives she meant some tiddly village near Cambridge that nobody from my part of the world would ever have heard of, and not the real St Ives in Cornwall that I'd gone to as a kid? The one with a beach.

- *Sending BF text meant for BFF calling him a selfish dick. Yeah, that one didn't go down well, and him reading about it on my blog the next day went down even less well. But the reader responses were brilliant. And he was a dick, we'd outgrown our relationship about a week after it had started – but neither of us could be bothered to admit we were romantic failures. Who on earth convinced blokes that sticking their tongues inside ears during sex would make a girl orgasmic? (That made the blog as well – He threatened me with an injunction, at the same time as asking if I could give him a plug on my blog and asking for the key to his place back.)*

We'd started with 'Yorkshire girl in the City' (Northumberland was considered too much of a mouthful, and I'd had that temporary job in Yorkshire after uni so she thought it was close enough). As I had recently transplanted, Carla thought I'd be a novelty, as well as publicly fulfilling the requirement to consider northerners as real people (I do realise that this could be why she employed me). Then we moved on to 'Confessions of a Single Girl in the City' (the Yorkshire bit had backfired on her when there was a regional uproar about her taking the piss out of everybody who wasn't from the south, and confessional stuff did hit all the commercial boxes, and I worked really, really hard to prove even without the northern angle I was still worth keeping on). From there we went on to 'Confessions of a Bad Girlfriend', 'Confessions of a Girl Who Can't Say No'. You get the drift?

Anyhow people love reading about my (slightly dramatized) cock-ups, and how I always manage to survive and dig myself out of the holes.

Well, they did. Things have kind of stalled a bit lately. Carla is right (though I hate to admit it), the 'office gossip shit' has got a bit boring. So, what am I on now? Confessions of a randy commuter?

'And Millie?' Carla stops me in my tracks as I'm trying to escape. 'Make it funny. Right? Not farcical, relatable.' I get her gimlet stare.

'Cool. Sure. Got it.' I mutter the last bit under my breath as I head back to my own desk. Funny, ha ha.

'And.' I freeze, and then when she doesn't carry on talking, I turn to look at her. 'Make them root for you, Millie.' Her tone has softened, and if I didn't know her better, I'd say she'd gone a bit dreamy. 'Why can't a meet-cute lead to love?'

Why not indeed?

'Well, it can, exactly!' It could, yes, with a guy like him! But, oh my God, that's the last thing I need right now. I don't need all the complications of a real, you know, full-on relationship on top of everything else. My head would explode.

It really might be better if I don't find him again, have to make it all up, and avoid the risk of things getting too hot to handle.

'Unlikely of course.' She's gone back to her normal brisk self. 'But we can all dream, and you're supposed to be a journalist, so make it happen!' She's off before I can think of a reply.

It is only when I sit down again that I realise she's totally blanked me about having a chat.

Alongside my decision to write about the sexual attractiveness of random strangers in train stations, I decided that I definitely need to spend more time with Mum. I need to actually act on the random comment I'd made to her about being there for her.

I don't need to be in the city every day to do my job, I can work at home one or two days a week. My childhood home.

This does not have to affect my career.

Well, actually it could. Which makes it hard enough to broach different working hours because I'm really torn about whether it could work or not, but Carla makes it impossible. Short of locking her in her office, five minutes alone together when I actually get to talk and she listens is practically impossible.

Maybe I should just email her?

I dither for a moment, hands over my keyboard. Then

grab my mobile. I will message Dale because whilst he can be a dick, I can rely on him for an unemotional response to whether my request is reasonable, and how I can broach it short of handcuffing Carla to her desk.

I'd rather chat face-to-face when I see him, like we always did when we first knew each other, but I don't know when I will next see him. Our diaries seem to have got out of sync, and the last time I saw him it was more of an executive meeting than a mates' night out, because one of his bosses had invited him to dinner, and dinner in Dale's world is a euphemism for 'promotion interview'. He needed a plus-one to show he is steady, reliable and not afraid of commitment. Ha ha.

Anyway, he might have some suggestions about how to tackle this; he's used to dealing with uber-busy people like Carla.

Hi stranger! Mum needs me, but not sure how to broach subject of working from home more with Carla. Any suggestions? Millie S x

I have to put my name; in case he's forgotten which Millie I am. It's not that I think he's playing the field and has many female best friends, more that he's not playing at all.

I hit send, then jump as my phone rings. It is Dale. This is not like him at all. He must have some very strong views on this subject which emojis and three-letter acronyms just won't cover.

'What do you mean, your mother needs you? Is she ill?' There's a taut edge to his voice. Dale doesn't like ill health.

He's the first out of the door if there's the slightest hint he might be needed to look after somebody. He actually went away for the weekend last time I had flu and asked him if he could warm some soup up for me, and left me a list of 'tip-top takeaways that delivered'.

'No, I think she's just struggling since Dad…' I can't say it. 'If I could spend more time with her, you know work from there the odd day.'

'Work from *there*? The *north*?' He sounds horrified, as though I've suggested working from Mars, or the Moon. I think he's been watching too much *Game of Thrones*. 'Why on earth would you do that?'

'To keep her company, to er, change plugs?' I don't tend to change plugs for myself – I'd rather buy a new appliance. But you know what I mean.

'I'm not being harsh, Millie, but it's her life. You've got here. She won't thank you for throwing your career away.'

'But I'm not throwing anything away, lots of people work from home. Hybrid working is the future!' I read this somewhere. I'm not one hundred per cent sure about the idea of *never* being in the office, because I do like people (and how could I write what I do without them?) and sometimes you do need face-to-face meetings, but I do buy into the 'happiness breeds productivity' angle.

He sighs. 'Not successful, dynamic people in this industry. Not when you're an unknown. You need to be in their faces. Present!'

'You can't say that, Dale!' I'm not sure what is annoying me the most, being classed as an unknown, or the sweeping statement that successful people have to be in an office. 'That's rubbish these days.'

'And what happens when she dies?' He carries on with his one-sided conversation, ignoring me. 'Which she will, and you'll be stuck in the back of beyond, no career, nothing.'

I think I have misjudged this. I am talking to completely the wrong person. 'You do know they have high-speed broadband and Aldi north of Birmingham now? *Peaky Blinders* isn't a documentary.'

'You know exactly where I'm coming from.'

'No, I don't!'

'Oh, and while I've got you on—' as though I'm the unavailable one! '—I know it's tiresome, but can you come to Edinburgh with me the weekend after next? I'd completely forgotten but my sister is getting hitched and if I go on my own, I'll have to put up with all the comments.'

Edinburgh? I love Edinburgh! Maybe I could combine it with a visit to see Mum? I could even take her! We could pop in and see Lou. It's not that far and…

Shit. What the hell am I doing? Why am I even thinking about going with him?

'No.'

'Sorry?'

A wave of disbelief and shock hits my eardrum. He is more taken aback by this than by the possibility of my moving north of Watford. Okay, I guess I can understand it. I've been too much of a pushover. I felt a bit indebted to Dale when I moved into his flat.

He'd shown me the fab, amazing side to the city, instead of the lonely, hard side that so many people had told me to expect. I'd not wanted to believe them, I'd been positive, it was what I wanted – but sometimes you can't help letting the jitters in for a bit, can you? Without him I would have found it tough, so I felt a bit duty-bound when he asked the first time if I minded being his plus one to an event. And then it kind of escalated. Lots of events. But if I'm honest I've enjoyed it; it is nice to get out. I was a bit of a billy-no-mates in the early days and Dale goes to some cool places.

He's not used to me saying no. But friendship works both ways, doesn't it?

'No, I can't come, Dale. I'm busy. With my mother. Grabbing some time together before she *dies*.' I end the call.

What on earth was I thinking, or more to the point not-thinking, when I'd contemplated crossing the line and nearly suggested we turn the idea of being together into *being-together*? He isn't bothered about me not being in London for work, this isn't about any imagined damage to my career, he's bothered about not having me on tap for when he needs a plus one.

I shake unpleasant, self-centred Dale out of my head and stare at the blank page on my screen.

All men can't be like him, can they? One day, when it's the right time, surely there's a chance I'll bump into the guy for me.

Can a meet-cute really lead to love?

Chapter Five

MILLIE

Friday 11th March

'Amelia!'

I've got one foot in the office, the other still in the lift, and freeze in panic, then shoot forward – practically into Carla's arms – as the doors threaten to close around my ankle. Luckily, she is off at a fair clip before I actually cannon into her.

'Come on, come on. What are you hanging about for?'
I scurry after her.
I was hanging about for two reasons—

1. She called me Amelia, I have learned from past experience that if anybody calls me Amelia – other than my mother, other (normally old) relatives and anybody working in an official capacity (including dentists and doctors) – then it

is bad news. She is not about to give my teeth a polish and scale, or (heaven forbid) grab a speculum, and she does not share my DNA, so there's a good chance she's about to sack me. Or give me a bollocking for something. And,

2. She has been lying in wait for me, and I'm not late.

Carla reaches my desk before I do, perches on the edge and points at my chair. Surely she isn't about to sack me, or give me a dressing-down in front of everybody else? Carla might be a total cow, but she is not stupid. Carla is hot on employees' rights. Carla is not about to fuck up by humiliating me in public. Is she?

'For fuck's sake stop twitching, you're making me edgy.'

I'm making *her* edgy? I sit down abruptly. On my hands. Nobody wants to make Carla edgier than she already is when she's in this mood.

She folds her arms. Defensive. I feel ill.

'You need to find that guy again.'

'Wha—?'

She leans forward slightly and speaks more slowly, like she does to any juniors before declaring they are inept. 'You. Need. To. Find. The. Guy. From. The. Train. Station.'

'But I don't know if…'

'It has to be him.' She has me fixed with her gimlet stare, but it doesn't matter. Carla doesn't actually *scare* me, unless she's about to sack me, and I've just realised she isn't. Phew.

I mean, being made redundant, and being sacked before I hit the big thirty was *never* part of my life plan.

'You said I should please myself!' I uncover my hands and fold my own arms. 'I could find some other guy.' Not that I am against hunting down train-guy, I just don't think it's possible.

Her eyebrow disappears under her fringe. Carla always knows best. Unfortunately, most of the time she actually *does* know best, so it's very hard to make the case for doing things my way. My alternatives have to be foolproof, not vague ideas.

'You said just find any guy, Carla. A series of guys. I was thinking about a variety of fall-on-top-of-them scenarios, then we could mark them out of ten on their response.' I had spent all evening, and most of the night, wondering how I was going to come up with a series of posts about sex on a suburban train. Or even a TransPennine Express. I was still at the 'very, very, vague ideas' stage. Not good.

'A variety of fall-on-top-of-them scenarios? Are you serious?' The sarcasm positively drips off her tongue. She's as good as saying, 'You've finally lost your marbles.' And okay, I have to agree, it does sound a bit wacky and lacking in development potential even by my standards, particularly when it's said in that tone of voice.

'Well, no, I'm not being totally serious, but…' To be honest, every time I've thought about my train journey, and how the hell I'm going to turn it into a weekly giggle and shock-fest, I've thought about him. Train-guy. He's messing with my head, and he barely knows I exist.

He also has inescapable potential. He's just the thing my readers want in their lives right now.

Let's be honest, he's the thing I want in my own life.

'Thank fuck for that. Right—' she bangs my desk decisively '—some other also-ran won't do. It has to be him.'

'But I...' I don't want to actually admit it to her, but chances of ever seeing him again are close to zero. I've done the maths (when I couldn't sleep, or work, or been sitting on the loo folding the paper into an origami bird). I have worked out just how many times I have caught the train to go home since I moved to London. It's a lot.

I have never seen my train-guy before. I'd have remembered. I know I would.

I have also not seen him since.

So that means I have seen him once in many hundreds of train hours. Not good odds. Unless he has only just started to commute on that route and will be doing it every week from now on, at precisely the same time as me.

See? Not good.

'Track him down, ask the station for CCTV or something.'

'You know I can't do that! It has to be illegal.'

'Well use your initiative. Investigative journalism.'

Oh my God, she's not expecting me to shimmy over the station fence and break in, is she? I'm not the shimmying type. Last time I tried to climb over a wall for a dare I got stuck on the top and had to be rescued by a passer-by who grabbed my foot and hauled. He had drunk four pints of

Stella and collapsed in a heap the moment my weight parted company with the bricks. At least my fall was cushioned.

'I'm a confessional journalist, not investigative. I suppose I could hire a PI or something...' My voice drifts off as I see her eyes gleam. 'If you could pay, I think they're quite expen—'

'Huh. You should be fine on your own. You're pretty resourceful.'

Wow, I think that's a compliment.

'I'll get you some new trainers on expenses if you wear them out.'

'Wow, you'd stretch to trainers?' I mutter under my breath, trying to at least get some joy from the backhanded compliment. Carla does not like handing out praise. I don't think it was actually praise though, I think it was a way of saying that I am only worthy of twenty quid tops in expenses.

'If you find him and write something decent, I'll throw in spare laces. Anyway, the exercise will do you good.' She gives me a quick look up and down.

See? Something nasty always has to follow something nice.

'But why the rush, Carla? Why does it have to be him?'

'Check your emails. Your falling-on-top-of him post—' she does air quotes '—went down quite well. I didn't say anything yesterday in case it was a fluke, but it just blew up over the day and last night. I've sent you the stats – read them, then come to the office and tell me if you're going to do it, or—' there is a significant pause '—I need to assign it to somebody else.' Assign him to somebody else? She can't just give away train-guy like that! He's mine! I think my jaw has dropped. How dare she!

'I'm sure you'll be able to appreciate why we need him when you see the facts and figures.' She stands up abruptly, and is striding off across the office, in her very-designer sneakers, before I have chance to even close my mouth.

I open the email.

'Wow, Millie! Look at that!' Zoe has scooted round and is peering over my shoulder.

I am looking. It is rather alarming, in a shockingly good way.

'I can see why you don't get to please yourself! If you don't want to climb aboard, I'll do it for you, and I don't even know him. Shit, look at the comments!'

She has a point.

It seems that people love my brief encounter by the tracks. They are practically gagging for Episode 2.

Apparently, for some people, throwing myself headlong down an escalator and into a stranger's arms isn't enough. It is just the beginning. And hot. They are panting for more, presumably the bits where I'll climb aboard and snog his face off (randy readers) or stand lovelorn (other, more romantic, readers) under the station clock until he appears carrying a red rose and declaring undying love.

Either way, it isn't going to happen. Is it? I don't have a hope in hell of bumping into him again. Shit.

I bury my head in my hands. This could have been my

big chance. Can I wing it? Just pretend? He's real enough in my head. I have a good imagination.

'Find him. Do it,' hisses Carla, in a tone that suggests it is an order not an option, and nearly making me spill my coffee. I don't know how she does that, sneaking up on people the way she does. It adds to her power. It makes gossiping about her impossible. Unless you want her put-downs, and demotion. 'Come on, I haven't got all day. Now you've seen the response, let's talk.'

I follow her into her office, in a bit of a daze. Feeling strangely excited, as well as a bit daunted. I would quite like to see him again. But what if he was only sorry that I was wet, but doesn't fancy me at all? He did seem very polite, and considerate.

This only worked because of the spark I'd felt. If I see him again and he doesn't remember me, or I discover I only thought he was dishy because the water in my eyes had blurred my contact lenses and at a second glance he's as ordinary as every other guy I've ever bumped into, then I'm screwed.

'That is the best response to anything you've written that you've have had for…' Carla pauses for so long I wonder if she's forgotten about me, 'well, for ever. It trumps every "Confessions" post.' She tilts her head and regards me. The way an owl studies the mouse it has in its talons. It is a bit unnerving. 'It's authentic. People respond to that. You're ambitious, you can't let an opportunity like this pass by, can you?' Carla being nice is definitely scary.

'Well, no, but…'

'Exactly.'

'But what if I can't find him again?' There's a flutter of mild panic starting up inside me.

'Of course you will,' she says dismissively. 'He was as hot as hell the way you've written it. If that isn't an incentive, then I don't know what is. It's not like I'm asking you to find a mangy dog you spotted in the underpass, is it?'

'Well no, but…' Why does she think I'm more capable of finding him because I fancied the pants off him? If I was a hound-dog capable of sniffing down hot-as-hell men I'd have been getting a hell of a lot more action than I have.

'Millie, do stop saying "but", you know "but"s are banned.' She is starting to look annoyed rather than positive. Carla's mood can flip in an instant.

'Well, he was hot, but to be honest I can't really remember *exactly* what he looks like,' I say apologetically. I know exactly what his eyes are like. And his hair. And the warmth of his hand that burned through my clothes as though they didn't exist.

'What?' Carla's tone has turned a little bit glacial.

'It was hurried, he was in a hurry, I was in a hurry. I only got a brief glimpse before he rushed off, and I think I might have made it up a bit.' I gabble. 'Exactly how he looked, that is.' It was the connection we had that threw me. I just felt like I knew him. That it was supposed to be happening. It was internal, it was emotional.

I wasn't exactly studying his appearance and marking him out of ten. I was just gazing into his eyes and hoping he'd stay a while. 'I'd spot him in a line-up though.' I cross my fingers. I'm pretty sure I could. Providing I could gaze into his eyes.

'Great. So, we're fine if he's a criminal and gets arrested.' Carla sits back, and her tone is heavy with sarcasm again. 'Look, play it how you want but don't screw it up, Millie, just screw the man. Got it? Not any man, that man.' She jabs at the email. 'He's the one they want. The one I want.'

I have a sudden, hysterical, urge to break into 'You're the One That I Want' and fling my arms about, John Travolta style. But I don't.

'Make it up if you have to, but I didn't say that. Now can you go and find him or something? I'm meeting Daniel later and I need a pedi, he's got a thing about feet.' She waves me away as she busies about, dropping her laptop into her tote bag and shouting out orders as she marches across the office. 'You've got just under a week! I might even move you to a better slot if it performs as well as the first one,' she yells over her shoulder just before barging her way out of the door.

It is only 8.45 a.m. I am exhausted.

But I have the chance of a better slot!

Chapter Six

JOE

Friday

'What are you grinning at?' Sophie nudges my elbow, so I show her the photo that's just popped up on my mobile. It's my workmates – and a *wish you were here?!* message.

'You should have stayed, looks like you're missing out.'

I shrug. When the email came in yesterday morning I was torn. Really torn.

Subject: End of phase get together

I might not exactly be a party animal, but it's always good to celebrate with the team. Nobody else can quite appreciate the last couple of weeks leading up to a software release – the pressure, the arguments about which corners to cut, the late nights after disastrous test days. Let's face it, nobody else wants a convo about crap computer code and users with impossible demands.

So yeah, I had planned on joining the team for the end of phase celebration this afternoon and had been in the middle of typing a text to Mum to say I'd be getting back late Friday, rather than on my normal Thursday train, when her message to me had landed. The *I think your sister needs an evening out* seemed more important than hanging about for a self-congratulatory afternoon booze-up.

Mum doesn't do drama. If it hadn't been important, she wouldn't have mentioned it at all. Her 'I think' equates to most people's 'get over here ASAP before something disastrous happens'.

So I just typed back: *Sure, see you tonight, might be a bit later than normal – work is busy. I'll tell her Friday night is date night – if you can babysit?*

This project has been a nightmare at times though. We've earned a beer – and it seems the celebration has stretched into a night out. But there'll be others, and there'll only ever be one moment exactly like this one in Sophie's life.

Sophie doesn't often need me; she doesn't often need anybody. Mum must have been seriously worried.

'This is just a normal night out, small-town-sis.' I wink. 'Every night is party night in the big city.'

She laughs, the first proper laugh since I got home last night.

'Oh yeah, cosmo-boy?' She leans in across the table, pushing her empty glass my way. 'Well let's get this par-tay started then.'

I head over to the bar, glancing back over my shoulder while I wait for the drinks to be poured.

She looks knackered. Fragile. I don't know about baby blues, I reckon landing a newborn means you're asked to double your normal work on half your normal sleep, with a background of screaming and smells. I guess they have to have moments of cuteness overload, or they wouldn't survive.

Soph has never been one for a simple life though. She doesn't do anything by halves – not even her love life or her future. She's been brought up in a landlocked farming family and decided to go one better and marry a guy who spends most of his time at sea. Go figure.

Her husband Mike is a nice guy, but he's in the Royal Navy so it's stints of six months and more away, then he's back long enough to make her think she's got a regular life. Before he goes again. It's a good job they love each other enough to survive both – the absences and times together.

He was back for the fun part of baby-making, of course, away for a short stint, then back for most of her pregnancy, then deployed unexpectedly a week after baby Ben arrived.

They talk, but long distance FaceTime isn't that much help when you've got a body raging full of hormones and a mini-me that needs to be nurtured 24/7, I guess.

'Your little Sophie coping okay?' the landlady asks. She

knows us. We all know each other round here. It's the way it is.

'She's fine.' I smile. 'You know Soph, doesn't let anything get her down.' Because that's what you say, isn't it? Not 'Mum is worried', or 'the nurse is keeping an eye on her', or 'I wish her bloody husband would get his arse back here, this is a two-man job.'

'Aye, I know your Sophie. Now, you make sure she doesn't do too much.'

'We will.' I nod, hand over the money and smile as I back away – before I get caught up in a conversation. Spend five minutes too long at the bar in here and before you know it you've shared everything – from what you've had for dinner to your plans for the next twelve months. She's nice, she means well, she's the perfect person if you want to offload your worries, and don't mind them being shared.

'Getting the third degree from Ruth? I bet you miss her!' Sophie takes the drink from me and grins. She's actually looking better already.

'Certainly was, she'll be offering to babysit next.'

'Over my dead body!' Soph puts on a good impression of Mum, giggles, then immediately sobers up. She sinks back into the seat. 'It was good of Mum and Dad to offer to look after him. I needed this.'

'They're his grandparents, you noddle. They want to.'

'Like you wanted to come home last night as normal so that you could come out with me and sit in some country pub, rather than celebrate in the bright lights with your mates?'

'They're just guys I work with,' I say. They are, it was no big deal. And if I'm honest with myself, I had selfish motives as well – coming back to spend Friday night in the pub with Sophie gave me an excuse to skip the party and take my normal Thursday evening train. And maybe see the girl from the station again.

If I'd gone out with the team today, then caught the train this evening, my chances of seeing her would have gone from remote to non-existent.

I just felt the need to be there on a Thursday, just in case.

As it happened though, I had work that had to be signed off, so I got to the station later than normal – but there was still a chance she'd be there, running late, wasn't there?

I could have sworn that last Thursday after we'd gone our separate ways, I'd seen her sitting on the train I should have been catching. If I hadn't been delayed by some guy I used to work with and hadn't seen for ages.

Though I'm probably wrong. It could have been anybody gazing through that window as the train pulled out of the station without me. She could have been on any train, going anywhere. She could have just been passing through King's Cross and actually on her way to St Pancras, going to Paris.

What on earth makes me think she'd be on a train heading to the northeast? Really?

'What are you thinking about?'

I refocus, and Sophie is peering at me over the top of her glass. 'That Mum couldn't wait for some quality time without you interfering! She'll be tapping into his subconscious and planting the desire to be a farmer!'

'Ha ha, very funny!'

We share a smile. Mum never tried to influence either of us. She did what she did because she said it was all she'd ever wanted. Her farming parents hadn't tried to influence her, it was just in her blood. In her soul.

She also said, in brisk practical mode, that we weren't going to be lazy and let somebody tell us what to do, it was up to us to work it out. She had her journey and we had ours.

'So, city boy, what's next if this project is done and dusted? Coming home?' She's teasing; she knows that whenever I'm back here, a part of me is twitchy. Itching to get back.

'There's more work, I've got at least a couple of weeks, I reckon, but then...' I shrug.

'No guarantees?'

'No guarantees.' I've not got wanderlust, it's not that I want to be anywhere but here. Here is my second favourite place, but my favourite is London.

'You should try and get a permanent job down there. It's a bit of a lottery, isn't it, just hoping a suitable contract comes up?'

'True.' I've been thinking the same myself for a while now. The software house I work for gets a shitload of work in London, but there's always the risk that when this contract comes to an end, they could want me to go somewhere else. 'They're sending Steve to Bristol. I could be next.'

'Bristol's nice.'

'Sure.' I nod.

'Big city vibe?'

I'd never see my train-girl again. New digs, new job. New commute. The thought makes me feel empty inside. I've never felt like this about the possibility of moving on to a different job. I like the change, the challenge.

But I like where I am. I like my digs. I like train-girl.

I don't want to think about it right now. I steer the conversation away from me. 'How's Mike getting on out at sea then?'

'He's fine, loving fatherhood!' She laughs.

'I bet! Nappy-free, full night's sleep.'

She sighs. 'He wishes he was here actually; he says he's missing out, he's missing me and Ben.'

'I know.' Like I say, he's a nice guy. He's not an accidental father, he's solid. He wanted a family as much as Sophie did.

'I wish he was as well.'

'I know that too.' When he's home he's there 24/7 for Sophie. Looking after her, making sure she's got everything she wants. Making her happy. He'll be a great dad. It's just a shame he's away for such long stretches.

A shame that most of the time she has no clue exactly where he is, or whether he'll even get back.

'But I did know what I was getting into,' she adds slightly defensively, just to make sure that I haven't forgotten that she isn't blaming anybody for her current state of mind.

'Maybe it would be a good thing if Mum persuades Ben to get back to his roots!' I grin. 'At least you'll know where he is and that he'll always be home for tea!'

'Very funny. God help us if it's true about them taking after their grandparents rather than their parents – he'll either be a maths geek like Dad, a shit shoveller like Mum, or very confused! Want another?'

I glance down at my nearly empty glass.

'Oh, come on, don't cop out on me yet, Joe-bro! I need a drink!'

'So do I. It's been a busy week.'

She falters for a second. 'Or do you think we need to get back? I mean, we've been out—'

I push my empty glass towards her but hold on to it as she goes to pick it up. 'It's okay to want some me-time, Soph. He'll be fine.'

'I know.'

I watch her head to the bar and wonder what it would be like sitting in here opposite my train-girl. Would she go for a glass of pinot, or half a cider? Would she think this place is quaint and countrified, or would she feel at home? I live in two worlds, I love both, but I've no idea what she likes. Where she is comfortable.

Or whether she's dating some other guy. Was heading home to a cosy night in.

I just know that something deep down inside me says she wasn't. That I was meant to meet her.

I could be deluded.

She wasn't on the train last night. What makes me think I will ever see her again?

In a couple of weeks, I could be leaving London. Heading somewhere new.

Chapter Seven

MILLIE

Thursday 24th March. Two weeks later.

'OMG, you found him!' Zoe's sharp chin digs into my shoulder. 'Wow—' she digs in deeper '—this is scorching, even better than the first post. Carla is going to be wetting herself, this guy is so hot.'

Sadly, I didn't find him. I went to the station the Thursday before last after my chat with Carla, and again last Thursday. No sign. Nothing. But, hey, maybe like me he'd been travelling on a different day to his normal commute. Maybe he was a Friday guy normally. So, I'd also got to the station super early the last two Fridays.

I have never in my life chased after a man, but I skulked up and down every bloody platform. I accosted total strangers who had toned bums that resembled his. I relentlessly chased men carrying umbrellas and wearing red scarves.

I was propositioned by a creep who had 'been watching me for an hour' and thought I needed a good seeing to.

I was informed by a guitar-playing busker that the Lord would solve my problems. He'd then offered me half his takings and told me I needed to slow down and think before I took the wrong path in life.

It was at this point that I gave up, as I realised that I had more chance of being arrested by the transport police than of finding my sexy train-guy.

Do I really want to find him though? Maybe it's better not to. Better that he never knows he has featured in my column, because, let's face it, mentioning people I actually know has never gone that well for me, has it? There are three stages.

They're briefly flattered.

Then outraged.

Then take their revenge.

Well, my hairdresser did. I went in one day all jolly and looking forward to sleekness and shine – and came out with bright blue highlights and a choppy cut that I definitely didn't ask for… after she recognised herself. And as for Seb, my three-date wonder, I don't want to go there. He went absolutely ape-shit when I wrote about our drunken fumble that fell flat, or should I say floppy, after four hours of building up expectations (just to be clear, he was doing the building, I had the expectations). He let me off for mentioning the up-your-nostril snog the week before (date two), but he said this was a step too far. Unforgivable. Everybody would know it was him. Which does beg the question, how often has this happened to him if it makes him instantly recognisable? I reckon I had a lucky escape; it could be a good job I was dumped before things got even more disappointing.

Carla has really piled the pressure on though. She announced, on the Tuesday after ordering the train love-fest, that to give me more time to 'track down photofit man' we would run a three-week 'love on the tracks' column to ramp things up and 'engage readership'. Until Zoe pointed out that only rats get to have it *on* the tracks; any other kind of love would be short-lived when the first train steamed along and squashed it.

This did not go down well, and Zoe was sent to King's Cross to stand under the clock (the outside one, in the rain, not the inside, romantic, one) and do some consumer research i.e. question commuters about whether they'd ever got a shag out of a trackside encounter.

Anyway, it gave me some breathing space. But I still haven't managed to work out how to find train-guy.

In desperation I have resorted to writing the truth, because Carla needs something today so that she can run it on Monday.

Monday is my new prime-time slot.

There are lots of songs about Mondays. None of them end well.

But Carla has decided that this is what people crave after their disappointing weekends. Hot off the press. 'The weekend they wish *they'd* had instead of their sad reality' were her words.

I have written about my real first (one and only) brief encounter with train-guy, and the umbrella. 'Confessions of a Randy Commuter' (okay, I've just added in the randy bit, and I'm not, honestly, but we all know what everybody is after) has to work, because if it does then:

a) I keep my column (and maybe even go up in the rankings), and…

b) I can raise the matter of working from Hexham on a Friday and Monday, so that I can support my mum and save my childhood home from the clutches of evil estate agents (I stand more chance with Carla if I ramp up the drama).

I'm panicking if I'm honest, worried that if I don't move quickly Carla will change her mind, or Mum will make a rash decision and talk to Sam again before I can persuade her that we can sort this. Not that I can turn into a gardener overnight, or possibly ever (who wants to go to bed with soil under their fingernails, fretting about slugs and fertiliser?), but I'll worry about that bit later.

I got a message from her this morning saying, *You're right. I'm going to take him up on his offer, you have to grab these opportunities while you can! See you Friday x.*

I'm right? What does she mean I'm right? I never bloody said she should sell up. I might have said Dad would have understood, but I never said this was a not-to-be-missed opportunity.

I also didn't commit to going this weekend. We'd left it open.

I called her. She didn't pick up – on her mobile or the

landline. I messaged her a *Got time for a chat?* and got back *Can it wait until later? I'm having my highlights done!* This can only mean one thing: she is making sure she looks her best for Sam!

I'm not proud of this, but I panicked. I went straight onto Trainline and booked a ticket home for this afternoon and messaged. *No probs! Decided to surprise you and come home tonight rather than tomorrow. Chinese takeaway? X p.s. it's quiet at work!* Which would stall any objections. I was right, I just got a thumbs-up and smiley face back.

Smiley is the last thing my face feels though.

'Flippin' heck. I bet he is one hell of a shag.' Zoe cuddles in closer, bringing me back to the here and now, and reads the rest of the post, which I have almost finished. I have reached the climax, as it were. He is just about to run off to jump on some train and leave me gagging for more, throbbing with unrequited lust. My heart, not my, er, bits.

'Er, how much of this is actually true?'

'All of it.' I nod my head slowly. Including (I imagine) the bit she has just said, about him being one hell of a shag. I bet.

I'm pretty honest and open with Zoe, who is my only true work friend. 'Some of the first post was a bit, er…'

'Made up?' She grins.

'Not exactly made up, more—'

'Manufactured?' The grin is broader than ever. Zoe is blond and bubbly. Fun, but totally supportive. We help each other out.

'Shut up. I might have embellished it a bit to make sure it was as commercial as possible,' I say primly.

'Yeah, yeah, yeah. But this?'

'It happened; he was…' I can't quite get the right words to describe him.

'Hot.' She's dropped the grin and has gone a bit swoony. 'Wow, Mill, this is dynamite. It's awesome that you found him again.'

I shake my head slowly. Typing as I do it. Letting him walk away from me.

'Shit,' she frowns, 'you haven't found him?'

My fingers stop, and a little sigh escapes from between my lips. 'Nope. This was when I first met him.' Tweaked slightly, because of course at this point he has to recognise the imaginary girl he imaginary-caught as she fell headfirst down the imaginary escalator and headfirst into love. 'The only inaccurate part of this is where he recognises me. He didn't. It's the first time we've seen each other.'

'Oh God, you have got to find him again. You need him, I need him. Shit, we all need him.' She taps the screen. 'This is so sexy. I don't know what he's done to you, but…' She fans herself dramatically, which makes me grin – despite the fact that my insides have started to churn. Not with lust, with panic.

'I don't know how to find him.' The problem isn't just that I scoured the station on Friday, and there was no sign of him, but that there was also no other guy who I thought could give me palpitations, or that I even fancied a quick snog with. Or a peck on the cheek. Or I'd be happy to even brush pinkies with.

There was nothing I could work with.

This is one of my problems. I can half-fancy somebody after a few drinks, but I've never before bumped into a guy who has given me chills and a hot flush at the same time just by looking at me. Let's face it. Most hot guys don't look at me anyway.

Luckily my 'things to achieve before I am thirty' list does not include being pregnant, married, engaged or even regularly dating. It does not include men at all.

Anyway, the station was heaving with the normal commuters during my stalk-fest on Friday. Hot, sweating and impatient – but not for sex. Whoever in their right mind would think it was possible to find love at King's Cross? They must be mad.

'Don't know how to find him, or don't want to?' Zoe is not grinning now; she is looking at me intently. She knows me better than I'm sometimes comfortable with.

'I do want to!' I say, my cheeks heating up.

'I know you, Miss Workaholic, and—' her eyes narrow '—my guess is you're scared to find him, because that—' she points at my screen '—is from the heart, girl.'

'Oh rubbish, I'm a writer, I—'

'I can tell the real thing when I read it, Mills, and that is real!'

My heart is pounding slightly harder than it should be doing. The thing is, I did look. I wasn't avoiding him, but some tiny part of me was half-hoping I'd not find my train-guy and I'd just have to make it all up.

Not honest. Not authentic.

'I reckon you need your train-guy, he could save your life!'

'Oh, stop being melodramatic! This all belongs in your secret novel and—'

Zoe freezes as I feel a presence on my other side.

It can only mean one thing. Carla.

We await judgment, like two rabbits caught in the glare.

'Shit hot, girl! That is what we need!'

'See!' Zoe says triumphantly, winking at me. 'Just what you need!'

I ignore her and glance up at Carla, who gives me a thumbs-up and the type of smile you reserve for photographers. This is the Carla-equivalent of extreme happiness. I take it she likes train-guy Part 2. But what the hell am I going to do for Part 3?

'Except he doesn't go off and get on some train and possibly meet some other girl, does he?' Her smile has dimmed down. It is sweet now, dangerous. So is the saccharine tone.

I can feel the colour rush to my cheeks.

'Well, er.' How does she know that this was where it ended?

'Whether he did, or did not, he is not doing today.' She leans over me and hits delete, delete, delete on my keyboard, until train-guy is back where he belongs. At the entrance to the station. Under the clock. 'And now, Amelia, he turns to look at you. Gazes into your eyes. You –' she emphasises the word '– are going to be the heroine, not just some random. Right?'

I nod vigorously. 'Deffo. I am not some random to him.'

'And that is where it ends. For now.'

I gulp, nod, my cheeks burning even brighter.

'Perfect!' Her proper smile is back again, and so is the thumbs-up. 'Get it polished and over to me ASAP.'

'On its way!' I smile back, as happily as I can, and return the thumbs-up. I'm not sure she sees it as she is already on her way back to her office.

Zoe sniggers.

Fuck.

I go to the top of the document, and optimistically put 'Episode 2' to cheer myself up. Because this is going to work. One way or another, I am going to make this work.

I'll find my guy (or some guy), fall in love, keep my career firmly on track, spend more time with Mum and be living my best life when I hit the big three-o.

Course I will. Never stop believing in yourself, as Dad would say.

The thought of Dad makes me pause for a second. It always does. Which is when I notice the time.

Double fuck. I need to get a move on. I grab at belongings, shoving them in my bag.

'I'd better go, Zoe. Had some weird message from Mum so I said I'd go home today. I've booked tomorrow off.'

'Sure. Is she okay?'

I shrug. 'I'm not sure. I really should spend more time

with her. She worries about everything, but then tells me she's fine.'

Zoe smiles, but this time it is soft, not a grin. 'Like mother like daughter, eh? What time's your train?'

I glance at the time again on my mobile before I shove it in my pocket. 'Oh bugger, I'm going to miss it if I don't run.' Thursday used to be a quieter day to travel than Friday, so it was nice to do it when I could, but these days it seems busy every day. 'Have a good weekend.'

'You too! Say hi to the sheep for me, my little country bumpkin.'

Zoe thinks that Northumberland consists of moors and sheep, and very little else. She'd probably be shocked to know there are beaches, and reliable WiFi.

I suppose that's one better than Carla, who (if she ever ventured north of the M25) would expect to find Blackpool Tower there.

The station is rammed. But even though I'm late, and it's not even my normal commuting day, I can't help myself. I scan the crowds, looking for train-guy. Hoping for a glimpse of a red scarf. Somebody jostles my elbow, I catch sight of the umbrella out of the corner of my eye and it's like déjà vu. I stop, my heart in my mouth, oh my God! It's happening. It's really happening!

I spin round, the laugh already bubbling out of me.

'Soz mate.'

My grin fades as our gazes meet. The eyes aren't his. They're brown, the face framed by dreadlocks, a hefty rucksack banging for a second time against my arm as he winks and pushes on.

Arghhhh! I shouldn't be disappointed, but I am. I'm gutted.

Because of course I need to see him for Part 3. That is all. Without him it won't work.

I do a quick time check; I haven't even got time to grab a coffee. I'd better get a move on. Get on the train. Live my normal life, one that definitely doesn't involve hot guys crushing me against their manly chests. Whatever Zoe thinks.

I will wing it with my 'Confessions'. Definitely. I can do it. It's worked before, it will work again. There's so much material to work with in a busy place like this. So many other people actually living out true-life romances, with all the bad bits as well as the good.

I just need to cherry-pick the highlights.

The platform is as packed as the rest of the station, which is odd. Specially for a Thursday. I glance up at the announcement board and grind to a halt.

Bugger. It's running ten minutes late, and, even worse, the previous service didn't run at all. Everybody who was waiting for that train is now about to clamber on to mine. I probably won't even get a seat, which means I won't get the work done I was hoping to. I can't polish the post up for Carla. She'll kill me.

Travelling mid-afternoon means I get there for supper at

a reasonable time, but I rely on getting a seat with a table and being able to do a few hours work.

I fish my mobile out, to message Mum and warn her I might be late, when there's a surge forward towards the edge of the platform as the train appears in the distance. I pocket my phone and move forward ready for the scrum; no way am I standing all the way to Newcastle, where I have to change trains.

Christ, it's a bloody good job I didn't get a coffee, this is an elbows-out-shove-your-way-on boarding.

I'm carried by the crowd as we all pile on, but I've got my fingers crossed. Please, please, please, let my reserved seat still be free! I'm not up for a stand-up row with somebody who had the same seat booked on the previous service, or who really, really needs it because they're old, infirm or just too big to argue with. I hate confrontation over silly things.

My feet ache, and my head is beginning to ache too, as I'm swept along knowing that I've potentially got three hours of standing on a swaying train.

Or sitting on the floor in that tiny, smelly space by the toilet. Yuk.

The train starts up abruptly before we've had chance to get to our seats, and there's a rolling wave of humanity as we all stagger forward. I've never been gladder that I'm wearing flats.

I have also never been more pleased to see a reserved seat that is still empty. It is mine! Yay!

I shimmy past a very large man who is half-blocking the

way and sink down smugly, gazing round at my fellow commuters happily. I have a seat. I have a table. I can work. Is it too early to have a celebratory G&T from the on-board refreshments?

There's just enough room on the table to squeeze my laptop in, but for once I do not care that the woman opposite is using all of her table-top space and probably a third of mine. Well, I do care a little bit, because I am having to hold my stomach in to make room for my keyboard, and I can't keep that up for more than three minutes tops – well, thirty seconds if I'm honest. And I probably look slightly deformed, trying to type with my thumbs resting on my boobs and my chin jammed down so hard my neck is bulging.

Not a good look. Good job train-guy isn't actually… my thought processes grind to a halt as I look at the latest email. From Carla. Thanking me for train-guy Part 2, reminding me she needs the final version like right now, and she needs Part 3 ASAP, and asking when I'll be able to get some lip action in.

I might have a seat, but I do not have train-guy and I have never needed a man so much in my life. Not of course for sex or love, for other more practical – essential – reasons. Sexual gratification is not essential, it is an add-on. Which is perfectly acceptable for a modern woman.

I do not have a clue what I am going to write next. I've barely got enough elbow wriggle room to type, my shoulder blades are pinched together so tightly they hurt, and I have just waded through a station that was like a rugby scrum, where Cupid wouldn't have had a chance of hitting anything with his little bow and arrow.

Oh my God, this is depressing. How can I even pretend that anybody has a chance of falling in love? More chance of tripping onto the tracks. I should call this Commuter Crush, 101 ways to body-slam a man and possibly die, not fall in love.

I stare out of the window, giving up on the pretence of tapping on my keyboard.

This is real life, and I'm fucked.

I'd fall down on my knees, risk ridicule and pray for him to reappear if I thought it would help. But I'm not convinced.

There also isn't enough room.

And are Carla and I feeding into some false hope?

Is there really somebody out there for everybody, lurking just round the corner? Or is it dangerous to daydream, better to bury yourself in work? In family? Hook up with somebody you've known all your life?

Which reminds me. I need to message Mum with an update.

The train clatters into Newcastle on schedule. Well, not the proper schedule, its new schedule given that we set off late. As it pulls in, there is an announcement to warn passengers in carriage E (my carriage) that the rear door is not operating correctly and that we need to exit via the door in the next carriage.

I fight my way between the passengers who didn't manage to get a seat, and are blocking the corridor, a flutter of panic in my chest that I am about to be stuck on the train. That I will be in Scotland before I know it.

'Excuse me, excuse, sorry...' People move slowly, reluctantly. Why don't they get out of my way? It's pretty obvious that the train is about to stop, and I'm trying to get off.

My heart rate slows slightly as I catch up with the girl in front, who is trying to get off as well. If there's a stream of us, they can't slam the door shut and trap us half on, half off, can they?

Not even officious guards can do that.

There's a slight clatter as she drops her phone. It bounces off the table, falls to my feet and I awkwardly bend to grab it – hoping the train doesn't choose this moment to grind to a complete halt leaving me headbutting her bum.

It doesn't.

'Hey, you dropped...' I tap her shoulder, hold it up. She turns, a puzzled look on her face.

'Not mine!' She waves her mobile. 'Think it's his.' And points over the man in front's shoulder to the one in front of him. I can only just see a head.

What do I do? I can't leave it here, but I can't clamber over bodies. And I'm not sure lobbing it would work. I don't have a very good aim, and I could get arrested for throwing dangerous objects at strangers. 'Could you pass...?'

She gives a dramatic sigh. 'No. I'm busy.'

I'm tempted to suggest she could stop chatting just for one nano-second, but the fierce look puts me off.

'Give it to him when we get off.' There's almost, but not quite, a 'duh' at the end. But she is right, the train is stuttering to a stop.

The doors open, letting in a whoosh of wonderful clean fresh air.

'Hey! Hey!' I push past Miss Unhelpful, hitting the platform at a jog. I just need to keep the top of his head in sight, not confuse it with another head, but it's so bloody busy.

And he is doing his best to disappear into the crowd. He's striding out, ducking and diving as though he's got a train to catch. Ha ha.

I could take it to lost and found, but it's so bloody annoying if you lose your phone, isn't it? I'd hate to get out of the station and discover I hadn't got mine. I have to at least try.

Oh bugger, people keep getting in my way, and he's getting further in front. There is only one option left to me. Sorry, Mum, but a girl has to do what a girl has to do, however unladylike. I stop. Take a deep breath. And bellow.

'Oi! You in the red scarf!'

I have to admit, it must have been quite impressive, because quite a few people stop and stare. None of them wearing a red scarf.

Actually, what is it about red scarves? I've never noticed any man wearing one, until train-guy, and now they've suddenly become a feature in my life. Is there some strange significance? Anyway, he seems to have forgotten he's got one, or he's deaf.

Luckily, I am not embarrassed, because I'll be on my next train soon, I'll never see these people again.

Unless they get on the Hexham train.

Shit, he's not heard me. But a very large gentleman behind him has. He points at 'red scarf man'. I nod. And he taps him on the shoulder with the type of force designed to send him flying off his feet.

The prat doesn't fly. He does however stop and half turn. Hallelujah!

'Yes, you! Red scarf man!' I splutter. This mobile better had be his, it's bloody hard running after men and shouting that loudly. His hand goes to the scarf around his neck, and he looks down as though he had no idea that he had it on. 'You dropped your phone!'

And then he looks straight at me.

Our gazes lock as he pats his pocket, realises it is empty, starts to stride back towards me.

And with each step my world seems to shrink.

My breath freezes in my body.

Chapter Eight

MILLIE

'Hey.' The softly spoken word as he reaches me, stops in front of me, sends a shiver down my neck.

'I think this is yours?' I croak out.

It's him. It is really him.

It is train-guy.

He's here, within touching distance. And I want to touch him, just to check he's real, that he won't fade into thin air.

Then his fingers close around mine, and his phone, and my whole body seems to perk up.

This is Zoe's fault. It's ridiculous, I do not need him, I am not responding to him in any unusual way at all.

I am.

My throat has dried up. My fingers are trembling.

He smiles. 'You have saved my life!' The deep voice is instantly recognisable. Then he pauses. Does a double take. 'Oh hell, it's you! It is you, isn't it?'

My hand tightens around the phone, and I stare at him.

How could I ever think I wouldn't recognise him again? Those eyes, that smile, that voice.

I'd recognise him if he was half a mile away on the other side of a dark stadium, in a crowd of people. Well, okay, I wouldn't recognise the back of his head, on a train. Obviously.

My train. Bloody hell we've been sharing the same train for the past three hours. We've been metres apart and I didn't know. He was in the next carriage!

He's got the same worried look he had after he gave me an impromptu shower; he's slightly awkward in a way that makes him even more attractive. 'Sorry, I'm the guy who tried to drown you a couple of weeks ago? You probably don't remember me.'

We're practically nose to nose. Both still clutching his mobile between us. I want to yell out that of course I remember. 'Are you kidding me?' I think I just said that out loud. But I want to grab him, kiss him all over frantically. Because he has just saved my career. Absolutely no other reason at all. Zoe is wrong, I'm just reacting like this because of the anticipation that has built up inside me – the hope I'd see him again, and what would happen if I did. This is gratitude, relief – not lust. 'How can I forget that umbrella!'

'Ha ha, I'm never going to live that one down, am I?' He shrugs slightly bashfully.

'It's fine, I got over it. I didn't shrink!' Okay, I have totally put him on the spot. Any second now he's going to run out on me. 'Honest, happens all the time!'

'Not quite that disastrously! But hey, moving on, let me get you a coffee this time?'

I'm torn, I'm really torn as I glance up at the station clock.

This is not me being pulled into a relationship that will churn me up inside, show me a happy ever after that includes everything I ever wanted, and then leave me wrung out and doubting anybody can ever love me and stay with me because I'm a career-obsessive who doesn't know how to prioritise properly.

This is work.

So why am I all shaky on the outside and fluttery on the inside? Why do I want to hold onto this moment as long as I can?

'I've got to get another train, a connection.' Even my voice wavers. Why does this have to happen to me? Maybe we could just stand here for another few seconds, hands wrapped around his phone?

'So do I.' He is still standing in front of me. Waiting.

There's a booming announcement, of the 'next train on platform' type.

'That's mine! There's normally a longer transfer time, but it was late and…' This is so unfair. Normally I have ages to waste. I can be hanging about at this flaming station for thirty minutes or more. More than enough time to have a coffee with a stranger.

Should I miss it, get the next one? But I can't do that to Mum, not for work. How can I even think it?

'That train is yours? You're kidding? Mine too.' His

smile broadens. 'I reckon I've just got time to grab one for you if there's not a queue, and I'm gasping so I'm getting one for myself anyway, and…' His voice tails off. He's smiling straight at me. Gazing into my eyes earnestly, waiting for a response. Oh my God, how can I say no?

'If I'm quick.' He tugs at his phone gently, to make the point. Bloody hell, what am I thinking (or not thinking), I'm still clutching his phone, like a lifeline. I let go.

'You're on the Hexham train? On this platform?' Bloody hell! This cannot be happening. He is about to get on MY train. Again. This time we will not be a carriage or two apart. This time he is mine. This is fate. I'm a great believer in coincidences, in not walking under ladders, in white feathers that tell me Dad is still with me. In signs.

I'm sticking with him, even if I have to sit on his knee, or dangle from the luggage rack.

Whatever it takes. He is not going to be the one that got away.

'Sure! The one that arrives in er—' he checks his watch '—four minutes!'

I grin. 'Go then! Quick, what are you waiting for?'

'Talk on the train?' I nod. 'Don't let it go without me!'

No chance.

If this train arrives before he gets back, I might have to straddle, one foot on and one off, or more likely just refuse to close the door because I am not – even for love, lust or the chance of promotion – risking being ripped in two. But I am not going without him. With or without the train.

'Sure, er, I mean, no! I won't. Definitely not.' Why am I rambling on? He needs to get a move on. 'Go!'

'Hey, what's your name? For the cup! And how do you take it?'

'It's Millie, and an americano please.'

'Milk?'

I shake my head.

'Don't go away, Millie!' He takes a step back, never breaking eye contact, grinning. Then he waves a finger and jogs off, glancing back over his shoulder once as he goes.

I stand hugging myself, grinning like a simpleton. Go away? He must be kidding.

I grab my mobile and open up a note.

Ep Three. And that's when it happened. I saw him again. So it seems like fate is telling me that this could be it. That it was meant to be, that I need to make sure I see him again...'

Chapter Nine

JOE

I cannot believe it. What are the chances of bumping into the girl you've been daydreaming about when you jump off your train, racing so you don't miss your connection?

I'd been desperate to get off the crowded train, forced my way through the scrum to try and replace the heavy smell of body odour with semi-fresh air. But then I turned and saw her, and in a split second I forgot all about that. None of it mattered.

For a moment I thought she might not recognise me, but then she smiled, laughed, looked genuinely pleased to see me!

And now she's within touching distance. We're getting on the same train.

'I won't be a second, don't let it go without me!'

She laughs, and her chestnut brown hair swings around her shoulders. She's even prettier than I remembered. I hover, like some idiot, but I don't want to stop looking at her. But I'm being a jerk, what's she going to do? Disappear into thin air?

Well, yeah, if my imagination has conjured her up, because, let's face it, she's been pretty constantly in my head since I first saw her.

But the touch of her hand, her soft skin, was real. It feels like the imprint of her fingers still lingers on my own skin; the smell of her perfume is still in my head.

She remembers me! I'm gawping like a simpleton. I take a step back, then another, unwilling to break eye-contact with her. The girl I thought I'd lost for ever.

'Hurry up, go!' Her soft voice vibrates with laughter, and I grin back, before giving her a thumbs-up and jogging off to get the coffee.

There's a queue, there's always a queue, but today with the mess-up with trains the station is even busier than ever. If the train goes, will she wait for me?

'Black americano, for Millie, one with milk for Joe.' I'm so edgy, I snap out the order. Then force myself to take a deep breath. Chill. Stop my fingers tapping on the counter.

How does she spell her name, with a 'y' or 'ie'? The guy doesn't ask. He's busy, under pressure from people like me who are in a hurry.

I'm normally pretty chilled. I don't mind waiting for my connection, I like public transport. It's fine when I can chill, gaze out of the window and let my brain loose on some knotty problem I've not been able to solve in the office. There's something freeing about being on the move, with only silent strangers around and the scenery whizzing past in a blur. But this is different, I'm on edge.

It is so unreal. It is weeks, three weeks, since I bumped into her at King's Cross station, and I'd pretty much given up hope of ever seeing her again. I mean, three weeks is like a lifetime. But now here she is, completely out of the blue, and it is just like the first time.

But better.

I'd been a bit scared that if I did see her again it would be a complete anti-climax. That she wouldn't be as pretty as the image in my head, that I'd realise I'd blown our first meeting out of all proportion and there was nothing between us at all. No connection. She'd just be an ordinary girl.

Or she wouldn't recognise me. Wouldn't remember me at all.

'Here you go, mate.'

'Cheers.' I grab the coffee cups. An announcement booms over the tannoy, the train is about to come in.

This feels a bit like I'm stepping into the unknown. It doesn't feel at all like any feeling I've had when I've met up with a girl before. Not that it's even a date, but something inside me is saying that I need to go for this. Make things happen.

I do it at work all the time, so why not with Millie?

Dad has always told me to get out there, to see the world, to never look back – always forward. That actions speak far louder than blowing my own trumpet or trying to impress people with words.

He's been right professionally, but right now I think I'm going to have to find words. To ask her the questions that I've been dying to.

To show her that I'm the guy she'd like to date.

It's making me nervous as well, but strangely hyped up. Normally I'm the guy on the train who has got his head down, working. I've always been happy just people-watching, but today I want to talk. I want to talk to her. There are so many questions I want to ask her. But knowing me, my mind will go blank when I'm with her. If she waits.

Although if I don't get my arse into gear, I'm going to be the guy left on the platform with two coffees, no girl and a ticket that isn't valid on the next train.

Chapter Ten

MILLIE

Luckily, train-guy comes just as the train starts to draw into the platform. I do not have to make the decision whether to risk life or limb.

We jump onto it, laughing, shoulder to shoulder and sink down onto the first two seats we come to.

'You saved my life, finding my phone!' he says.

'You've saved mine with this coffee!' I laugh.

Our gazes meet, and the smile fades from his face.

'I was hoping I'd bump into you again,' he says softly.

I'm about to say, 'So was I', when the train lurches into action and we both reach for the coffee cups to stop them flying off the table.

He raises an eyebrow and speaks again. 'Well, not bump!'

'Maybe not.' I laugh. He's funny. He's smart. 'Oh, you're kidding me?'

'What?'

I hold my cup up, then spin it round, so that he can see, and point at the name on it. 'Jilly?'

He looks at his own, and chuckles. 'Oh, shit, Mo? Jilly and Mo?'

'So, I take it you're a Joe really?'

'I certainly am.' He holds out a hand to shake awkwardly, given our cramped situation. 'Joe Greenwood, pleased to meet you.'

'Millie.' I smile back as I clasp his warm hand.

'With an "ie", or a "y"? So I know for next time!'

Oh my God. He's already thinking 'next time'.

'Millie with an "ie"!' It takes another lurch of the train to remind me that I need to let go. I don't really want to, but I do. I try and stop gazing into his eyes, glance down and sip my too-hot coffee as a distraction. 'Come here often?' Corny lines are allowed when you're stuck on a train with the man you've been waiting to reappear in your life. If not waiting all your life, at least waiting a few weeks. I can't help myself; I look back up at him.

'Every Thursday, back to my homeland, for my sins.' The corner of his mouth quirks up. He's beautiful. He can't be real. 'I missed the train last time I saw you, got held up by some guy from work and had to get the later one, or we might have got to chat then!'

So that's why he was staring across at the platform as it pulled out. He wasn't looking at me, he was looking at the train. The train he was supposed to be on.

'You're kidding?'

'I thought I spotted you on it, then convinced myself it

had been wishful thinking.' There's a tinge of pink along his cheekbones that makes me pause.

He's been wishfully thinking. About me. Wow! I wriggle in my seat, then realise I'm edging a bit closer – and shuffle back abruptly.

'I've not seen you since. Is this like a regular trip?'

Has he been searching for me, in the same way I've been looking out for him? 'Oh yeah, I head back this way a lot. Not every week, but a bit more lately. I usually do Fridays; when I saw you on the Thursday it was a one-off. Well, a two-off because here I am again.' I smile back at him. I'd been right to come back to the station on a Thursday; it *is* his day, even if, somehow, I managed to miss him two weeks on the run.

The first time was a Thursday, not my normal going-home day. Because it was Dad's anniversary. If it hadn't been for that, we would never have met at all. It really does feel like we were meant to meet. That this is right.

He turns his coffee cup round self-consciously. 'I haven't been able to get it out of my head, being such a clumsy idiot. God knows what you think of me. I don't normally soak gorgeous girls.'

'It's fine.' He called me gorgeous. He's not been able to get me out of his head. Well, the fact he drenched me, we can work on the rest.

'I did wonder if we'd bump into each other, but then I've been caught up with deadlines at work the past couple of weeks and had to catch a later train than normal. But you wouldn't have been here anyway, if Friday is your normal day.'

'No, true.' I can't admit that I've been here the last couple of Thursdays, stalking, can I? Heck though, I might have missed him by minutes. I might have been giving up and leaving the station seconds before he rolled up. 'But great that we're both here at the same time today!' Better than great, nothing short of a miracle. Meant to be.

Work though. This is a work opportunity, that is all. Must not forget that bit. Part 3 coming up. This could be brill! A nearly missed connection, a shared coffee, our first real not-so-brief encounter.

'Anything planned for the weekend then?' I really need to brush up on my chat-up lines or he'll make sure he avoids me for sure.

'More work!' He grins. 'I go back to help my folks out with the farm. Well, Mum really, Dad's a townie at heart who likes to hide out and do complicated maths equations with his online pupils.'

I raise an eyebrow. Not about the maths, I could see him with a studious father, but I can't quite see him as a farmer. His hands are too warm and gentle, his fingers long, his look slightly earnest.

'You're a farmer?' This could be a bit of a disaster. I'm not sure that farming talk is what Carla is after. She will definitely sack me if I write about turnips and sheep.

'Oh God, no!' He grins.

Phew.

'Do these hands look like they work the land?'

He holds his hands up, his grin broadening. It gives me the opportunity to study a part of his body without feeling I shouldn't. Okay, they are only hands, but they are still worth staring at. His hands are broad, without being chunky, his fingers quite long but they're strong. Workmanlike, rather than artistic. I can see the farmer hidden in him, even if his skin isn't scarred with old blisters and the dry roughness that comes with working outside.

I bet they're warm hands, capable hands, gentle. Those fingers won't just skate over skin with a feather-like touch, they're hands that you'll know are there. Searching. Firm.

I blink, suddenly aware that even with the invite, I've probably been staring for a bit too long. And fantasising. 'No soil under those nails as far as I can tell!' I rasp through my dry throat. I'm very tempted to grab one, so that I can check out the dirt situation, and feel his skin against mine.

He chuckles. Moves his hands away. This is a good thing, and a bad thing. Probably good, on balance.

'It's not my thing really, it isn't Dad's either, but Mum was born and bred to it, and she won't let go.'

'She's always lived on a farm?' I need to stop thinking about fondling hands. Try and act like a normal person.

'She has. She's always lived on the same one actually, she was born there.'

'But your dad?'

'Dad was brought up in the next village, but he went to the private school, played cricket, had holidays in France and is obsessed with algebra and probability. When they met, the only experience he had of working the land was mowing the lawn. They couldn't be more different, considering they were born only a few miles apart.' He pauses. 'But they found each other and that was that.' He shrugs, and when he speaks again his tone is soft. 'Dad says if the farm makes her happy, then it makes him happy. The things you do for love, eh?' He shakes his head, and another part of my insides melt. This guy is a true romantic, but in a totally matter-of-fact, isn't-this-normal kind of way. 'I sometimes wish she wasn't so bloody stubborn though, and they'd sell up and retire. They could go on holiday, buy a nice little place.'

'And take up bridge and coffee mornings?'

He laughs. 'Okay, okay. You're probably right, she'd be bored stiff. But it's bloody hard work, and they never get a day off to just chill. Dad always told me to use my brain, get out and live.' A hint of a frown clouds his features. 'He's so bloody clever, really smart,' he says, thoughtfully. 'Really, really smart. But you'd never know it, he's not one to do stuff to impress other people, he does it because he wants to. He just quietly gets on with it, does it for himself, and that's what he always told me to do.'

'So you did, you do?' I don't think Joe would show off either. I can see him quietly getting on with it. 'Get out and live?'

'I did, I do! Exactly.' He grins. 'And I have to say, I'm loving it. It's like, freedom.' He throws his arm as wide as the crowded space will let him. 'New, exciting stuff every day.' The grin broadens, the dimples deepen. 'I bet I sound like some overexcited kid!'

'Not at all.' I smile back. 'I'm the same, it was totally starting over again when I got my job.'

'So you do come from Northumberland, not London?'

'I do! Can't you tell? The accent, the not-quite city clothes and hair?' I hold my hands out to the side, palms upwards self-consciously, inviting him to look. Criticise.

'No way! You look like you're a total convert!' His smile is soft at the corners of his mouth. 'But a nice one,' he adds gently.

This pleases me far more than it probably should. I am positively glowing, as though he has paid me a huge compliment.

'Did you miss home when you moved down here?'

'A bit, but I can get on a train, be home in time for tea-ish! It's not that far really, is it?' I've never really thought about how far I've gone. All my thoughts have been about the distance in terms of achievement, lifestyle – not miles. And I still don't feel like I've done enough, gone far enough.

'Just a lifetime.' He studies his hands on the table, his tone thoughtful. For him I guess it must have been a bigger leap. I guess in my head I've lived in London since I was a kid, so I never thought about the actual move. It's only now, since Dad went, that I've felt I'm a long way away from Mum. From my old life. 'It feels like a different world. Different rules.' He catches my eye, and I nod – wanting him to carry on. This feels important, this feels like he is telling me who he really is. Letting me see the real him, even though we don't know each other at all. 'It was odd without my lot at first. It's always been us, the farm. Mum and Dad have always kept themselves to themselves a bit. Well—' he laughs softly glancing up again to meet my gaze '—a lot. It was odd sharing a flat with a stranger, feeling like everyone knew my business when you're used to privacy, but—' he shrugs '—they don't really know, do they? Nobody cares really what you're up to or where you are. Only family, well, some families. I guess I'm lucky I've got the ones I have. So yeah—' he suddenly laughs, self-consciously '—I missed my lot at first, but I got to know people, got on with my job and it's totally amazing. I could never go back. At first, I told myself to get a grip, not fail, but now I'm there because I like it so much. I want to be in London. Dad was right about always looking forward.'

'And your family are happy for you?' I think I'm asking because I'm trying to justify to myself that leaving was okay. That parents are happy when their offspring fly away. As long as they're like homing pigeons and come back now and again.

'Oh yeah. One hundred per cent. Proud as punch, first one on Mum's side of the family to ever go off to university and get a degree.' His cheekbones are pink-tinged, I guess he doesn't like talking about himself, bigging himself up. 'Dad's done it all of course, but she said this is different. I've got her genes.'

I can hear the happiness in his voice, the pride, the affection for his mother, and I want to hug him. That could be me talking about how Dad made me feel when I got my job.

That was me, when I still had him there to boost my confidence, when I wanted to please him, show him I could do it. 'And you go back when you can?'

'To be fair they never actually ask me to go back, and my sister normally does a lot for them, but she's just had a baby and her husband works away and...' He shrugs. 'It's market day on Saturday so Mum needs a hand with getting ready for that. Dad helps but he gets distracted and starts to put things in the wrong boxes. He's more into theoretical problems than practical solutions!' Affection tinges the tone of his voice.

'So, you take after your mum more than your dad?' I want to know, and this is not about work. I really do want to know what he's like, what makes him tick – it's like I need to soak up as much of him as possible. Just in case I don't see him again.

'I guess I'm a bit of a mix. She'd never survive the city, an office, and I love it.' He shrugs. 'But I love getting out on the moors as well, and– ' his eyes twinkle '—I can still work out coding problems while I'm packing homemade chutney!'

'Multi-tasking eh?'

'I can even play the piano and do different things with my two hands!'

I find myself staring at his long fingers and my pulse picks up pace, heat rushing to my cheeks.

'What about you?'

I tear my gaze away from his hands guiltily.

'How often do you get back? Do you miss home?'

Oh, he's asking about that, not multi-tasking and what those hands can do! 'I love London, I used to dream about working in the big city from when I was a little kid. I'd bore everybody with it, telling them how brilliant I was going to be, how I'd have it all. Insufferable brat.'

'I doubt you were insufferable.'

'Okay, obsessed.' We share a smile. 'But I guess—' I've paused, it's something I've only just realised '—I do miss home a bit. I probably don't get back as often as I should,' I finish softly. 'I've been really busy with work—' I try and justify myself '—and my sister moved up to Edinburgh a while ago, so I don't often see her, but I'm going to see Mum. She's struggled since we—' I hesitate, study my hands. I've not talked to anybody about Dad. 'Since we lost my dad a couple of years ago.' I glance his way, and his steady gaze is on me.

'It must be hard.' His tone softens. It feels intimate, as though as he cares, as though he really is listening and nobody else around us matters. 'Did you get to say goodbye, with being away…'

'I did,' I murmur and stare out of the window for a moment, my eyes misting over. 'But I wasn't ready to say goodbye. I wasn't ready for him to go; I never will be. Anyway…' I take a deep breath. I need to move on, not dump on a man I hardly know, however much he looks like he's happy for me to. He's probably just being polite. 'I don't spend enough time with Mum. I normally head home on a Friday, but I decided to go a day early this week.' Before she has a chance to do something she'll regret.

'That's nice.' Nice might be an over-used word, but the way he says it, it means something. 'Oh hey, really sorry, but this is me!' He's already half out of his seat. 'Almost missed it!'

I glance out of the window. How did that happen? We're already at Corbridge – the stop before Hexham. How can forty minutes pass so quickly? It isn't long enough. It isn't anywhere near long enough. I've just quizzed him about his family, I've been trying to work out if I'm doing the right thing, if I should have left home, left Mum. I've not found out anything really about him at all. Not even where he lives, or his phone number!

He stands up, stretches. Straightens his trousers. Reaches up to grab his bag from the overhead rack and hesitates for a second. 'See you next week, maybe? Talk more?'

'Maybe!' Then I watch as he strides down towards the door. He's on the platform. Looking for me, raising a hand. Watching as the train leaves, and I twist round so I can look back, watch until he disappears from sight.

'Maybe.' Why the hell did I say 'maybe'? Why didn't I say, 'Yes, great'? Why didn't I check whether he'd be here on a Thursday or Friday?

I study the passing scenery – without seeing it.

Maybe it's because I don't want to make a big thing of this. I don't want it to be big.

He's lovely, he's perfect for my column because I do actually fancy the pants off him. But he can't live up to the hype in my head, can he?

But talking about hype, how truthful should I be in this week's column? Do I own up to how he actually made me feel – how much I want to touch him, how much I want him to touch me? The flutter of anticipation he's caused inside me – do I want to share it with the world?

So far I have around four sentences, saying this was meant to be.

Is it?

Chapter Eleven

MILLIE

OMG who knew our street was so long? Okay, this could be because I'm staring at my feet as I march along. But I dare not look ahead, because if I do, and there's a 'For Sale' sign, I won't know whether to stop and cry or run back to the train station.

At least meeting train-guy, sorry, Joe, in the flesh totally distracted me from all my worries about Mum. But then he left, and I got off the train, and now I can think about nothing else.

It's weird, I'm practically having palpitations, my heart is pounding so hard. But whatever, I can solve this. I will not panic because I can solve this. But, oh shit, I'm here. Out of the corner of my eye I can see the gate, and even if I couldn't, I'd know I was here because I know every kerbstone, every crack in the pavement, every misplaced garden gnome and badly tended bit of topiary down our road.

I drag my gaze up and let out a huge sigh of relief. There is no 'For Sale' board. Although maybe they don't act that quickly. Maybe they've booked a man to come round tomorrow. Maybe I should check on Rightmove? I'm reaching for my phone when the front door opens.

'What are you doing standing out there, Millie? It's cold, and I went and picked up the Chinese takeaway as soon as you texted to say you were at the station, so it's keeping warm in the oven. Come on, hurry up! Honestly, you're such a daydreaming Delilah!'

I hurry up. And am half out of my coat when I realise that she has not gone to dish out the dinner, she is standing watching me. Arms folded.

'What?'

'I think you better tell me what the hurry was, don't you? You're disrupting my life with all these impromptu midweek visits! You're supposed to come on a Friday, or not at all!' She smiles, to show she's not really cross, but she does want an answer.

'It's not midweek, it's Thursday,' I object. 'Thursday is the start of the weekend. And what do you mean, Friday or not at all?' My insides are all stirred up. This is not going how I thought it would. It's like the biggest anti-climax ever. I'm on the verge of changing my working day, and she doesn't want me here? Maybe I should have discussed this with her, but I just assumed. I mean, that's normal, isn't it?

'You know what I mean, Amelia.'

'I don't.' I am all hot and cold. I am also Amelia, which is not good news.

'You've always just come on a Friday,' she says softly. 'It's not that I don't like seeing you.' She squeezes my arm, but I don't want squeezing. I feel tetchy. Edgy. 'But it's just what works for both of us, isn't it?'

'What do you mean, disrupting your life?' I back off a bit and look at her suspiciously.

'I do have a social life, you know.'

'Really?' I frown, finish taking my coat off and hang it up. I mean, not being funny, but I know she has shopping trips, and coffee with friends, and the occasional lunch and stuff. But she doesn't go *out* out.

'There's no need to sound so surprised, you cheeky thing!'

'I'm not, it's just…' I look her in the eye. I'm not here because she does or doesn't have friends. 'Don't sell the house, Mum!' I blurt out.

'Oh Millie, I told you I wouldn't rush into a decision, and I won't,' she says, her tone soft as she moves in for a hug. 'Is that what this is all about?'

'Your text.' I feel like crying, but instead I bite my lip and hold it together.

'What text?'

'The one saying you were going to take him up on his offer, and it was too good an opportunity to miss! Oh Mum, I know you're worried,' I blither on, even though she's waving a hand as though she wants to interrupt. But this has been building up, I have to say it. All of it. 'And I don't want to interfere, but I don't want some stupid estate agent to bully you into doing something—'

'Millie!'

'... that you don't really want—'

'Millie, stop right there!' she practically bellows, so I do, jaw hanging open. It's the kind of bellow she used when I was a kid and she wanted an emergency stop, because I was about to run out into the road or grab a hot pan. 'What on earth are you going on about? I never said I was going to do that!' There's a tinge of pink along her cheekbones and she looks flustered, or cross, I'm not sure which.

I thrust out my phone, right in her face, and she does the last thing I expect. She sniggers like a naughty schoolgirl. Then stops and looks self-conscious.

'Whoops, I am getting stupid in my old age! That wasn't meant for you, it was meant for Linda!' Her cheekbones are pink, the colour is flooding into her face.

'Linda?' This is worse; she wasn't even going to tell me!

'I must have hit the wrong button, and I didn't even notice. How ridiculous is that? I didn't even realise I'd sent it to the wrong person. Oh, for heaven's sake, I'm so stupid, I need to tell her. She'll be thinking I'm ignoring her now that I've not answered. Hang on, I'd better text her and...'

'Mum, stop! It doesn't matter who you meant to send it to, it says offer—' I point '—and opportunity!'

'Well.' There is more than a hint of pink on her cheeks now, she is crimson. She looks embarrassed, shy. Then sighs and covers her eyes. 'Oh, for heaven's sake I don't know why I'm finding this awkward. You're a grown woman, even if you are my daughter.' She meets my eye. 'Somebody, a man—' she pauses, to give it time to sink in

'—asked if I wanted to go out for a drink and I automatically said no, because, well, you know…'

Mum and Dad met when they were young. I think she's only dated one other man in her whole life.

'But then I thought, why not?'

Oh wow, that's a relief! She wasn't talking about selling up.

'He's very nice.' Her tone is soft. 'I've known him for ages, and it's not like I'm past it, or your dad would have expected me to give up on life, is it?'

Another man. This is weird. How do I feel about this? I shake my head slowly. 'No, he wouldn't.' Not give up. But my mother, out with a man. Possibly kissing, possibly… Eurghhhh. And she just called it an opportunity. An opportunity to what exactly? Oh my God, I feel a bit queasy.

I shake my head to clear it of all the yukky Mum-snogging-a-man-and-worse thoughts. I can't go there. I must not.

'So,' I croak out, 'you've not spoken to Sam, you're not selling?' Quite honestly, it's tons easier thinking about the house than it is to even consider my mother *dating*.

'No, I've not spoken to Sam, but no, I can't say I'm not considering selling, Millie. I haven't decided, I really don't know what to do.'

I suppose one advantage of her seeing a man is she might be distracted (though hopefully not too distracted) and far too busy to talk to estate agents.

One has to look for the positive side of everything.

'But I do know I've got a date tomorrow, so you'll have to sort your own tea out!' There's a glimmer in her eye that tells me this one is non-negotiable.

'Fine. I am capable, you know. You go out and enjoy yourself, after I've come all this way…'

We laugh together.

'I do want you here, you know that, don't you, Millie? Whenever you want. I just don't want to be a burden.' She kisses my cheek.

'You could never be a burden, Mum. And I don't want to get in your way.'

'Well, I can't say you never do that.' She laughs again. Then she wraps her arms round me and I know I'm home.

Chapter Twelve

JOE

Friday

Normally I quite like packing the van for Mum in preparation for the market tomorrow. The repetitive task of stacking trays of eggs, boxes of jars and trays of veg is quite soothing, methodical, lets me think about other things.

Tonight, it is not what I need at all. This evening I'd be better off in town, drinking with workmates. Laughing about work, life. Swapping moves on the latest games we're playing. Talking about the footie.

Tonight, I am like Dad – except it's not some knotty maths problem that is on my mind. It is Millie.

Not that I don't like to think about her. But before, it seemed like a crazy obsession. Slightly unreal. I wanted to believe our meeting had been meant to be, but I could hide behind the odds that it wasn't at all. That I'd never see her again.

It was safe to daydream about her.

But now I have seen her again. And chatting to Millie came so naturally it was scary.

I have never, ever talked to a stranger like that. Told them things about me, my family. Shared without feeling awkward or self-conscious.

I have never wanted to.

But I spent the best part of an hour talking about me, me, me, and I know hardly anything about her at all.

What on earth is wrong with me?

All I know is that she's lost her dad, she works in London, and she loves her job.

And she normally commutes on a Friday, not a Thursday like I do.

Would it be mad to swap things round and come home a day later? Or would that be stalkerish? I don't even know if she likes me. I mean, we had a good chat, it seemed to come naturally to both of us. We shared a laugh. But maybe she was just being polite.

She didn't exactly race after me and offer me her number. And when I asked if I'd see her next week she just said 'maybe'. I mean, maybe means no, doesn't it?

I guess if I do swap my commute day next week, and 'bump' into her again, then she'll soon let me know if I've read this all wrong. I need to, I guess, or I'll spend the next few weeks wishing I had. Realising I was an idiot for not at least trying.

What's the worst that could happen? I find out she's not interested. She thinks I'm a creep.

I grab a box of 'country relish' and swing round, then stop myself just in time before I drop it onto a tray of 'ethical eggs'.

'Joe!' Mum wrestles the box out of my hands and sets it down gently on the other side of the van. 'I swear you get more like your father every day!'

'Sorry, I...'

'Have got things on your mind?' She studies me, in much the same way her free-range hens study worms just before they grab them. Then she ruffles my hair. 'Ahh!'

I duck out of the way. 'What do you mean, ahhh?'

'That's the look he had before he asked me to marry him!'

Heat rushes to my cheeks. 'Rubbish!' I choke out. 'I haven't even got a girlfriend at the moment!'

'The trouble with being a thinker is you're sometimes several steps ahead of the rest of the world, you know. Don't plan out the future in your head until you've shared what's in your heart, eh?'

Oh boy, if she knew what a sharer I'd turned into on the train, she'd think I'd completely lost my head.

'I bet you didn't say that to Dad!'

'I did the first time he asked.' She chuckles. She's got a mischievous look in her eye that I don't often see. 'As your grandad used to say, it takes time to grow a proper crop, even if the seeds germinate on the first sunny day. There could be a drought or a wet week ahead!'

I raise an eyebrow. 'Very prosaic.'

'Though I'd say that you need to make the most of any sign of life if you get the chance!' She laughs, then squeezes my arm. 'You tread carefully though, Joe. You only get one heart and I'd hate anybody to hurt yours. Now –' her voice recovers its normal brisk edge '– if you can concentrate for long enough, could you go and get the traybakes I've stacked up on top of the fridge?'

'Sure.'

'And I won't buy a hat yet!'

'Very funny.' Her laughter follows me as I head back into the house.

Is it really that obvious that I've met somebody who I can't stop thinking about?

Chapter Thirteen

MILLIE

Friday 25th March

'What's the matter? Why are you answering Mum's phone?' There's a hint of suspicion, and a lot of impatience in my sister Lou's tone.

'She's out.' It is a Friday evening, and I am home alone while my mother is out on the town. I might have what appears to be a glitzy lifestyle in the city but right now she is the one with a date. Whilst I have a pizza and a bottle of wine. On my own.

'Out?'

'With a man.'

'Oh, right.'

'Does that seem okay to you?' Lou does not seem bothered about the fact that our mother is out on the razz.

'Well, it is Friday, and she's single, so isn't it normal?' I can almost hear the shrug of her shoulders in her tone. 'It's what people do.'

And this is what Lou does. Avoids talking about it, avoids mention of Dad and the part about 'single' and 'widowed' not feeling the same.

But I don't want a row about it right now.

And I guess it is normal to go out on a Friday night.

What isn't normal is that although my social life isn't bad, my dating life has hit a period of drought. Well, let's be honest, I haven't had a Friday night date with a man since I moved down to London.

I hadn't thought I missed it, until I watched Mum get ready nervously. Trying to hide her excitement as she checked her lipstick for the third time.

'So when will she be home?'

'I'm not sure, she told me not to wait up.' Is it wrong to feel jealous of your own mother? She'd said it with a laugh, so I'm not quite sure if she was being serious or not. How late is too late? When should I start to worry?

'Well, there aren't that many places round there that stay open past eleven o'clock, are there? Tell her I'll call her in the morning. Stop it!'

'What?' My sister has a very commanding tone.

'I'm talking to the dog, not you. Cracker, stop, I said. Oh, for heaven's sake. I've got to go, the cat's brought something dead in and Cracker's grabbed it. I'll have blood and guts all over the lounge, and… Cracker, don't you dare! I told the kids to keep the door shut. If she spreads that all over the new rug, I'll kill her.' The phone line goes dead.

I should be feeling smug. My life is neat and ordered. There is a good side to not having Friday night dates – they can lead to a husband, children, pets, blood and guts all over your soft furnishings.

I will relax, watch a nice romcom movie, enjoy my wine. Do whatever I like without interference.

Scanning through the movies, I don't feel smug. The trouble with romcoms is they are about romance. Something I am trying to avoid. Unlike my mother.

I could watch a psychological thriller, I like those. The description of the first one doesn't sound like it will be chilled watching, more like I'll be awake all night listening out for the sound of a car stopping. Nope. Oh my God, the next one is worse. What kind of twisted mind thinks up this stuff? How can a guy you don't even know decide to poison your water supply because he thinks you'll make a beautiful corpse? I pour another glass of wine. I can't drink water.

I'm fine watching stuff like that if I'm with somebody else, somebody big, strong and sensible, who can reassure me that I did actually leave the bedroom in that state – it was not some stalker guy who has been in looking for knickers to steal. And that the creaking is the central heating, not a stranger in the house.

I think I'll find something funny to watch. Or a re-run of *Sex in the City* or something, where everybody is strong, and happy, and supportive, and doesn't need a man.

Except I know I don't need a man. I know I am strong and independent. It would just be quite nice if Joe – well, somebody like Joe – was here to add a bit of sparkle to my Friday night now and again.

I'm sure he'd add sparkle. He was funny. Cute. He was a great listener, and so gentle, possibly an excellent kisser… No. I must not think about Joe. Or kissing. This is ridiculous.

I'm just being irrational because my mum has something I haven't, and I stupidly feel like I might be missing out.

I pick up the TV remote control again and flick through the channels. But it doesn't work, I am not distracted. I used to like my Friday date nights. When I was the one going out, not waiting in. Feeling restless, I wander through to the kitchen, in search of some snacks that might make me feel better.

I've been so busy, so determined and single-minded about work and making my own way in life, that it's not hit me until now how much I miss my life as it used to be.

This house, this place, the countryside. Having a boyfriend. Because there's always plenty of time, isn't there, for stuff like that?

Although according to the new plaque next to the pinboard and above the biscuit tin, which is my current destination, I should 'Live in the moment'.

The biscuit tin is empty. So much for that particular moment. I think I am going to go to bed early, read, make a point of not waiting up for Mum.

I know I was thinking I should be here for her, look after her more, but this is taking role reversal a step too far. I might have to open the Pringles and take them up to bed with me. Very daring.

It's a bit pathetic that even after faffing about in the bathroom for ages, and doing all the cleansing, toning, moisturising, teeth flossing and eyebrow plucking that I don't normally have time for, it is still only ten o'clock.

I might have to take up hoovering and dusting.

What counts as late, and not waiting up?

The sound of a car engine slowing outside the house takes me scurrying to the window. Luckily my room is at the front of the house. I hold the curtain shut and peep between a small gap. She can't think I'm spying on her!

It is a nice car, a shiny, new, rather big car, and it has stopped at the bottom of our driveway. It's a bit disappointing actually, I'd half-hoped that it would be some tatty van belching fumes (mean, I know) and then I'd be able to advise Mum that this is not a path she wants to go down.

Instead, this car is silent and fume-free.

Why isn't she getting out? What are they doing in there? I slide down, my nose slipping along the gap in the curtain and squint, my head on one side. I can't see inside the car! What if they're kissing? A flutter of panic starts in my chest. I should have stayed downstairs; I would have been able to see what they were doing then! But do I want to know? Should I know? I can't help myself though. I'd be hanging on to these curtains with my fingernails if anybody tried to drag me away.

The interior light flicks on, the driver's door opens and

this giant of a man gets out. What's he done with my mother? He walks around the back of the car. He's actually quite handsome looking, though it is dark, and I am watching through a sliver of a gap from a funny angle.

He opens the door and holds out a hand for Mum to take. She is smiling! No bloody wonder. I let the curtains slip from my grasp and rest my chin on my hands – peering over the windowsill down at them.

I'm holding my breath. Waiting for him to lean down, kiss her, but actually hating the thought that he will. I want her to be happy, I really do. And this is so romantic, but I want to shout down to her to be careful, take it slowly. Like I'm her mother. Even though she seems to have her life better sorted than I have mine.

She takes a step away from the car, and he closes the door. I'm holding my breath, waiting for her to invite him in – at which point I might have to dive into bed and put the pillow over my head to block out the sound.

She lifts a hand, but it's not to take his – it's to wave him goodbye.

I breathe a huge sigh of relief, which mists up the window, just as he takes a step back towards her. Heck! I wipe frantically, and as he says something she glances up. Bugger, she must have seen my hand. What do I do, pretend I was waving, disappear behind the curtain?

She laughs, and shakes her head at me, then still laughing turns to says something to her date. Who also laughs and turns back to his car.

How embarrassing is that? Caught spying on my

mother. Well, spying on her at all is pretty bad. I'm not quite sure whether to breeze down the stairs asking how it went, or shout out goodnight.

But I think she's happy. Content. She might not have everything – for a start she's not got Dad any longer – but she seems to be getting her life sorted fine. Without my help.

I crawl across the bedroom floor to the bed, and prop myself up with my back against it. I've not been looking for a happy ever after since I moved down to London. I've never pined for babies. I've always wanted a career more than anything, not exactly to be famous but to be good at what I do. To have a bit of glamour, go to the 'in' places. I've wanted to prove I'm good enough. I've been fighting to prove I'm good enough ever since the doubters got under my skin.

But right now, I'd love nothing more than to have a simple date night. A walk across the moors holding hands with somebody that I really do care for – not a Tuesday night hook-up. A chance to look up at the inky sky, dotted with bright stars, and share it with a guy like I used to share it with Dad.

'Fancy a nightcap with me, Millie?' Mum's voice drifts up the stairs.

'Sure!' I head to the top of the stairs, stretching and doing a fake yawn, but I know she isn't taken in. She just laughs, then catches me as I jump down the last couple of steps.

Chapter Fourteen

MILLIE

Sunday 27th March

'Where are you?' Dale's petulant tone gets ripped away by the wind, and I clutch the phone closer to my ear.

'At home.'

'No, you're not! I've just come from there and—'

'*Home* home, as in Hexham, with Mum.'

'Oh.' There's a long pause. 'I thought you were there last weekend?'

'I was.'

'But you only go once a month.'

I try not to sigh. 'I've been trying to come every weekend lately. I told you, Mum needs me.'

'Oh, don't start that again. She's a grown woman, she doesn't need you. Has she asked you to?'

'No, but...'

'I thought we'd been through this, Millie? You will totally ruin your life if you spend any more time in the back of beyond.'

I gaze around. According to the app on my phone, the weather is positively *balmy* in the rest of the UK. Here though it is neither soft nor soothing, nor warm. It's bloody cold, with an icy wind that could freeze my fingertips off if they weren't inside my woolly mittens. As it is, I feel like I'm in a dinghy on the Atlantic during a storm. My nose is so cold my eyes are watering, I've lost the feeling in my feet, and my red cheeks probably look like they've had a slapping.

I drag the zip of my jacket up the last few millimetres and lift my face to the wind so that I can smell, feel, as well as see the hills.

The scene is as breathtaking as the weather, and it suddenly hits me that right now, in this moment, in this place, I'm happy. Really laugh-out-loud happy.

I've been barging my way through life, determinedly going after what I want, but I've taken all of this for granted. Not thought about it at all. It's just somewhere I come back to every now and again.

But after seeing Mum so happy last night, after feeling a heavy lump form in my chest that doesn't seem to be going, I realise I do miss it. I'd not really stopped to think about it until Joe asked on the train. I'd just been going through the motions of coming back, of thinking I should come back more often for Mum's sake. But he's made me think about it. Properly. And now I'm seeing it through different eyes.

I do want my career; I do want the city. But I also want this place. And I want to feel happy. And I want to date – but a man who understands me, who will support me, like Dad did with Mum. I feel like I've been missing out on a chunk of life, and it's time to reclaim it.

And maybe I need to come back here to do it, although I'm still not sure how I do that.

'It's not the back of beyond, Dale,' I say softly, making do with a grin. 'It's home.'

But let's face it, Dale will not get it. He's as likely to stand on a windswept moor as he is to take up knitting. Actually, he'd probably consider knitting.

'I was expecting you to come to brunch with Ant and me. Charlotte is busy and I need a female perspective so we can deep dive—'

'I don't want to deep dive anything with you and Ant, Dale.' I hold my chin higher, so that the wind hits me full on, blows the hair out of my face and scorches my cheeks and chin. Who needs blusher when windburn comes additive-free? I close my eyes and I could be posing like Rose on the Titanic, but without a Jack at my back.

It's more likely I'm a doomed ghostly Catherine, wandering the moors as I wait for my Heathcliff to appear. Wrong moors though.

'Millie? Millie, are you still there? It's an incredibly bad line, don't they even have proper reception there?'

'It's the wind.' I wish he'd go, I am so over Dale, but too polite to tell him. I should feel lonely out here, with the wind in my hair and not another soul in sight. But I don't.

I've never felt lonely out here. This is where I want to be right now. In my heart.

'Well, it's a bloody nuisance. Look, Mill, I'm not being funny but if you're going to keep disappearing, I don't see how this is going to work.'

'What do you mean, *this*? We're friends.'

'Friends are there for each other, they don't just piss off to play nursemaid.'

'And they don't just use each other when it suits them. Look, I've got to go, Dale.' Not sure exactly what I'm rushing off to do. Maybe a sheep needs me. 'Was there anything else?'

'Will you be here next Thursday night to be my plus one at the art gallery opening?' He's got an edge to his tone and sounds a bit huffy.

'Unlikely.' I pause, my eyes wide open as I stare at the distant clouds. 'I'm planning on coming out here on a Thursday night and working from home every Friday.' As long as it doesn't interfere with my mother's new social life. That thought makes me smile.

'That's ridiculous. But fine, if you want to play silly buggers with your life and wreck what you've worked so hard for then that's fine. I'll ring Charlie, or Rach.'

'You do that, Dale. I'm sure they're much more reliable than me. Bye!' Has Dale ever been any good for me? Have I learned anything from him? Or has he just reflected back at me the bright-light dreams that I'd craved, but like a child never questioned?

Things are never black and white, are they? It has just

dawned on me that I have never needed to choose between being a country girl and a city girl. It's not like I want it all, but I don't have to just stick with strawberry creams, I can have the chocolate caramels as well.

I turn away from the distant hills and look back the way I came.

My hair whips around my face, and I tuck it behind my ears as a flash of white catches my eye.

It's a feather. A sign.

With a smile I pick it up and closing my hand around it I set off back down the slope.

I know what I need to do. I've just told Dale I was planning on heading home on a Thursday, and that is what I am going to do.

I need to travel on Thursdays. I need to. For Mum – well, okay, maybe I'm kidding myself a bit there, she does seem to be coping quite well on her own, but I'm sure she'd like to see more of me and have somebody to call on when her latest date lets her down. For my career. For the train-guy.

But more than that, I want to. I want to do this for me.

How can Carla say no? She can't now that I can tell her that Thursday is Joe-day! It makes perfect sense.

Fate is telling me to do it. To write this column. To see more of him, Joe. Except – I frown, – I'm still not sure what I can make out of our forty-minute coffee break. I don't want to write about what I told him. About Dad. About life choices. Or maybe I should. Maybe I do need to be more authentic, as Carla said. But funny as well. Hmmm.

I can't out him though, put his name in print, can I? Because I've already been stung on that front. It's fine if he wants his life – warts and all – made public. But he didn't really seem like that type of guy. In fact, he was the total opposite. We might not have had much time to chat, but it was pretty obvious that he comes from a family that value privacy and don't like to brag or show off about what they are up to.

Seb, the three-date-wonder, was pretty out-there, but he only wanted to be shown in a good light. Which I suppose is only human, but not how my column works.

Could I call him Mo? No. Sorry to all the Mo's but not sure on that one. I'll have to come up with a name, so that if he did happen to read what I've written he wouldn't realise, and things wouldn't get wrecked like they have in the past.

I could just call him train-guy. At least for now. Mystery is good.

I can write about saving a guy's life – well, by finding his phone. The modern-day equivalent of heroics.

My mobile judders in my pocket and I grab it, fully prepared to tell Dale exactly where he can shove his selfish, opinionated, controlling idea of friendship. But say it in a way that won't lose me my tenancy.

'Millie?' It is Mum. 'Where are you, darling?'

'On my way back.'

'You sound a bit breathless, are you okay?'

'I'm fine!' I suddenly realise that I've been striding out faster and faster, as the ideas whirl round in my head. The decisions.

I am breathing quite heavily. Zumba in the living room isn't quite the same as tramping in the countryside with fresh air and actual hills. I stop and try and catch my breath. I've always carried a little bit of weight because I think life is for living (and eating and drinking), but I've been fit enough to get away with it. Either the crisps are going to have to go, or I'll have to join a gym. 'Totally fine. I just ended up walking on the moor and lost track of time!'

'That's a fun walk in this wind.' She chuckles. 'You're getting more like your father every day!'

Maybe I am, maybe I'm looking for whatever he had. 'I needed it.' I come to a halt, smile even though she can't see me. 'Mum, it's your decision, about the house. I just want what's best for you.'

'I know, darling.'

'I want you to be happy. I don't want you to sell up if you don't want to. I can help, I'll be round here more. I can find another gardener, look on Facebook. But if you do want to move, I get it. It's your life, I can help you move.'

'Thank you. Now, hurry up back, dinner is nearly ready, and it won't eat itself, you know!'

Chapter Fifteen

JOE

Sunday afternoon

It's kind of a relief that there's only a handful of people in the last carriage on the train when I jump on, and nobody on the platform as we start to slowly pull out of the station. Nobody to see me walk past all the empty seats and into the next carriage, then the third one, then the fourth. Glancing around as casually as I can.

Feeling more and more disappointed, and silly, with each step.

She's not here. There's no way I could miss her if she was. Millie.

I'm being daft. Why am I even looking? Why the hell *should* she be on this train?

Actually, seeing her again on Thursday was amazing, nothing short of a miracle. I'd more or less given up hope.

And then she was there. Prettier than I remembered and so funny, so easy to talk to.

If I thought I had it bad after our first brief encounter, this has made it even worse.

I never even asked what day she headed back to London, I just kind of assumed that there was a good chance it was on a Sunday. What a complete dork. If I had any sense, I'd be heading back on the first train on Monday, like I normally do. But I made excuses to Mum and Dad, and to myself, that I needed to get back today. That I had a load of work to do tomorrow, and an important meeting, and all kinds of bullshit. Okay, it's all true but I could have done my normal commute. I could have stayed over, instead of eating my Sunday lunch then heading to the station.

But I want to see her. I'm going to admit that to myself, even if I won't to anybody else. That's the only reason.

Thursday seems far too long a wait.

And will she even be there on Thursday? I mean, she did say her normal day to travel was Friday – but if I swap to a Friday like I was thinking of doing, then what if she'd decided to swap to a Thursday? Slim chance. But possible. This is ridiculous. I'm ridiculous.

Why the hell didn't I ask for her number, or where exactly she lived, or worked? I'm pretty pathetic, the worse she could have done was said no, thought I was a creep and avoided me for ever after. Which wouldn't have been difficult. Now, I might never, ever see her again.

My track record, ha ha, with her has been so bad, she's

as likely to hide from me as grab a coffee. That journey whizzed by so quickly, and – from what I can remember – all I did was ramble on about the farm. Mr Interesting.

I slump into a seat and stare out at the passing countryside.

Each creak and sway of the carriage is taking me nearer to the city. The normal buzz I get when I head back is on a bit of a dimmer switch though right now, because all weekend I've been thinking about Millie and her gorgeous smile. The fun shining in her eyes. And although it's ridiculous, I'd kind of thought, hoped, she might be sitting on this train. Grinning at me. That she'd tell me all about her weekend, we'd swap tales and I'd get to know a bit more about her. About the father she obviously misses like hell. About what she does when she's in town. About maybe how we could meet up some time in the week if she was up for it. I'd been counting on it.

Which is totally ridiculous. My whole life is about logic, about probability, not about chance meetings.

Why the hell didn't I at least ask her about where she goes in town? What kind of food she likes? Give her a proper impression of the current me, instead of lapsing into introvert farmer mode. Gah.

Gawd, if Sophie could see inside my head, she'd dine out on this for the rest of her life. Rib me to high heaven in front of everybody who'd listen.

But I wouldn't care. If Millie was here.

Shit. I have to stop fantasising like this. She's just a pretty girl, with a cute smile that I've bumped into twice.

That I nearly drowned. Who chased up the platform after me.

Not that she knew it was me. She was just being kind.

I need to get a grip and stop being such a silly sod.

She's probably married, or seriously dating, or just wasn't interested in me. Though she did seem to be. It did seem more than just being polite.

Gah. My phone beeps, cutting through the music that I'm only half listening to.

Hey man, you still up for a beer tomorrow night?

Sure thing, I type back, smiling. Al is a bit of an idiot, and when it comes to work, he's a liability, but he knows some cool places to go to. He introduced this country boy to Sticks'n'sushi, and killer cocktails. The stuff you need to know if you want to sweep a girl off her feet. If you can find her, that is. *Be good to celebrate my birthday with a mate!*

Shit, it's your b'day? No way, man! Why didn't you say?

I just did! I grin.

Cool. C U in Borough Market at seven?

I send a thumbs-up.

Taking no prisoners bro, this could be a late one.

This could be dangerous. I know Al. Any excuse for a party. When it was his birthday a couple of months back, he made sure that everybody knew, and the party went on all weekend. But I'm not like that. Yeah, I like a booze-up, but I don't announce to the world that I'm celebrating anything. My birthday's not exactly a secret, but we've never been an oversharing family. Two hundred 'happy birthdays' on Facebook isn't really me. I must have one of the smallest social media trails out there for a guy my age.

Mum and Dad were totally shocked when a neighbour congratulated them on their grandchild, after Sophie had posted pictures on her Insta page. They were pretty gobsmacked that a shitload of other people they didn't even know had seen my nephew within hours of their first viewing.

Sophie is definitely the black sheep of the family. I'm more white with a few flecks. But I like it that way.

I turn the volume of my music up.

A couple of mates on a Monday 7-10 p.m. with Al will turn into a big group partying past midnight, I reckon. But that's one of the things I like about my new life in London – the freedom and independence, the not needing to think about getting up at daybreak to milk cows and muck out stalls. It's cool.

I guess I'll never be the type to broadcast to the world what I'm up to, or share my breakfast on Insta, but actually being able to eat street food, fusion food that could come from anywhere and tastes of everywhere, 24/7 is amazing. Way different to our family routine of Sunday lunches, bacon butties. Fish on a Friday and shepherd's pie on a Tuesday. Not that I'm dissing that. I love the food I was brought up on, but the stuff that's on my doorstep now blew my mind at first. I felt like every day was Christmas Day.

And I love the fact that I walk up a street and there are people from every part of the globe, that the place is buzzing with buskers who are amazing, and street artists who can chalk the pavements and make you feel like you're in New York City.

My phone vibrates again.

You back tonight country boy? K x

I grin at the message from Katherine, my landlady. And project manager. She's at least ten years older than me, divorced, flamboyant and loaded. We have an ongoing tussle about how much rent I should pay. She doesn't want my money, I insist, she puts it to one side and treats us both to takeaways and bottles of expensive wine, not giving me the option to say no. It's a weird relationship, but it works.

On my way.

Got tickets for some stand up night, Charlie's pissed me off, you up for it? I'll throw in nachos and a beer?? K

I'm up for it. I'm up for lots of stuff. I'm a tart. She gets a thumbs-up. It's my most overused emoticon.

Sophie's right. I really need to get my finger out and get a permanent job down here. Not just rely on the software company I work for finding me projects that need more staff. It's worked so far, it was a great way to find out if it was what I really wanted, but it's kind of precarious.

Any day now they could yank me out and send me to Scotland to work on something totally different.

I guess, though, I've carried on because it's handy. It's not too demanding, leaves me time to develop games – the kind of stuff I'd really like to be working on.

I grab my phone and bring up a recruitment agency. Okay, I know this is all displacement activities, I'm trying to stop thinking about how I might have lost the girl I felt an instant connection with.

So much for love at first sight.

But hey, I'm definitely never ever going to see her again if I leave London, am I?

Chapter Sixteen

MILLIE

Monday 28th March

E pisode 3
Confessions of… is it meant to be?

Something amazing happened to me on Thursday. I bumped into train-guy again, when I wasn't even looking, and I practically saved his life!

You'd think I'd have learned by now, that when you look you don't find. Wouldn't you? Remember when I wasted half my Saturday morning looking for my credit card so that I could go out and treat myself to breakfast pastries? Then, when I had given up and raided the cupboard to see what I could scrape together it was there, right next to the empty marmalade jar – which I'd noticed when I'd got in the day before. Which was why I was treating myself to pastries. By the time I got to the patisserie there was a double decker bus rammed into the plate-glass window. Luckily nobody was injured but imagine if I'd got there five minutes earlier and had been busy sorting through cinnamon swirls and maple and pecan plaits.

And the time I couldn't find my favourite scarf which I totally needed for a hot date? I was late for the date, and he was chatting up some other girl by the time I got there. I found it the next morning hiding in my shoe. I mean, that's a sign that the date was doomed, if ever there was one. He was as worthwhile as something I'd scrape off the bottom of my shoe, and twice as stinky.

Well, I reckon guys are like that. If you're meant to be dating them, they'll turn up. If you're not, they'll be out of sight until the day you're snogging some other guy and you'll have lost any chance you had.

Anyway, I'd had a pretty crap day. I'd had a weird message from my mum, was panicking to get my work word perfect, the station was rammed when I got there, and my train was delayed and then totally heaving. When it was time to get off I was spat out like the contents of a zit that's been popped.

And that's when I saw it. A mobile phone that somebody had dropped. I couldn't not pick it up — I mean, how would I feel if I mislaid mine (unlikely)? It would be like losing an arm, an entire child. Worse.

I was on a mission, I was dynamite, clutching my boobs as I went for it — partly because I'd miss my connection if I wasted too much time. Pah to my PE teacher, I thought, as I put in the best fifty-metre dash of my life — she said I would never catch a fly, but who cares about flies when a mobile phone is at stake? — I had that bright red scarf of his in my vision and I wasn't giving up. Well, not until I suspected from the chafing that my F cup and my boob had parted company.

So I resorted to what my mother would call 'shouting like a fishwife'.

A guy whacked him on the shoulder for me, and he turned. Looked.

And it was him. Yes, him!

OMG the world stopped turning. I had that dizzy moment again. He is even better looking than I remember.

I could hardly believe it when he told me he was catching the same train as me. He bought me a coffee, told me his name, and we chatted. Like really chatted in a non-drunken, normal-person way – the last time I remember doing that with a man I fancy was when I was in the sixth form and he was a teacher and it was way out of order and completely one-sided. The crush, not the convo.

But this is different.

I've flattened the guy, he's drenched me, and now I've saved him. Is this what modern-day love looks like? I reckon I've got to go for it, it seems like fate is telling me that this could be it. That this (whatever this means) is meant to be, that I need to see him again. Could it be on Platform 3 next week?'

'Fan-bloody-tastic. Sorry but you're going to have to work from the sticks on a Friday if he catches the train on a Thursday. I take it that isn't a problem?' I get the Carla gimlet stare.

Wow! No argument from me. I've not even had to ask. 'No, er, not at all. I'll make it work. Sure.' This certainly is fan-bloody-tastic. I cannot believe my luck. I emailed Carla late last night to pave the way a bit. I confirmed that I had found train-guy and gave her a sketchy outline of how I saved his bacon (well, his mobile phone) and how we'd progressed to nudging knees and swapping names. And itineraries. I'd made a point of saying it was a Thursday just in case she'd missed that.

I didn't get a reply, but now I'm in work she's practically wetting herself – and practically begging me to travel back to Northumberland on a Thursday. Result!

'I think he catches the train back here on a Monday evening.' Does he? Fuck, when does he come back here? Why didn't we talk about return trips, so I could stalk him properly? What kind of journalist forgets her objectives and rambles on about coffee, her parents and total dross like that? What was I thinking? Or, more to the point, not thinking. I got carried away and gooey. Though to be fair to me, I did only have forty-five minutes. But really, the fact that I didn't even check the times of his bloody commute is bad even for the over-excited (at finding him again), goggle-eyed (at seeing his gorgeousness again) version of me. I need to get a grip. It's almost like I forgot what my mission really is!

Shit. Anyway, I can work that one out later, but right now I need Mondays with Mum as well as Fridays. This is about her (we did establish that she was kidding about me interrupting her hectic social life, she'd love to see more of me), not just my career, and the possibility of a love life and sex. 'Would Mondays at home work for you as well? If that's when he travels? Then I double the chances of getting a good story each week?' I think I might be pushing it here, but what the hell. If you don't ask, you don't get.

And now that Dale has ghosted me, I've got one less friend and many fewer social engagements in town anyway. He was entertaining, and he did attend a lot of 'openings' and stuff like that. My social life is going to shrink down to postage-stamp size. I really might as well be in my wellies on the moors or drinking coffee with Mum. If she's in.

There's a pause. Carla is frowning.

Have I gone too far? Been too eager?

'I like the red scarf bit.' Phew, she's just concentrating on the story. 'But maybe some yoik didn't have to grab him, I reckon you were faster, keener.' She peers from under her black fringe with a judgemental stare, so I just nod.

'Keen, I was very keen.'

'You ran, sprinted—' I nod again, even though I'm not really a sprinting type and my body isn't equipped for spurts of energy. I'd probably need an incontinence pad and oxygen, as well as a good sports bra. I'm more the gentle jog type. '—after him, grabbed the scarf breathlessly, and he spun round. You reeled him in, oh yes, I like that, reeled! Put that in, it shows you're being assertive, involved, the main man here. You're leading this, Millie, but also being swept off your feet by his heroism.' I'm not quite sure what's heroic about being strangled by some strange woman, but we will hold that thought for now. I can work it in, somehow. 'You were nose to nose, practically snogging?'

'Maybe,' I say, aware there's a note of doubt in my voice – which Carla will not like. But I'm still trying to work out her angle here. He's heroic, I'm heroic. Is that one hero too many?

'And I'm not sure about red?' Her voice lifts with a question. The frown is now a mini-scowl. 'Is red an actual thing? Does anybody actually buy red scarves these days?' There's a note of distaste. If you can't buy a label red scarf, then one does not exist.

'I think his mum bou— I mean knitted it for him. He was wearing it for her, because it's the decent thing to do.'

'Oh well, that's okay then. But maybe a child made it? We don't want a mummy's boy vibe in here, do we?'

'Oh, definitely not. Although does it matter? Maybe we need to keep this about him? And me? Not, er, complicate it with other stuff?' Like a made-up family.

'Whatever, I'll leave the detail to you. We'll monitor the response during the day each Monday as soon as it goes out, so I suppose you might as well work from home. I've got no use for you here, you're just taking up desk space.' Thanks, Carla. 'Then we can tweak on Tuesday and make sure we get the next one spot-on.'

'Right.' Result though! She can diss me and my space-taking capacity all she likes. I get my column, and I get my time with Mum.

'And Millie?'

'Yes?'

'How long do you think it'll be before you screw?'

'I have absolutely no—' Idea? Intention?

'Park that thought for now. We need to weigh up the romance and suspense side. I'll do some number-crunching when we get the latest stats back. I'm thinking your crowd right now are more will-she-won't-she-snog-him rather than when-she's-going-to-jump-him. More *Brief Encounter*, less *Cosmo*. Leave that one with me.'

I'm not sure I want to leave any aspect of my love life with her. I'm also not sure that I like that summing up.

Is she suggesting I am past the age of impulsive action and hot sex, and the most that my readers are hoping for is some lip action?

I'm a hot and sexy young woman, with lust and love pounding through my veins as I wait for a man strong enough to sweep me off my feet – and not be afraid of being taken the piss out of in a very public way.

Okay, maybe not. She could have read me right. These days all I'm really up for by the time I leave work is a glass of wine and a bubble-filled bath followed by a good Netflix binge. Or all three together. There's no room for sex in my tub.

Actually, I need to write that down. I might use that at some point.

But if real-life Joe could live up to the man I'm painting in my column, then I think I could let him squeeze in at the tap end.

And I might even ask him to get hot and steamy with me, because right now even writing 'pretend' hot and steamy would be a bit of a challenge because I can't actually remember how it feels.

Maybe it's a good thing that my readers don't have any great expectations.

'My office, 3 p.m. to go through the feedback for this week. Looking not too shoddy so far.'

Not too shoddy is high praise in Carla's world.

'You need to keep them hooked though, one slip and they'll be back to reading real-life tampon reviews. Zoe, my office now, I've got more customer survey bollocks to do, and you shone last time. You're my first choice.' This is Carla in high-flattery mode because she knows it's a shit job that Zoe will hate.

Zoe rolls her eyes.

That could have been me, I remind myself. It could still be me if the magic between me and Joe fizzles out like a damp squib.

It's all well and good trying to write something that people relate to, but they want better than real life, don't they? Or what's the point?

When Zoe marches out of Carla's office her cheeks are pink, and her shoulders scrunched up with anger. I go out for pastries to try and defuse the situation, but I don't think it is working.

'Fucking stupid little shit machines.' She is jabbing at her keyboard and talking through a cinnamon swirl.

'Shit machines?' What the hell is Carla interested in now?

'Frogs.' She splutters through her pastry and pulls off another part of the swirl with a vicious jab. 'Who gives a flying fuck how inconvenient it is, they shouldn't bloody get them if they aren't happy to walk.'

'Frogs?' I am confused.

I am treated to an eye roll, and an angry glare. 'Dogs.'

Ah, this makes a bit more sense. Dogs. Walking. 'Happy to walk where?' I ask tentatively. Zoe is a sunshine and showers person. Right now she is in full-on storm mode and I don't want to get hit by a lightning bolt at my desk. I have work to do. I have a relationship to nurture.

She folds her arms. 'To a frigging doggy doo-dah disposal point!'

'You're asking people about poo bins?' It is hard to keep a straight face, even though I am sympathetic.

'Turds,' she spits out with distaste, and I assume she is talking about work, and it isn't an insult aimed at me.

'You're asking them about the actual poo?' A muscle in my face is twitching. I must not laugh, I really must not.

'Don't you frigging dare laugh at me or I'll track down your train-guy and tell him you're a frigid virgin soliciting for your dominatrix sister.'

'Not sure it's what Carla and my readers are after, but I could use that, I guess, if he isn't interested?'

'Huh. I hate you, have I told you that before?'

I blow her a kiss and push the rest of the pastries closer to her.

Zoe glances over her shoulder to make sure nobody is in earshot. 'Apparently now that everybody in the universe has got a pooch, waste disposal is a *massive* topic.' She mimics Carla almost perfectly.

'Unless you've got a chihuahua, in which case it's a tiny topic?'

'Shut up, you're not funny. Do people want more bins? Better located ones? Bigger ones? How important are bio-degradable poo bags on a – oh my God, you have to be kidding me, I cannot actually ask this – sliding scale from one to ten?'

I snigger, I can't help it. But it seems better not to comment, I think these are rhetorical questions.

'Do normal people, sorry, non-dog owners if there's still such a thing, want a total ban apart from in tiny dog parks, or would they favour compulsory nappies? Favour? Favour!' Her tone goes up a couple of octaves. 'How can anybody favour anything to do with excrement? Fuck, she really thinks I should ask about dog-diapers? The woman is bonkers, a complete wombat, what is this shit?'

'Dog shit?' I pull what I hope is a sympathetic face, then duck as it looks like a pencil-shaped missile is about to head my way. 'I'd better get back to work, I guess.'

'Yeah, yeah, course you should. You get to think about being fucked, I am fucked. I've reached a new low. I am literally scraping the shit off my shoe.'

'Not if you get more poo bins,' I say in my most reasonable voice.

'You wait,' she says in a threatening tone, waving the pencil about. 'Mess that up and this could be your next assignment, a series of articles about dog owners in the city, starting at the arse end.'

Luckily my phone pings with a message, and Zoe stalks off to the ladies for a sulk.

She spends the rest of the morning messaging her best mate about what a shithole this place is and trying to work out how she can skew the results in a way that she will find amusing.

I spend my morning daydreaming about Joe, and reeling him in by his red scarf, and tweaking our brief encounter to make it more marketable.

The trouble is, after I'd got over the shock, and huge sense of relief that I'd actually found him, I forgot all about the fact he was 'work', and all about my worries over Mum, and just enjoyed talking to him. I don't want to tweak it. I just want to remember it as it was.

It was just a shame we had less than an hour to chat, and that all I really know about him is that there's a good chance he'll be on that same train on Thursday.

If he's not, I'm buggered. I could well, as Zoe so kindly pointed out, end up being demoted to writing about the smelly end of dog ownership.

Chapter Seventeen

MILLIE

Thursday 31st March

He's not by the entrance as I saunter in, trying to nonchalantly scan the crowds but avoid bumping into anybody. My normal thing is to arrive last minute, dodge through the crowds and collapse on the train seconds before it pulls out – feeling and looking like I've run a marathon. It requires full focus and determination.

Today I am fifteen minutes earlier than the ten minutes early that I always attempt but never manage. This is nothing short of a miracle.

I have also found time to brush my hair, apply the most expensive non-fuzz serum my hairdresser stocks, reapply my lipstick at least seventy-eight times and give my armpits a quick sniff. I am good to go. I even have perfume on, skin-tight jeans that are doing their best to cut off the blood supply to my legs and stop me breathing, and I am wearing my best imitation silk top that he won't even get to see unless it is super-hot on the train and I've got enough elbow room to wriggle out of my coat.

I glance at the board, to check the train is coming into the normal platform, and I feel slightly sick. I'm not sure if it is all nerves or also down to the tight jeans and the fact that I shortened my bra straps so much I'm practically eating my own breasts. This was not for flirtatious purposes; it was to stop them escaping if I have to chase him again.

It's like a first date. No, it is worse. It's like going to prom night when you haven't got anybody to go with but you're hoping the hot guy who has been looking your way across the maths classroom in a significant fashion actually meant it.

There is no sign of him, and my heart is starting to pound as I search for a glimpse of red scarf, for his sun-streaked hair.

I'll go and get a coffee, waste some time seeing as I'm so early.

No, I'll go over to the platform, go to the loo. Comb my hair. Again.

Yep, I'll do that, then if he is there, I won't miss him.

If he shows.

Maybe this week's column is going to be all about the huge disappointment of losing him after I've just found him. Do people want disappointment? Not according to Carla. They want a fairy tale, they want to know that anything is possible, that fate will provide, that I have got it all. I am a beacon of hope.

I'm not sure I want to be a beacon of anything.

'Love.' A woman heading in the opposite direction points down towards my feet. Shit, I am a beacon of hope dragging a swathe of toilet paper that has snagged on her heel.

'Cheers.' Bugger, I hope it's clean. Maybe this is another avenue that Zoe can consider. That I might soon have to consider.

'Hey!'

I wobble, one foot still in mid-air, toilet paper dangling and glance up. Then nearly fall over.

Joe is standing in front of me, with a cup of coffee in each hand, and a broad smile on his face. He is a vision of male hunkiness – even taller than I remember, and sexier. Those twinkling eyes, that smile, could melt icecaps as well as kneecaps. Mine seem distinctly wobblier.

For a moment I am stunned into silence. One hand full of second-hand tissue, my mouth open. Definitely not a vision of womanhood – well, not a good one.

Then he raises one eyebrow. 'Problem?'

'Oh God, am I pleased to see you!' The words tumble out. All that nervous anticipation that has been rocketing round my body and giving me the jitters disappears into the air as I grin back at him.

He's here! And all I feel is happy. And slightly stupid. I hop a couple of times, then remember to put my foot down, then do a little slide and nearly end up in a heap at his feet.

'I thought I was doomed to a life of asking people about pooper-scoopers.' It is out before I can stop it. Must be the shock, or relief, or excitement, or something.

He half frowns, the smile dimming slightly.

'Sorry, ignore me, busy day, spaced-out brain. It's a work thing. I need caffeine!' I grab at the cup to stop myself burbling on and making an even bigger fool of myself. 'But really, it's so good to see you!'

It is. The pooper-scooper comment was ridiculous. Nerves.

'Great to see you too! I thought I was going to be left looking like a complete saddo with two cold coffees. Not that I'd mind, that's not just why I'm pleased, I mean... I didn't mean...'

'No, fine, I know what you mean. I think.' Well, at least we're equal on the feeling-an-idiot stakes. 'Great!'

'I really wasn't sure if you'd be here,' he says, his look intent. 'With you saying today wasn't your normal day to travel. I...' He hesitates. 'I nearly swapped over to tomorrow, but I'm glad I didn't.'

'So am I,' I say softly.

I stare at him, look into his eyes. I *am* pleased to see him, and not just because of work. I'm pleased to see him because I really wanted to.

If he'd not been here, because he'd thought he had a better chance of seeing me tomorrow, it would have been sweet, but terrible. Because I wouldn't have known.

I would have thought he wasn't interested.

But he is. And here we both are. Same time, same place.

It's nice just looking at him. Gazing into his stormy-sky eyes.

I might be happy to write about poop if I also had a man like Joe to go home to. No, rewind. I would not. My career is important, and I have absolutely no intention of writing about poop, even if I do have a man to go home to. Which I won't, at least not for ages, and as far as I know my lovely Joe might be just another Dale. Or another three-date Seb.

He holds his cup up, breaks the silence. 'Anyway, cheers.'

'Oh wow, you're a lifesaver. I was just about to go and buy one.'

'I read your mind.' He winks. I feel all warm and fuzzy, important, ridiculously happy. 'There are times when nothing beats a coffee.'

'For sure! Oh my God, you're a keeper, there are *so* many people that don't get this!' I'm rambling again.

He chuckles. 'Don't get coffee? You're kidding me.'

'Dale told me I had to move on to matcha!' I'm still rambling.

'Dale? Boyfriend?'

Rambling in a bad way. I have verbal diarrhoea. 'Oh God, no! He's my landlord.'

'With a matcha habit?'

I nod. 'He likes to be…' I pause. What does he like to be? 'On-trend.' Is that Dale in a nutshell? 'And he's a friend, well he was a friend. I'm not sure now, he seems to have ghosted me.'

There's a silence. 'We disagreed about my career

choices.' Joe still doesn't say anything. We just fall into step, walking towards my platform, *our* platform.

'Are your career choices any of his business? It seems a bit—'

'Bossy?'

'I was going to say controlling. And weird. But if he is, was, a good friend...'

'Well, I did think he was a good friend, he helped me a lot, and I suppose it wasn't exactly my career choice, more that I think I need to spend more time with my mum, and he thought I was ruining my life.'

'A bit extreme,' he says, his voice mild. I think Joe is a mild, measured type of guy. The opposite of Dale. 'Is your mum okay? I guess it must be hard since she lost your dad.'

I blink at him, then remember that we swapped 'going home' stories last time we met. He's remembered. 'It is, she's just... well, I just think I need, no, I want...' I'm rambling, I do that when I'm nervous. I take a deep breath. 'I want to spend more time with my mum, but that means spending less time in the office—'

'Sounds good to me.' He smiles, encourages me to carry on.

'I can work from home more and I think she'd welcome some company, and a helping hand. I didn't really realise until the other day after we'd chatted—' we share a look '— that I would actually quite like to be there more for her and for me, for both of us.' And for Dad.

'That's nice.' He motions with his cup. 'I think we need to get our skates on, looks like the train will be going soon.'

'Oh heck, yes!'

'There! Quick!' Joe points to some empty seats.

'Oh my God, we need to get them!' I dive down the train, trying to beat the people who are coming from the opposite direction.

'Quicker, quicker!' He's right at my back, his hand on my waist and even though it is sending shivers through my entire body, it feels just normal, like we've known each other for ever. We're giggling like a pair of kids as I fling myself into the space. 'Fantastic, nothing worse than having to stand,' he says, plonking himself down next to me then turning to look – straight into my eyes.

We grin at each other for a moment, then I glance down self-consciously. This is weird. I hardly know him. Why do I feel like we've been buddies for ages?

'You're telling me.' I sink further down in the seat and wriggle myself free of my coat, trying to give myself something to do that doesn't involve looking at him. Keep myself occupied.

Then I busy about in my bag, waiting for everybody to settle. Which is all to do with me, and not to do with being sat next to a man I can't seem to take my eyes off.

'You didn't mind me sitting…?'

Shit. Joe thinks I'm freezing him out now. 'Oh no, no, not at all. I've got this weird thing where I can't talk properly on a train until it's moved off. Odd, eh?'

'I get that when I'm on a plane. You know, that bit from when it pulls back until it's in the air?'

I nod. 'You're like in limbo?'

'Waiting for it to actually happen.'

'It's so nice to see you again.' I pause. 'I'm really glad you didn't hang on until tomorrow.'

'That would have been terrible.'

I glance, to check he's not taking the piss. He's not. His face is serious.

We both sit in silence. Not chatting. Then I let out a sigh of relief as the train judders into action.

'You said—'

'Any plans—'

We both speak at the same time. Both stop and grin. He shakes his head, a slow, lazy smile teasing the corners of his mouth.

'You first,' I say.

'So, you've got the type of job you can do from home? Sounds cool.'

'Yep, I'm a writer. What about you?'

'Similar!' He grins. 'I'm a games developer.'

'Wow! That's…'

'Nerdy?' He chuckles.

'No, no, it's impressive.' He grins self-consciously. 'Okay, I guess to do that stuff you need to be a tiny bit geeky but in a good way. I'm geeky about what I do, I want it to be good.'

'Okay, I'm going to 'fess up here. I'm actually bigging myself up, I'm more boring than that, I'm actually an IT consultant in the day. I thought games developer might impress you more!'

He's trying to impress me. It's cute. It's, well, impressive.

'Both impress me! I love my apps, but the thought that somebody can actually put that stuff together is a bit mind-boggling.' I can picture him at his laptop, all studious and clever, creating whole new worlds to give the rest of us something to do when we need a diversion.

'It's not that clever.' He's modest as well as smart. 'I moonlight as a games developer, but in my head that's what I am really. My sister reckons she finds out more about my state of mind from what I'm writing than from what I say! But anyway, I was trying to impress you!'

'You have, with both.' I guess he's not one to unload, more a giver than a taker. Not the type of guy who wants his fifteen minutes of fame. He'll think what I do is horrendous.

'Your job sounds much more exciting.' He sits back, twinkling eyes fixed on mine. If only he knew. 'What kind of writer? Hang on, let me guess!'

I can't not tell him. That would be weird. 'Okay, you get three guesses!'

The train lurches.

'Are you secretly a famous author who is going to kill me in your next murder mystery, for drenching you?'

'Ha ha. Now there's a thought!'

'Was I close?'

'Not really, much more boring!'

'I can't believe you'd ever be boring.' From anybody else that would sound like flattery. From Joe it just sounds like he believes it. 'Okay. So, more journalist than novelist?'

'Closer! One guess left!' I feel like this could be make or break. I don't want it to break. I want to find out more about him.

'That wasn't an actual guess!'

'It was so.' I suddenly realise I'm leaning in, even though I'm scared of where this is going. I can't help myself. Our upper arms are pressed together. I'm grinning at him, because I can't help it. He's fun. As well as smart.

'You are just like my sister.' He shakes his head. 'Right, last guess. If I get it right, the next round of coffees is on you!'

'Sure.' I suddenly feel nervous.

His eyes are twinkling. He runs his fingers through his hair, and I can imagine my hand where his is. I can imagine my hands resting on his shoulders, his chest, feeling the ripple of his muscles. My mouth is dry.

'So, you write for some paper or mag or something.' He holds up a finger. 'That isn't a guess, I'm thinking out loud!'

Oh boy. My throat is suddenly tight for a different reason. This could be tricky. I can't lie. My heart is pounding faster in a not good way. Not an 'I fancy the pants off you' way, more an 'I'm a rabbit looking for an escape route' way.

I can't admit I'm the stalker from hell who has already shared our meet-cute with more people than inhabit his hometown and mine combined, and my career depends on me being able to dramatise, romanticise and hilaricise every trip we make together. Can I?

This man doesn't wear his heart, and his life, on his sleeve. This man is quiet, considered. Private.

My pulse slows very slightly. I need to keep this simple. Not quite the whole truth, but the truth.

'I know! You're an agony aunt!'

I can't help it. I laugh as all the tension leaves my body in a rush. I shake my head. 'Oh my God, you're kidding me? I'd give rubbish advice, or just tell people to get a grip.'

'And drink coffee?'

'And drink coffee, and gin. Lots.'

'So?'

'So, well, I'm far more humdrum. No scandal here, I just write a weekly column about everyday life.'

'Ah.' He chuckles. 'Well, that explains your pooper scooper comment!'

'It's not all glamour, you know!' I'm relieved now I've said it. But playing it down is definitely the way to go.

'I bet it's a bit like, er, what was it Sophie used to read?' Sophie, who is Sophie? 'Oh yeah, I know, Slummy Mummy, I think that was it?'

'Er yes, there was a column like, ages –' aeons '– ago called that. Is Sophie, er, your aunt?' Surely, he can't have a girlfriend who read that column, like ten years ago? Mum used to read it out to me. She could relate, apparently. At least I know where I inherited my accident-prone side from.

'Soph's my sister! I have so got to tell her you thought she was my aunt.'

'Oh my God, no! No, don't say that, she'll hate me.' I don't want her to hate me.

'No way! She's a pain, but she's always been a bit weird.'

'Weird?' Does he think people who read columns like mine are weird? Oh God, this is getting even worse. No way can I tell him the whole story.

'I think that stuff she used to read was aimed at people like who she is now, not who she was all those years ago. She must have been mentally preparing herself for her thirties!'

'Ha ha, yes!' Phew.

'She loves stuff like that.' Shit, I'm not exactly unique but there's not that many people write columns like mine. If I don't own up, and we carry on meeting – which we must – then what are the chances she'll read one of my columns, recognise him in it, spill the beans and he'll be upset and that'll be the end of us.

My stomach hollows out. I reckon my smile has changed to a grimace.

I guess it could still please Carla. Reality. The big break-up. As long as we get the snog and sex first.

Although does she really want 'real' this time? I think she's more into fantasy. I think she wants happy, feel-good, relatable but unlikely. Not jangling nerves and feeling sick.

'Are you okay?'

'Fine, sorry! Coffee went down the wrong way.' I splutter to make it sound authentic. 'So what else does

Sophie read?' I shove my spare hand under my thigh and cross my fingers.

'All that "Why Mummy Drinks" stuff, the books, y'know?'

'Oh yes, they're funny, hilarious!' Why have I adopted a posh London drawl?

'Is that the type of stuff you write?'

'Kind of, but about other people more than myself.'

He grins. 'Oh God, yeah, can't imagine anything worse than writing about myself!' Shit. 'I mean, who wants to tell the whole world about their lives? I don't even get the whole dumping on social media thing about private stuff. Weird.'

'Weird.' I nod. This is going from bad to worse, I really have to 'fess up, or otherwise if he finds out he'll be gutted. I don't want him to be gutted.

'Mum would die if she realised how much Sophie shares on Facebook.' He grins. 'I'm pretty sure when she was pregnant, she shared her scans with her mates on there before she even showed Mum and Dad. They'd be horrified if they knew.'

Horrified. If I get through this unscathed, and we ever get to the 'meet the parents' bit then I am doomed. 'They're not into social media at all?' Just to be one hundred per cent clear on this.

He shrugs, a bit self-consciously. 'It's not really social media, they're just not into sharing full stop. I guess we're dyed-in-the-wool farming folk who don't talk about personal stuff unless it's absolutely necessary, and it definitely doesn't go outside the family. Not that they've got a huge social circle, just a handful of people that they really like.'

'Apart from Sophie?' Sophie might like me.

'Apart from Sophie, she's a total rebel.' He chuckles. 'The touchy-feely one who'd pal up with somebody she found on a park bench.' I can practically see his fondness for her oozing out of him. I think I quite like her myself. 'But even she was mortified when somebody told her she'd made it into the local newspaper!'

'Oh wow, what did she do?'

'Passed her Bikeability test at school. She was mentioned on page 9 in a long list of others. Mum was chuffed and tore it out, Sophie was mortified and refused to use her bike again for two weeks in case she fell off and got ribbed about it.'

'So you're not chasing public adoration then?'

'Can't think of anything worse, can you? Or—' he glances down at his coffee, avoiding my gaze '—understand why *anybody* would want that.'

I stare at the top of his head. He's sweet, he's nice, he's sexy. And he's also funny and clever. He seems straight-up and honest, but he's the type of guy who shares with the people who are close to him. In real life.

I think getting to know Joe and writing about falling for a guy on a train are two mutually exclusive events.

He has stopped talking, he looks up. Straight at me.

'Oh shit, that's not what you do, is it? Look, I'm sorry, I didn't mean… okay, I did mean I'd rather die than share all my shit in public, but I mean, I get that some people like that stuff. Lots of people. Like Sophie, er, everybody. I mean, look at how popular all that reality TV is. Ignore me, it's cool. Great. People want to be famous. If they want to share everything then that's cool. That's... I sound judgy, I'm not, honest. I need to shut up, don't I?'

'It's fine.' I smile. 'You don't sound judgy, but it is kind of what I write –' I smile apologetically and blunder on '– but it's not exactly people wanting to share.' I think I need to be careful here, he'll think I'm totally whacko. Or a nosey busybody who follows people. 'I write this "Confessions of a..." column which is about me a bit, but about people I come across as well.' He nods but is looking confused. I'm a writer, and I can't even explain what I'm writing. I need to start again. 'I started off with "Yorkshire Girl in the City"—'

'Yorkshire? I didn't realise, I thought you...'

'I'm not from Yorkshire.' I grin. 'It looked better as a headline, I mean Northumberland is a bit of a mouthful isn't it?' He nods. 'And my boss thought it was close enough.'

He shakes his head, but he's smiling. 'If you told Mum that Yorkshire and Northumberland are close enough, she'd have a duck fit!'

'So would mine! I had to explain to Mum that it was because I'd worked there briefly.' Very briefly. Disastrously.

'What made you go down to London then? Yorkshire not as good as they say?' He's grinning, looking cheeky. His dimples deepening.

Phew. I think we might be okay here.

'London was the dream, Yorkshire just a stepping-stone,' I say breezily.

'Mine too,' he says. His words are soft, but you can tell he means them. 'And has the dream been everything you'd hoped for?'

'Oh yes! I got the job on the local newspaper because there didn't seem to be any jobs for people like me in London, and I wasn't sure I could cut it. I mean, everybody said it was just a fantasy.'

'What do you mean, people like you?' He sounds genuinely interested, not patronising, or like he's taking the mickey.

'Wrong accent, wrong degree.' I shrug. 'Wrong – well, no – connections. It helps if you know people.'

He nods. 'I can imagine. Different in my line of work, logical, black and white. You can do it, or you can't. But hey, I can't believe your family didn't think you could do it!'

'They didn't. It was everybody else, but, well, I proved them wrong, didn't I?' I smile, triumphantly. I'm proud of what I've achieved.

'You did. I bet you're formidable when you're challenged!'

We share a smile. I like that he thinks I might be formidable.

'So hey, what is this dream job then?'

'Well, the dream was London, and a big publication, and, well, to be killing it, but not necessarily quite what I'm doing.' He doesn't comment, just raises that eyebrow again. We both know I'm dodging the issue. 'So—' I take a deep breath '—yeah, the column, it was originally about kind of what I found strange, or odd, or funny when I moved to London, and how people reacted to me because I saw stuff differently and cocked up a lot.' This sounds lame, it is not going well, I need to change the subject. 'And then it kind of grew to more general stuff about everyday life. Commuting, falling in love, watching people on dates—' I'll just drop that one in there '—people's strange hobbies, funny convos. I people watch a lot, it's interesting.'

'Trains must be a brilliant source of inspiration.'

He's looking straight at me. Is this a test? Did he pick up on the 'falling in love' bit, does he know and he's waiting to see if I'll be honest?

But he can't know. That's impossible.

'It's hilarious the stuff some people come out with.' He grins, laughter lines fanning out at the corner of his eyes. They're deep. He smiles a lot. Genuine smiles that fill his whole face, not just change the shape of his mouth. 'It's like they don't think anybody can hear them.'

'Worse on the underground!' Phew, it's fine.

'You're telling me. They've got headphones in and are shouting about personal stuff that you wouldn't even talk to your best mate about.' He colours up a bit. 'Well, I wouldn't. You know…'

'I know exactly what you mean.'

We fall into companionable silence

'Well, anything juicy you hear that might work for me, let me know!'

'You got it! I'm your man. Hey, our stop, I think!'

I quite like the sound of that. Our stop. I cannot believe we've got to Newcastle so quickly; the time has flown by, and I've not had a chance to worry about Mum, or work. Or what I'm going to put in the column this week.

'All change.' I smile as I grab my bag. 'My turn to get the coffee!'

His own smile is apologetic. 'Look, I'm sorry, I'm afraid I'm meeting a mate here, so I'm not getting the connection until later.'

'Oh.' The train noisily grinds to a halt, just before the final pull into the station. I can't believe how disappointed I am that he's ditching me. That we won't get on the next train together.

'Bit of a bugger really, but too late to cancel, it wouldn't be fair.'

'Oh no, heavens no, don't cancel. It was great to see you again!' Oh my God, he's funny as well as sweet, and earnest and all the rest. He's the type of guy I'd really go for if I had time in my life.

Hell, what if I never see him again? Do I ask him for his number? I dither. This is not like me, I'm not a ditherer, I'm a doer.

So why have I gone all fidgety, and don't know what to do?

'Same time next week?' He pulls his bag down from the overhead rack as he speaks. 'Or will you be heading home on Friday instead?'

'No, no, this is going to be my regular train from now

on. Thursday. Hopefully see you, unless I get caught in traffic or by my boss or something.'

'Wow, that's brilliant. The Thursdays, not missing the train!' He grins. 'You can see more of your mum?'

'Exactly.' And I can see more of you, if you want to, that is?

'Fantastic. I'm really pleased for you; it must be a real relief.'

'It is.' I grin back at him as I follow him down towards the door. *Does* he want to see me again? The train lurches back into motion, slowly chugs into the station.

The door is opening, he's stepping off. Shit, why did I just say I'd 'hopefully' see him again? Why didn't I say I wanted to see him, as well as spend more time with Mum? He'll think I'm not interested. I need to say something quick. What's the worst that could happen if I ask about doing this again? He could say, 'Thank you, but no, thank you.' Gut-wrenchingly disappointing. That is all. And I'll be screwed as far as my column goes. But it's the thought that he might not be interested that is causing the flutter in my stomach. I know it is.

That I might have already put him off with my job choice. Or just put him off by being me.

He half turns, waiting for me to follow him off the train. 'Cool. Erm, you don't fancy grabbing a drink at Hexham sometime, do you? I could stay on the train? Or here in Newcastle? If you're not busy, or I guess your mum will be expecting—'

I grin. Result! I am that kid who's been offered a giant

bag of sweets. And a pony! A unicorn. 'That would be cool! I'd like to.' Like? 'Love to! Mum wouldn't mind at all, and Hexham sounds fab if you don't mind staying on?' I would like to grab a drink with him. I really would – and not just because it will send Carla into spasms of delight. 'Next week?' Oh my God, I'm being pushy now. Why can't I strike a happy medium? But it is a *whole* week until then.

'Great!'

We hover on the platform. People having to swarm around us, but I don't care.

'There's a nice bar quite near the station.' Should I ask for his number?

'Sounds good. We better move, I guess, or you'll miss your connection.' He's edging away, but slowly – he doesn't seem to want to go. I don't want him to go. I'm following him like a puppy. 'Same time next week then, Millie?'

I like the way he says my name. 'Fab! It's a date, Joe!' His name rolls off my tongue as though it was always supposed to be. It doesn't sound strange to my ears. And I don't need his number. I'll see him on the train, and if I don't it means we're not having a drink anyway.

He's just a guy on the train that I've chatted to, not a date. Yet.

'Okay, sure.' He hesitates. 'Hey, what day do you usually head back? Sunday?'

'I always used to, but—' It's my turn to falter. I'd love to see him again. Sunday, if that's when he travels back to London. But I've got Mum to think about. He's a stranger, even though he doesn't feel like one. I promised myself to make more room for my mother in my life. 'I've started to stay over sometimes and catch the early train on Monday, if Mum needs me, or head back late on Sunday if I need to be in the office. I think it'll be Sunday this weekend but...'

'That's nice.' He smiles. My God, he is gorgeous. 'No worries, I just wondered. I tend to head back Sunday morning, or just after lunch. I like being back in London.' There's the slightest of shrugs, the lightest of pink on his cheekbones. 'It would just be nice, if we bumped into each other or... But Thursday is great. Something to look forward to.'

I nod. 'I am already looking forward to it.'

We're not holding hands, but if we were we'd be at the arms outstretched stage, our fingertips keeping contact until the very late minute.

'Go!' He grins at me and breaks the contact. 'Go on, you'll miss your train!'

'I'm going. See you next week! My turn to get the coffee.'

He doesn't reply. Just smiles, and winks. I watch as he strides off, willing him to turn round one last time.

He does. He waves, a small self-conscious wave that I return. Still smiling.

My phone pings. It's a message from Mum, and I suddenly realise I've not worried about her, or work, all the way home like I usually do. It's been fun. A total distraction.

Chapter Eighteen

JOE

Sunday 3rd April

'What do you mean, you need a lift to the station in half an hour? I thought you were going in the morning? You go home earlier every week; don't you love us anymore, you city slicker?'

'Of course I love you, little sis.' I smile at Sophie and ruffle her hair, just to annoy her. She does have a point. By the end of the weekend my mind is already half back in London. I'm deciding what to grab for my supper and looking forward to wandering round the flat in bare feet and PJs with a beer in my hand knowing I don't have to get up at 5 a.m. to help sort the cows.

At my parents' home the cold seeps out of the stone floors leaving your feet freezing even with socks on. The only cosy room is the kitchen, where the Aga is on 24/7, the internet is too slow to run games on and it's lights out at 10 p.m. because of the early start.

I love it here and I love my family. I'd miss them if I didn't pop back at weekends, but maybe Sophie is right. Maybe a part of me has gone city slicker. I just love my new life. It's weird really because I'm not a party guy, and I like peace, and my own space. But London gives me the lot. It's a totally different kind of freedom, the kind of feeling that anything is possible. Whereas here on the farm there are immovable boundaries. They've been set in stone for centuries. Or at least that's how it feels.

I wonder what it is about London that made Millie dream about making it there? For me, it just kind of happened and now I wouldn't want it any other way. My biggest dread is that my company hauls me out and sends me somewhere else.

It sounds like Millie was determined to go after a permanent job there and managed it. Maybe it's time I was a little more pro-active. Sure, I've signed up with a couple of agencies, I've talked to a mate, but I need to get on the case, chase people up. Make it happen for me.

We could be the dream team.

Oh gawd, where am I going with this? She looked quite pleased when I suggested we meet up again, but maybe we need to go on a proper date before I get too carried away.

'You're doing that not-listening thing again, where you go all misty-eyed!'

'What?'

'You stare into the distance. Have you got a new girlfriend, or are you just thinking about computer code?'

'Ha ha. Anyway, I don't go back earlier every week. It just feels like that because you pine for me so much when I'm not there!' I put my hand on my heart and a pained expression on my face.

'In your dreams, and did you know you look like you've got constipation?'

'Awww I do love your maternal side!' I tease. 'You're on the lookout for signs of distress!'

'Or maybe it's wind,' she says sweetly, 'and you need a good thump on the back.'

I swing round and wrap my arms round her before she gets any ideas, and we have a brief tussle until Mum walks past and tuts.

'I've got to get back tonight because there's an early crisis meeting tomorrow morning.' I unhand her, and Sophie straightens her top and smooths down her hair.

'Sure. Anyway, what are you reading?'

'Trying to read.' I elbow her out of the way so she isn't peering over my shoulder. 'Can't you butt out and leave me in peace?'

I smile to soften the words. But I do want to be left alone. I'm feeling antsy, because I've resisted all weekend but can't manage any longer. And this is something I need to do without my sister peering over my shoulder. It's private because it's embarrassing. And it's embarrassing because I feel a bit like a stalker. But how can I not do it?

Millie has been on my mind most of the weekend, and

even though I've only met her a couple of times, only had a brief train journey with her, not even had a drink with her yet – I need to Google her.

I've never, ever felt like this before. When I've asked anybody out on a date, the last thing on my mind has been looking them up on the internet – because private lives are private, aren't they? If somebody wants to share something with me about themselves, they'll tell me.

Is it normal? Or am I becoming some kind of weird obsessive, who is about to make a fool of themselves?

Either way, I don't want to share the experience with Sophie.

I flex my fingers nervously and angle my screen away from her.

Obviously when you don't have a surname to go for, don't know which publication a person works for, and are not sure if she has a pseudonym, you cannot have high expectations. But I type anyway.

And wow. Google has taken my lame offering of 'Millie Confessions Yorkshire' and has turned up Millie Shaw. Who bears a striking resemblance to my gorgeous commuter-girl.

Millie, it seems, is a busy girl – she's prolific as well as pretty. Hilariously funny, as I thought she was, and also endearing but down-to-earth and the total girl-next-door.

Well, no, I disagree with the last bit. She is not actually girl-next-door-ish, she is something far more than that kind of tag suggests. She is not ordinary at all.

'I know her!'

I jump guiltily. 'Soph!' It would seem that my nosey sister has not gone away.

'Budge over, let me see properly. Why are you looking at Millie Shaw?' She frowns. 'She writes that "Confessions" column, it's ace.' She squeezes onto the chair next to me. 'She's from Yorkshire, you know.'

'She's not, she's from round here. She worked in Yorkshire for a bit.'

'Really? Are you sure?'

'Positive.' I move to close my laptop, but she stops me.

'She wrote about moving down to London, and then she started to write about her train journeys back to...' Her voice tails off. There's a long pause. 'You're positive? What do you mean, you're positive? How could you possibly...' There's an even longer pause. 'Oh my God, it's her, isn't it?'

'What do you mean, it's her?' I can hear the defensive scratchiness in my voice.

'Oh my God! That's who you've gone all cow-eyed about. You've not been thinking about some boring computer game, you've been thinking about her! You've gone bright red. I knew there was a girl involved. You met her on the train, didn't you?'

'So what? I see lots of people, I was just checking...'

'What's she like in real life? Is she as funny as in the column? I'd totally love to meet her, she's like so smart and independent, but like real as well. If I didn't have my gang, I'd be so into the idea of being like her. So go on, is she just as nice, or is she one of those people who just switch it on for the crowds and are totes boring in real life?'

She is so not 'totes boring'. 'I don't know, I don't read the column!'

'But you are going to!'

'No I'm not, I was just reading about her.'

She folds her arms and stares at me. 'You never read stuff like this. You've actually really met her properly, haven't you? Or you wouldn't have known her name or the Yorkshire bit.'

I wouldn't. She is right. I never read stuff like this.

'Wow, you've got a crush on her! I knew there was somebody, what did I say?'

'You say lots of things. Can you just pipe down?'

She lowers her voice to a loud whisper. 'You've not kissed her, have you? Oh God, Joe.' She puts her hand over her mouth, but I can still hear her chuckle. Then she leans forward so that she's whispering straight into my ear. 'You do know that she wrote about her ex once after he'd been crap in bed, and he was like totally fuming, and dumped her, and she wrote about that as well? If you snog her, you are well screwed, Joe-bro. She'll tell the whole world what it was like! Oh shit.' She stops talking abruptly, so I look at her out of the corner of my eye. She's got her hand over her mouth. 'Oh shit, she wrote this column a few weeks ago about falling for somebody when she was at King's Cross. She really fancied him, practically wanted to shag him on the platform!'

Oh my God. My heart seems to have stopped; my skin is prickling. I'm not sure if I'm hot or cold. She wrote about me, about us, she did feel something. More than something. This isn't just me.

'She literally fell on top of him, fell down the escalator or steps or something.' She raises a questioning eyebrow.

'Don't be ridiculous!' I croak out.

My heart has restarted but there's this heavy lump of disappointment in my stomach. I feel slightly sick. She fell for somebody, but it wasn't me. We bumped into each other, then she walked away, and collided with – fell on top of – somebody else.

When she chased after me with my mobile, she was just being kind.

Meeting up again was just, well, what was it?

But she agreed to meet me on Friday, have a drink together. A date. So that has to mean something, right?

Cool. I'm not completely imagining the connection between us. It's not just me. The guy she met must have been nothing. Or something that just fizzled out straightaway. I can handle that. That's fine. Soph said it was a few weeks ago, so that could have happened way before we met. I relax slightly. A girl like Millie must meet and date lots of guys.

I'm just over-reacting because for a moment there I thought she'd made our encounter public! Phew, last thing I want is to be plastered all over the web.

Soph chuckles, interrupting the whirring cogs in my brain. But it's fine. My cold sweat has ebbed away. 'She is just so bloody accident-prone and funny; I mean who else could meet a guy that way? She's not had another column for what?' She pauses, frowns slightly. 'Like a couple of weeks. They've been running this "love on the tracks" stuff by some other woman, about whether the train's romantic or not. Surveys and stuff like that, you know? In fact, you've just reminded me, I've not read this week's episode, I usually do it when Ben's asleep and he seems to have forgotten about doing that at the moment.'

She groans and rests her head on my shoulder briefly, so I wrap my arm round her and pull her in for a hug. It's serious stuff when she's missing out on her reading. She pulls back after a few seconds, to prove that she's coping. And I get it. Soph might share more than the rest of the family, but she still wants us to think she's strong.

'She must be warming up to writing a whole series of stuff about meeting guys on trains. Wow, you want to watch out, she might be on the prowl.' She walks her fingers up my arm. 'She could have you in her sights to use and abuse! She might be luring you in!'

I flinch away, swatting at her hand, and slam the top of the laptop down. 'You talk such a load of crap at times, Soph.'

'My hormones told me you were up to something! Baby hormones mean I'm super tuned in to everybody, including you, ha ha.'

'You sound evil.' My stomach is feeling kind of hollow again now. But I can't believe Millie was just chatting to me for material for her column. No. I can't. It was so natural, we got on. There was a … feeling. A definite attraction.

'I am evil!' Soph chuckles, in a very evil fashion. Then

seems to sober up. 'You do know what you're doing here, Joe, don't you? You haven't done anything you're going to—'

'I haven't done anything at all,' I say firmly. 'Now, if you don't mind, I need to get my stuff together.'

'Gawd Joe, who'd have thought?' She is giggling to herself as she finally leaves me alone.

Bugger, bugger, bugger. Have I made a complete idiot of myself? I fancied her, I more or less came on to her, but she seemed to like me too. I didn't feel like she was working out if she could use me as material for her column. She never suggested that at all.

I could stand her up. Catch another train.

But I know I can't. I want to see her again. I need to.

Maybe I do need to read her column, find out what she really writes about – when Sophie isn't peering over my shoulder. Except she's not been writing anything recently. That's what Sophie just said. Surveys. It's just been surveys and general chat about finding romance on a train. And the story about her falling in lust with a stranger who isn't me.

I'm not sure I want to read about that right now.

Maybe it's better not to know?

Chapter Nineteen

MILLIE

Monday 4th April

E pisode 4
   Confessions of… we meet for real!
   I am beginning to feel like a schoolgirl with a hopeless crush.
My train-guy might have a name now (I'm superstitious, I can't
make it public until I'm sure this is real), but we still haven't
swapped numbers and all I really know about him is that he works
in IT, in London. That narrows it down a lot, doesn't it?

I spent all of Wednesday evening preparing for our encounter,
which meant I had sticky notes all over the bedroom mirror and a
checklist on my phone. I practised my smile, and a variety of
opening lines to cover every scenario.

Despite the fact that we were only (possibly) meeting on a
train I decided to treat this as a practice run in case things
developed between us. My father firmly believed in starting as you
mean to go on, so this is my new mantra. Although I'm not sure

that, when he said it, he was thinking about eyebrow and lady-forest tidying, or lacy bras that contain hidden extra-control (this is in case sprinting is required, before stripping – you have to catch your man before you can kiss him is also a new motto).

Anyway, I was scrubbed, plucked and trussed more thoroughly than any turkey before I headed in to work on Thursday. I had deliberated very carefully on footwear and decided that while flatties might be most sensible, he might not recognise me if I'd lost three inches in height since we last met. I'll have to work my way down once we get to know each other.

I double dosed on lippy and deodorant before I left the office, as I was sure in my worked-up anxious state I'd be sweating cobs (that means 'profusely' in London-speak) and even if my lips weren't destined to be mashed against his there's a good chance I'd have licked the colour off myself. Yes, I was a bit of a nervous wreck. Which is probably why when I got to the station, I didn't notice that I'd picked up half a loo roll on the bottom of my shoe, on my second emergency wee-visit.

My bladder is my stress-level indicator. On the outside I might be calm and serene, but inside my waterworks send out alarms every twenty seconds. How the hell am I supposed to meet the perfect guy/perform the perfect interview/give the perfect presentation if my bladder thinks it controls my life?

Anyway, confession coming up. All my preparations turned out to be a waste of time. When I spotted him, it was through my legs, my arse stuck in the air as I wobbled on one leg, grappling with a piece of dirty toilet paper of uncertain provenance.

In my dotage I am not likely to have fond, romantic memories of young love to look back on.

Anyway, to give him his due he recognised my behind, and had bought coffee!

Oh my God, it felt so good as we walked, shoulders brushing (well, mine brushed his bicep) to catch the, our, train.

I think I've met a good guy here. He didn't spend the entire journey talking about his ex, his job, how hard done by he is or how there's a global conspiracy and he's sure the world is going to end tomorrow (yep, I have heard them all). In fact, he didn't spend a single second of the journey talking about any of that shit. We chatted, we laughed, he listened, he even tempted me into talking about losing my dad. I've never found a stranger so easy to talk to – but he's not a stranger is he? It already feels like I've known him all my life.

The journey didn't last quite that long though. I didn't get to ask him about himself hardly at all before we hit Newcastle and it was time to change trains. And then when it came to catching our connection, he left me.

Yes, he had to go. I can tell you, the disappointment was real. I thought we had more time.

I am counting on the fact that he really did have another meeting arranged – probably as a get out in case I turned out to be a complete looney – and he'll be there next week.

———————

'Sweet. But you still haven't kissed?' Carla says in her judgemental tone, and frowns.

'No, but we have talked properly!'

'This has to be the slowest moving romance since we

wore bonnets and were chained to railings.' She rolls her eyes. 'When I said think *Brief Encounter* I didn't mean you have to be as chaste as they were in 1945. You're not married, and I presume he's not, so what's stopping you?'

This is one question that has bothered me. Why am I going so slowly, treading so carefully? It's as though every second counts.

Am I worried that I'll miss out on a good thing, or spoil one? Whatever, it is not something I am going to discuss with Carla.

'In case you didn't notice,' I say primly, 'commuter trains aren't exactly the Orient Express. There's hardly enough elbow room for you to drink a coffee without risking spilling it all over yourself, so there's definitely not enough room for a leg-over.'

'Doe-eyes only get you so far, girl. You'll have to up the pace or treat us to a "dumped him" episode.'

'How can I dump him, if I hardly know him?'

'Ahh, but you do, don't you? You want to jump him.'

She's right. I do want more. But I also like what we've got. Except I'm not one hundred per cent sure what that is.

I like him, he seems to like me. We have things in common, like Northumberland and London, like a sense of humour, like a coffee addiction. We also have areas of potential difference that scare me. Major things. Like the fact that my job revolves around sharing stuff.

He seems to be a very private person, and I share *everything*. Is that ever going to work?

'Well, we'll see what feedback we get on today's edition,

but early signs are that they're still hooked. They've got you saving his bacon, but I reckon next Monday they will want more action. So don't say I didn't warn you!'

I try not to roll my eyes. I also try hard to still the flutter in my stomach that is not indigestion from the pastries I stuffed in my face on the way to work – it is more like mild panic. Or 'I'm going to puke any second now', because she has just reminded me that Episode 3 went out first thing this morning. If Joe, by some weird totally unlikely chance (and they happen a lot in my life), actually reads the column, he will know it is him. He will recognise his red scarf; he will remember dropping his mobile phone. There is no way he cannot know I have written about him.

And then he might catch a different train, leave the country, yell at me about privacy and fucking up his life by humiliating him, or worst of all blank me. My stomach feels hollow just at the thought.

It's all happened before, but the difference is that this time I really care. It matters.

'We've arranged to have a drink together next week.' I drag the words out reluctantly. Saying them out loud, putting it out there, seems even more like I'm tempting fate. Bad fate. I like to know things for certain before I broadcast them.

I don't know at all whether this drink is going to happen.

'Good girl.' Carla smiles and marches off, not having a clue about what is currently going on in my brain.

'Shit, I thought that she was actually going to pat you on the head like a dog then,' sniggers Zoe.

'Sod off.' But so did I. Scary. Even more scary to think what she'll do to me if I am train-ghosted and never see Joe again.

Chapter Twenty

MILLIE

Thursday 7th April

'Had a good day?'

Oh boy, it has just got a million times better. Those eyes, that soft voice, those kissable lips – coffee! I am so relieved to see him I'm tempted to grab him and plant a smacker on his lovely lips. I don't, instead I smile weakly and stutter out, 'Sure, not bad. You?' with relief and grab the cup he's holding out.

My stomach is churning as I search his face for signs that he has read Episode 3, that he has recognised himself, that he hates me.

'It's just got better!' He grins. 'Am I allowed to say that? I'm not very good at being cool.'

'Me neither. I like not-cool.' I grin back at him, and the panic leaves my body and is replaced with the much nicer buzzy feeling of anticipation and excitement. I'm not sure my insides are equipped to cope with so much emotional turmoil. It's far easier to be single, detached and a workaholic. 'Not that I think you're not cool or anything, I just meant...' I raise my eyebrows and screw my mouth up in an 'eek, help me' look and he laughs.

He is mesmerising when he laughs. His whole face transforms, and the sound is addictive. I want to hear it again; I want to make him laugh. Is that odd? Wanting so much to make somebody else feel happy?

'I'm not cool. One hundred per cent not. Are you still up for that...'

'Drink? I'm counting on it!'

His shoulders drop slightly, and I realise that he's just relaxed. He was edgy, wound up and nervous as well, for different reasons. Or maybe they're the same one.

Wanting to know we both feel the same way.

Okay, I didn't want him to read my stuff and freak, but I just plain didn't want to lose the chance of getting to know him better, I guess.

'Glad we got that awkward bit over with!' I love the fact that he's so open, says the bits that a lot of us would gloss over. 'I was worried you'd bail out on me at Newcastle.'

'Never! How did your drink go last week?' I suddenly realise how bad that sounds, like I'm accusing *him* of ducking out. 'I didn't mean I thought *you'd* bailed out, you just reminded me!'

'I'd rather have got on the train with you actually! By the time I got on I was stuck with the happy hour crowd.' He grins, pauses to let me get on the train first. Waits until we are in our seats. 'It was okay, useful, I guess.' He shrugs. 'Had to see a man about a dog, or more accurately a job.'

Wow, a job in Newcastle. Oh no, that means he won't be on the train – but it also means he'll be closer if I spend more time in Hexham. Woah, what am I thinking? I've not even had a date with the man. One drink at a time, Millie.

'You're looking to move to Newcastle, closer to home?'

'Not really.' He pauses.

This is a bumpy ride. It's a bit like a rollercoaster.

'I love being in London, but my job isn't a permanent position, I work for a software house, they send me here there and everywhere.'

'Exciting! You're a globetrotter!'

He laughs and my heart does a little skip. 'Not quite the globe! It can be good, I used to love the travel when I started, but, in a way, I sometimes wish I had the certainty of staying in London. It feels like home, it feels—' he pauses '—like everything. Like I've arrived, if you get what I mean? My mum loves to be able to tell people that her son works "in the city". But I could get yanked out at any time and sent to the Outer Hebrides or somewhere remote and not exciting at all!'

He grins and I want to grin back, but my face feels a bit stiff. My heart has just dived off the platform. 'The in-place to be, I hear.'

He wants to be in London. Permanently. 24/7/365.

And I'm looking to spend more time with Mum, working remotely.

I never saw that one coming. Is this going to be a problem?

I think I want to be back home more than I want to be in London right now – and I never saw that coming either. Because it is home.

Though I do also want to be on this train. Because Joe is here.

He laughs. 'I guess. This guy recruits all over, he just happens to be based in Newcastle, and it was an easy place to meet. But who knows what the future holds, eh? Though listening to her—' he tilts his head towards a girl sat at the end of the carriage '—it could be worse.'

I turn my head slightly, glance at the girl a few seats down – shouting into her mobile phone.

'This is turning into a right 'mare, innit? I mean I gotta ask Shaz to be a bridesmaid, haven't I?'

'Yeah, but it's her sister's boyfriend's place where we're having the wedding and it's totally sick. I can't not go there now, can I? I'd look a right div if we changed to somewhere cheap.'

'I know, it's like she's bought her way in. She only told me about it so I'd owe 'er.'

'Well I 'ad only got five, so I s'pose six is like neater?'

'Oh yeah, babe, you're the chief one, deffo one hundred per cent like.'

'Yeah, but I can't put her at the back, can I? I mean her dad is like sorting the cocktails and stuff as well.'

'Shaz is going to demand centre stage,' Joe whispers in my ear and makes me giggle.

'Shaz has got her by the short and curlies,' I mutter back,

trying not to move my lips too much and let her know we're listening. Though I reckon she's oblivious to the rest of the world.

'I reckon she's more the Brazilian type of girl, looking at her.'

I splutter into my coffee.

'Well, look at those eyebrows, they've been taken off and painted back on! Maybe she's the same down there as well?'

'Tattoos?'

'Oh God, imagine the pain? But the question is—' he pauses '—did Shaz or one of her mates do it?'

'Joe!' I'm choking back the laughter; my eyes are watering. I put down my coffee with shaky hands and wipe the tears away.

'No babe, Daz's mate is doing the disco.'

'And what else?' mouths Joe. I bite my lip and study my fingernails; he's still looking at me and I know if our eyes meet I won't be able to help myself. I'll be laughing.

'I'm not havin' her mess with my music, man.'

'Yeah, he's the real deal. That thing last week was rockin', wasn't it?'

'But it was like just normal? This place is amazing and when he saw it, he was like saying the sound would be totally cool?'

'Can you imagine if she has to get married in somewhere just normal with no cocktails?' Joe says.

'The shame!'

He tips his head to one side, switches his attention to me. 'Do you think she actually loves the lucky guy?'

I sigh. 'Weddings often end up bigger than the romance. I guess it's easy to get carried away, not that I'd know.'

'Me neither.'

Ahh, so we've got that one out of the way!

He smiles. 'It seems a bit sad though. I guess I'd be happy getting married at the side of the road, if it was to the right girl.'

'You're a true romantic,' I tease, nudging his arm with my elbow and feeling a bit fuzzy inside. 'Not that many girls would agree to getting hitched at the side of the M6.'

'Really? You surprise me!'

'It could make a good story for me though.' I draw out the imaginary headline. 'From cold shoulder to hard shoulder – the perfect place to get married.'

'Ha ha, you're funny.'

'Thank you, kind sir, it's my claim to fame.'

The bride-to-be moves up the train to get better phone reception, still moaning on about Shaz.

'I guess the train is a romantic place to meet as well?' he says softly, but it seems like a leading question, and it's my turn to feel slightly on edge. Is writing about this, about us, going to be a deal-breaker? Could it spoil everything? Or is my imagination just working overtime because I'm scared it will?

'I guess.' I smile, hoping it will help me relax. Hide the jumble of nerves I'm feeling. 'Fleeting encounters, the will-we-meet-again feeling, strangers colliding.' I raise an eyebrow.

He half smiles in return. Looks slightly awkward and

embarrassed. 'Okay, I admit it, I couldn't resist looking you up and—' he cringes slightly '—I read some of your Yorkshire Girl posts, and I've seen all the surveys and interviews with people who think a train journey is the most romantic trip in the world, who want to find love under the clock at St Pancras.' He really has coloured up now.

Oh boy, does this mean he never got beyond that? That he hasn't read about when I met *him*?

'And I read your bit about landing on some poor guy, except I skipped over the bits when you said he was hot!'

It's my turn to look embarrassed. Do I admit it was really about him? That he did something to me right from that first meeting. Or is that too much, likely to scare him to death and send him running for cover? Oh, to hell with it. 'Okay, I've got a confession, I fell on him, but I didn't fall for him, I was think—'

'Stop!' He's laughing. 'Poor guy! I'm glad you didn't fall for him.' His gaze is steady; the laughter has died. 'But he'd probably be crushed if he realised the whole world had read about it, and he still didn't get the girl! You.' His voice is soft as he says the final world.

Shit. He obviously hasn't read Episodes 2 or 3 – the ones about him, us. And he's probably talking about himself, saying he'd be crushed if I told the whole world.

Do I tell him? I don't want to tell him. I'm selfish, I want this moment. I want this drink with him, this date.

'Shit, we're here.' He's on his feet abruptly, grabbing my hand. 'Come on, we've nearly missed our stop! I can't believe the time whizzed by so quick, it normally feels much longer.'

'It does.' I grab my bag as he chivvies me along. His smile is so warm, genuine. Happy. I want to spend some time with him.

I need to.

Then I'll tell him.

Before he gets a chance to do a catch-up and reads it all and hates me.

I'll tell him over the drink. That's what I'll do.

'Oh no, look!' I point up at the departures board, as we step off the train at Newcastle. 'Our train's delayed by thirty minutes, which probably means more like an hour.' I've spent many an hour at Newcastle, drinking coffee and people-watching. Fine on a nice summer's evening, not so fine in the middle of winter when it's freezing cold, dark and damp. At least it is April, there's a hint of warmth in the air, the days are getting longer. And I've got Joe for company. Still, I was looking forward to our drink, and at this rate it'll be rushed.

'Change of plan then, grab a beer near here and do Hexham next time? If that's okay with you?'

I grin, feeling much happier. For one, he's making sure we get our first drink together, and two – he's planning on there being a next time! 'Sounds good to me.'

'Go for the nearest place that looks okay, then plan to

catch the later train?'

'Sure.' We head down the platform in companionable silence, and I feel like I'm glowing, and practically floating.

I've not been able to get the idea of this date (if I dare call it that) out of my head all week, and the fact that we've been chatting happily all journey, and there's no sign of us hitting an awkward silence, makes it feel perfect.

I mean, how many first dates have you been on where however much you fancy each other, it has been excruciating? The whole 'I can't say that, he'll think I'm boring as hell', 'why didn't I wear my other jeans?', 'have I got a VPL or a muffin top?', 'will this lipstick come off if we kiss?', 'is he thinking about being somewhere else?', 'should we kiss?' nightmare is not on my mind at all. Well, apart from the kiss bit. I want to kiss him, I really do. And I don't care about my lipstick.

But is it really going to happen just outside Newcastle station after a quick pint while we're keeping an eye on the clock?

I did write a whole series of 'confessions' about first dates. They're easy fodder, so many turn out to be a nightmare. Even deciding what to wear and where to go is a minefield. But somehow, even though I've made this a big thing in my head, in reality I've not been through the whole 'will I be over/underdressed' thing because I had to be dressed suitably for work, and travelling home, and I didn't want Carla's sarcasm, or my mother in shock. And the 'where' was never in my hands anyway.

So, it turns out that there is a bar at the station, and it is actually quite a nice bar – though I'm fairly sure I wouldn't be that bothered if it wasn't – because I can't take my eyes off Joe.

I watch him as he goes to the bar for our drinks, I watch him as he talks, not being able to tear my gaze from his mouth and I don't care what Carla wants, what my readers need, what will keep my career on track. I just want to kiss him.

'So.' He sips his pint, his eyes never leaving mine. 'Deep down, country girl or city girl?'

'Wow, that's a big question for this early in the evening!' A question I don't think I know the answer to any longer. I was so sure, but now I'm not.

I watch the bubbles rise in my prosecco, then let my gaze meet his again. 'I guess I've always wanted to be in the big city and it's the best place to have a career like mine. But I do like going home. What about you?' I think I'm trying to sidestep the question. I wasn't expecting it. It's the question I should be asking myself, and instead he's done it.

'My sister calls me a city slicker!' He chuckles. 'Which isn't exactly true, but I guess I do feel comfortable there. You get a kind of freedom, don't you?'

I nod. You do. Freedom from the feeling that everybody knows your business, from the boundaries – city limits are far bigger than rural ones, mentally as well as physically. And I guess you can also get freedom from responsibilities. For him it might have been getting up at dawn to milk the cows, but for me it was from my family. And I don't want that.

'Penny for them?'

'Sorry.' I shake the thoughts away. 'I was just thinking about Mum. I guess I got too much freedom from my worries in that way.'

'But you're getting more time with her now. Fridays?' he says softly. His hand briefly resting over mine.

'I am.'

'I love the way she's so important to you, and you're prepared to do something about it. Not just say you wish it was different.'

'I'm lucky I'm in a job where I can.'

'It's still down to you making it happen.'

'I don't want to let her or Dad down.'

'I doubt you'd ever let anybody down.' He's looking at me so earnestly, his fingertips only inches from mine.

'I can travel back to London on a Monday evening now as well.' The words catch in my throat. I'm acutely aware of his skin against mine, of the gentle but firm grip. His gaze is on me when I glance up, steady, but his eyes are dark.

He is thinking the same as me. He has to be.

'That's great for you.' His words are barely there. 'Shame I usually have to go back on Sunday, or first thing Monday.'

'At least we get Thursdays.' My throat is parched.

'We certainly do.'

I am watching his lips move, not really hearing the words. I'm leaning in towards him, drawn in a way I can't ignore, and he matches me. Reaches out and tucks my hair behind my ear, his fingers lingering on my cheek with a pressure so light, so tempting I find myself pressing into it, wanting it to last. Not wanting him to move away.

I stare at his lips, slightly parted, and moisten my own. Aware of his breathing, matching mine to his.

'Millie?' It's a question and an answer all in one. The flutter in the base of my stomach scares me, but what scares me more is missing out on this.

I think we move at the same time; I think it is Joe who makes the decision, I think I'm trembling. But none of it matters. The warmth of his breath fans my lips as for a fraction of a moment he gives me chance to turn away, and then he kisses me.

I've been kissed many times. Gently, roughly, searchingly, badly, but never in a way that's made me so acutely aware of the way our lips meet and match so perfectly, the slight roughness of firm lips, the heat of his mouth, the taste of mingled coffee, tangy beer and something much more basic, the gentle burn in my throat as I ache for more. The tingle in my body as the back of his hand drifts down my neck, the heat in my belly as his fingers settle on my waist.

He pulls back slightly. Just enough to break contact. His thumb brushing the corner of my mouth as he cups my jaw with his hand.

'We should stop.' His voice is gruff. 'I don't want to.' His forehead rests against mine. 'But I think we're attracting an audience.' Our gazes meet, then his drifts towards the bar and I follow suit.

The guy serving drinks has his elbows on the bar and is grinning at us.

'Time for a hasty departure?' he says softly, still not moving away.

I grin back at him. 'The train pulling out of platform...' Then giggling like kids we pull apart, grab our stuff and hare off, my hand in his.

I don't realise until we're on the platform that we're still holding hands.

It just feels right. I just accepted it.

I glance up at him as he studies the departure board. Is this too good to be true?

He looks down at me, as though he knows. Does it matter? Can't I just live in the moment, enjoy this for what it is, even if tomorrow our trains set off in different directions?

Sometimes I think I spend too much time on regrets over the past and hopes for the future. And skip living in the moment. The most important time.

Well, whether it is too good or not, Carla is going to kill me. Our first kiss was not under the iconic clock, the romantic meeting point at King's Cross. It was not on Hadrian's Wall with the wind whistling around us.

Or at the top of Blackpool Tower.

It was in a bar.

At Newcastle railway station.

As we waited for our connection.

But you know what? I don't care. It was perfect.

So perfect that I'm not sure I'm ready to share it with anybody, let alone my readers, yet.

Chapter Twenty-One

JOE

Sunday 10th April

The last bit of the journey – when we caught the train at Newcastle – was strange. It was like the goalposts had moved. There'd been this shift. It wasn't awkward. It was just different. Like I'd stepped into her bubble, and we weren't two totally separate people any longer.

We didn't chat, we sat next to each other, me trying to steal looks at her without her noticing – and failing. She kept catching my eye, and grinning.

Millie is beautiful. It goes beyond being pretty, it's her whole being, her smile, the way she moves, her teasing voice. The way she's so heart-achingly lovely and vulnerable when she talks about her mum.

I guess family is important to me, and there are some values that you have to share. Or you've not got a foundation to build on.

Our shoulders were touching, our upper arms, our hands occasionally brushing against each other, and it made me realise I want, I need so much more. If I'd thought I was stupidly smitten before, it's gone up several levels of infatuation now.

I wanted to grab her, kiss her again. I wanted to beg her to meet up with me the very next day. I wanted to wrap my arms round her, touch every inch of her. But I didn't.

I did ask for her number though. I did promise I'd see her same time next week, and she laughed and said, 'It's a date!'

There were so many things I wished I'd said, so much wasted time, and I feel like I have to make every second count in case she slips between my fingers. Disappears back to where she came from.

What if she decides I'm uptight and boring? She's so open, so outgoing and happy to share everything. She writes about her cock-ups, her feelings. It's what she does, it's her job. It's her. We're just so bloody different in that way.

But I just felt completely on the same wavelength as her. Comfortable.

I reckon a part of my brain thinks that this cannot be happening. She can't possibly be real. That it doesn't make sense, bumping into somebody and feeling like it was fate – and then seeing them again and it being even better than you could imagine.

I'm not like this. Things like this don't happen to me.

Although I thought when I dated Lisa that we were

meant to be. There was no bolt of lightning, just a steadiness. A feeling it was right. That we'd stay together – after all we'd known each other for years. And look what happened there.

I had bought Lisa a ring. I was about to ask her to marry me. To start a new life with me. Instead, I found out she was planning a different life – for both of us. I found out she'd told her parents I was coming back, had told her dad I'd like to work for him.

And he'd mentioned it to my dad. And they'd been devastated that I hadn't told them myself first.

It had been a mess.

It was like we'd been on totally different wavelengths. There'd been no communication. I couldn't trust a word she said.

So, if I'd been so wrong with someone I'd known most of my life, how can I expect a random meeting with a girl at a railway station to turn out any better? It might feel like it's meant to be, but she might be just like Lisa. Thinking I'm somebody different to who I really am.

I don't know why I changed the subject after I'd told Millie about my job hunting. Why didn't I tell her that it's not just a more permanent position I want, I'd like to give us a chance and see where this goes?

Be open. Be completely upfront and make sure it is totally different from how it was with Lisa.

Because it's true, I have admitted to myself, I'm not just looking to turn my current contract into something more permanent because I love London. I want to do it so that in the coming days, weeks, before I've really had a chance with her, I'm not sent somewhere else. I'm not on some other journey. Some other path.

Why can't I admit it to her as well?

It does sound ridiculous even to me. I might have only met her a handful of times, but something deep inside me is saying that this is different. That this is important.

I need to make it different. I should have encouraged her to tell me about the guy she fell on at the station, asked her about what she's writing about now. About love on the train tracks. Found out more about her aspirations, and told her about mine, so that I'd know. We'd know.

I've been so wrapped up in my thoughts about seeing her again, I haven't even kept up to date and read her latest stuff.

'Okay lover-boy?' Sophie whispers as she drops casually onto the sofa next to me, cradling my nephew. Startling me back to the present. He's cute. I get why she can't resist showing him off on social media to all her mates. Is sharing so bad?

His tiny little fingers are closed into fists which twitch as he sleeps. His mouth so tiny and perfectly formed it's hard to know how he can make such a loud noise when he wants. I've never, like a lot of guys I guess, been really into babies. To be honest they just weren't on my radar, until little Ben came into our lives. But now I get why parents can be so fiercely protective, why they'd do anything to keep their kids safe. He's so tiny, so innocent, so totally vulnerable.

'I'm fine. You?' I whisper back, touching his little finger gently.

'Knackered.'

'You look it.' I grin back at her. She has dark shadows under her eyes.

'I would kill for a straight eight hours right now, or even six, or five at a push.'

'Can't help with that one, I'm afraid. Can't you get his loving granny to do a shift?'

She rolls her tired eyes. 'I daren't ask her anything right now.'

'What have you been tiffing about now?' I ask mildly. Sophie and Mum are always at odds, they're so different.

'Apparently I have been hanging out my dirty washing in public!'

'Nappies?' I pull a face. How do even doting parents cope with that?

'Worse! I posted on Facebook about the shit side of motherhood.' She looks down at Ben, the love radiating out. 'I mean I love him to bits; I'd never want anything different, but he is bloody hard work at times. But—' she gives a heavy sigh '—apparently I should only discuss it behind closed doors, not admit to failure in public.'

'You're not a failure.' I put an arm round her shoulders and give her a hug.

'I know.'

She really does sound worn out.

'How did she even know about the Facebook thing?'

'Nosey Norma at the post office has got a new iPad. Talking of which—' she shuffles into a more comfortable position '—you better be careful with that Millie, you know.'

'What do you mean, careful?'

'I take it you've not actually read her recent stuff?'

I frown. I can't exactly tell her it's on my to-do list, can I? 'Well, I had a quick look through her stuff.' I admit reluctantly. 'It's funny.'

'It is. She is. But I'd look at what she's writing now if I was you.' Ben stirs, then a second later is instantly awake, his fingers and mouth twitching. 'Hang on, the beast awakens, I better shove something in his mouth before he turns nasty.' She struggles to her feet, and I give her a helping shove. 'You need a lift to the station?'

'Dad's taking me in the morning.'

'Cool. Read it though, seriously.'

'Why?'

'It's you! She's been writing about you, Joe-bro!'

'Yeah, sure she has.' Shit. I wave her away casually as though I don't care, but my heart is pounding, and the smile is making my face ache.

I've put off reading more because I didn't want to read about any more random guys she might have met, in the search for love – even if she didn't actually *fall* for them. I mean, that had kind of reassured me, made me think that she wasn't writing about actual real life. That her private life would stay that way.

And the surveys weren't exactly my bag. So surely if she was writing about *us*, she'd have said something on the train? Even if our conversation was cut short when we arrived in Newcastle.

I wait until Sophie's left the room and has closed the door before I pick my laptop up, though my hands are shaking so much I can't type anyway. I take a breath and get over it. So what if she's mentioned me? She does this for a living, she told me she did.

Although she did also say that she people-watches, that it's about other people more than it is about her. But if she's writing about me, then she's writing about herself.

I need to get a grip, see what she's actually written. It can't be that bad. Sophie is just stirring because she's tired, and has fallen out with Mum again.

I peel up the lid of my laptop, click on a tab in the browser – the one I'd been looking at before when I'd read about her, scanned some of the stuff she'd written before. The funny stuff about a Yorkshire girl (who isn't a Yorkshire girl) who'd been uprooted and dropped into the city.

My heart is trying to hammer its way out of my chest, and my palms are clammy. She can't be telling the world about our kiss, can she? She just can't. That was special, that was between us. Well, shared with a barman and quite a few commuters passing through Newcastle station on their way home.

I take a long deep breath, look at the most recent episode. Episode 3. It is dated last Monday. Phew. Although what was I thinking? She couldn't possibly have written about something that happened on Thursday, could she?

I try and concentrate, read about her finding a mobile phone, chasing a guy in a red scarf. About what happened a couple of weeks ago.

I guess there are time lags in publishing. This isn't a news headline that has to be out within minutes of an event.

But the truth is inescapable. This is about me. My phone, my scarf. My feelings.

It's hard to take in – I mean, this is personal, something special between two people. This is, well, it's weird. Not natural. Not what I want.

And the next episode will be out tomorrow. There in black and white for me, and anybody else who might be interested, to read.

The queasy feeling in my stomach intensifies. This feels almost like betrayal. Why didn't she mention this? Tell me that she'd ditched her first train-guy, but moved on to talking about us?

Shit, what exactly happened a week ago, when I saw her? I cover my eyes with the palms of my hands. That was when I asked her if she was up for a date, a drink. Did I make a complete twat of myself?

I don't know what's worse – the fact that total strangers are going to have a step-by-step breakdown of our relationship (if I can call it that yet), or the fact that Sophie, and anybody else in my family, or friends can read about it.

I am totally recognisable; I am being made totally public. And without even opening up the comments properly I can see that I'm being coined 'sexy as shit' by one person, then 'a dithering loser' by another.

I put my laptop down and look at my hands. I'm trembling. I close my eyes. I need to be logical here. That is what I am good at.

1. I am not instantly recognisable; she hasn't named me. Sophie only knew because she'd seen me looking Millie up, put two and two together and made four hundred.
2. Lots of guys wear red scarves, work in London and catch trains.
3. This is not personal; this is just work for Millie.

Hell, is that all this is for her? Am I just some guy she can use to spice up her column? I open my eyes and stare at the wall. My stomach feeling like it has been gripped in a vice.

That really would be the pits. Worse than hitting the headlines and being displayed for all and sundry to have a pop at. It really would.

I just cannot believe anybody can kiss like that and not mean it though. I can't be that out of touch with my feelings that I kidded myself. It wasn't one-sided. I'm sure it wasn't.

This just cannot be Lisa all over again. I can't have made the same mistake twice, can I?

But I'd never noticed the warning signs last time. Never realised that things weren't how I saw them.

Maybe I need to ring Millie. See her before Thursday

and get this out in the open, because if I don't it's going to be bubbling up in my head all week.

I'm going to be wondering if I've totally cocked up again, if my dating radar is so bad that I need to accept once and for all that I'm better off being a single guy.

Chapter Twenty-Two

MILLIE

Monday 11th April

E*pisode 5. Confessions of… and then he kissed me!*
    I am having a real problem here. I have got the title line but have now hit a roadblock. I don't know how to write this, I don't know how to put something so special out there in a funny, engaging way. Because it was private. It was between the two of us. It was the best kiss I have ever had in my life. I could feel it lingering on my lips, in my body, all the way home. I don't want to share it.

It doesn't help that even though last week's column has only just gone out, it has already got zillions of hits (okay, quite a few) and a load of comments.

They cannot believe he left me at Newcastle.

They cannot believe I didn't chase him down the platform.

They cannot believe we didn't snog. They cannot believe

I have left them hanging, tantalising them with the prospect of maybe a proper date next week.

I mean, how do they think I feel? This is my life; I am actually living it! Honestly, do these people not consider I'm a real living person, and it is my beating heart that is at stake here?

There are demands for more action. I will, apparently, be responsible for the asphyxiation of half the female population if I don't make a move on him soon.

The pressure is real.

The fact that we actually did lock lips, but I don't want to tell anybody, makes it worse.

There is no going back, we have taken that step and it can never be untaken. From now on we get more involved, and it works between us, or it all ends. For ever.

This is scarier than any other relationship I've had. I mean, if you just meet and it's a date from the start then there's nothing to lose.

The normal order of things is chat, drink, drink, chat, more drink, minor grope, snog then dial it up or head for home alone. The normal order of things is let's-get-physical first, and if that doesn't work then there's no point in finding out more about each other.

But this is different.

We've bumped into each other a couple of times, fancied each other, chatted – and then kissed. It's more like a courtship than a fling. Everything has shifted now. It's upside down – like we mentally bonded first, and the amazing kiss was a bonus. Not the start of things.

I guess it's a bit like deciding to risk a friend becoming a lover. You feel like there is so much more at stake.

Not that we were exactly friends, or that I knew him at all. But it felt like that. And now we've crossed an invisible line, and nothing is ever going to be the same again.

And I am supposed to write about it!

It's a lot easier to write about dog-poo bins. I might ask Zoe if she wants to do swapsies. Except she is not having Joe. She'll have to start again, find her own train-guy.

I realised this afternoon as I left the office that it is now over a month since I first spoke to train-guy

My fingers still on the keyboard. I am still not sure about outing Joe. I run the name round inside my head. It's a nice, dependable name. Honest. Like he seems to be. He is also private.

It's weird, it makes me like him even more. He's a breath of fresh air – a guy who isn't an oversharer, an in-your-face 'what about me' type. Nearly all my dates since I've moved down here have been extroverts, what Mum would call show-offs. I'm so over all of that. Joe stands out. He's an individual, a guy who will stick to his guns, do what he believes in. I'm screwed. He's probably spent the weekend thinking about what I told him I do and has already decided that this will not work.

I can't name him, no way, or I totally lose all my chances. But if he ever reads this, he's still going to know it is him, even if nobody else does. And I've got this churning in the pit of my stomach that tells me he might not be happy.

Why the hell didn't I explain properly? Give him a chance to run before we kissed?

I've got his phone number now, so what the hell is stopping me ringing him? Explaining?

I take my fingers off the keyboard and rest them on my mobile. I'm scared. What if I tell him and he says that's it? And walks away, like other men have done before.

I wasn't as bothered about any of them, but with Joe it's different.

I can't risk trying to explain in a message, or even calling him. I need to see him face to face, see his reaction, be able to put this right if it's going wrong. I tap my phone nervously.

'Okay?' Zoe stands up. 'I'm going for coffee and pastries, want one?'

'Sounds like a good idea!' I put the phone down. Type some more.

and I have not kissed him until now – it must be a record! But I have also realised that one of those little sayings my dad had, 'the good things are worth waiting for', is totally true. This was worth waiting for.

I've got to admit, I've always thought that a kiss is just a kiss, and a first kiss.... well, a first kiss can be a bit like a New Year's Eve party – you look forward to it for weeks and then four drinks in realise that this is it. It's not getting any better. In other words, a total anti-climax. But this kiss was something else.

So does this count as a first date?

'Things still on track with train-guy?' She raises an eyebrow.

'Sure are! I thought you were getting pastries?' Oh shit, this is bad, I don't even want Zoe reading this yet.

'Sure am.' She laughs. 'So, is it all window dressing, or the real deal?'

'He's cute,' I say.

'That's a bit non-committal.'

'Very cute.' I sigh, bury my head in my hands and talk through my fingers. 'Funny, sexy, interesting.'

When I glance up, she is grinning. 'Oh my God, you have fallen for him! Is this love?' There's only the slightest hint of gentle mocking in her tone. She's asking for real, but leaving it open for me to just laugh it off or be rude back.

'Oh hell, I don't know what it is.' I slump forward and bury my head in my hands again, then peep back up at her. 'I don't know what to write, Zo. I just, well...'

'It's fine taking the piss out of things that aren't important?'

'Exactly.'

'Well—' she shakes her head as though the answer is obvious '—don't take the piss.'

'I can't do that either, it's too, well—' I pause as the words whizz round in my head '—exposing.'

'You can be authentic without spilling every single little bean, Millie! Come on, get a grip, you can do this. You've done it before! I expect you to be typing like mad by the time I get back with our breakfast!'

She's right. I can do this.

The truth has just hit me full on. It's not my fear of being authentic that's stopping me here – it's my fear of losing Joe. Because kissing him has changed everything.

Oh my God, that's a scary thought. If a kiss has messed up my head this much, if we ever make it to the bedroom will I spontaneously combust or something?

Chapter Twenty-Three

JOE

Monday 11th April

I have discovered one *huge* disadvantage to getting the 6.13 a.m. train back to London on a Monday morning. The first stretch is quiet, too quiet. I've always seen this as a bonus, until this morning when I had no distractions and so decided to see if the latest edition of Millie's column was online.

It was.

I am now in the office and finding it hard to concentrate on anything but her words. Written words.

At least on the train there was nobody looking over my shoulder to read what I was, nobody sitting opposite me to see my reaction. But here in the office I'm on display and I have already been asked by four different people if I've eaten something that has disagreed with me or had a disastrous weekend.

I surreptitiously swap screens, from a screen full of code to Episode 4 of Millie and Joe. I feel like the mouse that's being hypnotised by the snake, I can't back off, I'm drawn in. Not that I'm thinking of her as a snake. Bad simile. Must try harder. She's more siren of the sea luring the poor sailors to their deaths.

But this is our first proper chat, our first shared journey – just over a week ago.

I have to concentrate on the positives, not the bits that are making me cringe for England.

She had felt like she was a schoolgirl with a crush, she was gutted I had to leave her at Newcastle, she was excited that we'd set up a date for the next week. This is all good, this does not say 'girl doing it for her job', it says she feels like I do.

My first reaction is to feel chuffed that she feels like this. But it's swiftly followed by something that feels like fear.

It would be amazing, brilliant, if this was in a message that she'd sent me. A personal message. But is it right to tell *everybody*? It feels so wrong when we've only just met, when we hardly know each other, when we're just finding out.

This is uncomfortable.

My throat feels tight. If I'm honest, it really hurts that she never asked what I thought. And even if she'd warned me that she was doing it, I don't think I'd feel any differently.

This feels like she's reached inside of me, pulled out my innermost emotions and thrown them out to the world to see what everybody else thinks.

I don't want to be analysed. I don't want to be famous or infamous, I don't want to be *known*. Our conversations were ours, even though we haven't made any big declarations, or made any romantic gestures. Our touches, our kiss, were supposed to be between the two of us.

Shit. The kiss. I need to know what she's writing now, what will make the press next week. We kissed. If she's going to share my technique and timing something inside me will die.

How can I even think about things getting more intimate, if this is how it's going to be?

This is worse than the lack of communication between me and Lisa.

'Joe?'

I switch screens back, guiltily, and try and sound breezy. 'Katherine?' And stop thinking about kissing. Because that is bad on two fronts. One, it is turning me on, and two, it is giving me the heebie-jeebies because I am about to be outed. She is going to put it into words and make it public.

'You up for a bit of overtime if I can wangle it with your lot?'

'Sure.'

I have to talk to Millie. I've got to. Soon.

'I can push for Fridays if you want a good excuse to spend more time down here!' Katherine knows all about the farm, about how it sometimes feels like I'm back-pedalling when I go there even though I love my family. How much I love being here. I sounded her out on the possibility of a permanent job here and she made all the right noises.

'Ha ha.' Friday? Maybe I should do that. Stay. Work in the office on Fridays. Cut my losses before my heart is broken and served up on a platter to the masses. Or maybe not. 'Sophie is bouncing back, but she's still got baby brain so I could do with being there to give them a hand for a few more weeks. But after that...' I shrug.

After that, who knows. I'd been planning on suggesting to Millie that we meet up for lunch in London midweek, if Thursday went okay. That we could take another step forward, see more of each other – and then if I didn't get to see her on the train it wouldn't matter.

But I'm still like that moth to a flame. I can't not catch the train home on Thursday. And it is true about Sophie. She might pretend that she's got her normal bounce back, but she needs to know I'm there. That there's a back-up plan.

'Cool, I'll let you know how many hours we can stretch to.' Katherine gives me the thumbs-up.

My mobile vibrates noisily on the desk.

Hey! How's things? Hope you had a good weekend. Millie x

My heart kind of freezes in my body and for a moment all I can do is stare. Motionless. Then my thumbs go into a frenzy. *Great thanks!* J I get ready to hit send, then backtrack and add a kiss, then delete it, then add it back again. Then delete the J and add *Not as good as the train trip home though J x* Is that too much? Sod it. Send.

The whole world stops. All I can hear is my breathing.

Same here! Look, was wondering if you had time for a coffee tomorrow? Wanted to chat about something. And see you of course. Millie x

Funny, I was about to ask you the same J x

Shit, why does she want to meet up so urgently? Is she going to tell me that this is about to get messy, that Episode 5 is the one where she dumps the guy in a red scarf?

I wipe my clammy palms down the seams of my jeans.

Borough Market @1pm? M x

It's a date! J x

She sends back a big smiley face.

And just like that, the world doesn't seem quite as bad a place. She's not traipsing across the city to say she doesn't want to see me again, is she? If she wasn't interested, if she was just using me for her column then she'd just tell me she didn't want to meet up again when we saw each other on Thursday. She'd want some kind of dramatic ending that she could write about.

Shit, why was my first reaction fear that she was dumping me, when a few minutes ago all I could do was think I needed to walk away before she shared my innermost thoughts with her readers?

The feeling of panic had been real. So, what would be

worse, losing her or losing my pride, my dignity, my privacy?

I didn't explain to Lisa well enough how I felt. I can't make the same mistake with Millie. Even if I risk losing her now, I need to tell her how I feel her. Before I get in even deeper. Before my heart overrules my head.

Whatever it is she wants to chat about, I've got twenty-four hours to work out what I need to say to her. Because however much I panicked at the thought she was about to dump me, I still can't ignore the fact that I've read her column and it has made me a bit twitchy.

I've got twenty-four hours to come to terms with the fact that I am train-guy – well, train-guy Mark 2. Is it a deal-breaker?

Chapter Twenty-Four

MILLIE

Tuesday 12th April

This feels a bit weird, meeting Joe somewhere that isn't on a train, or at a station. It feels far more like a date than the drink-last-week date. This has been pre-arranged. An *actual* date, this isn't just a coincidental meeting. Or a filling-in of time.

Except it is also not actually a date. It is when I 'fess up and risk him finishing this before it has really started.

One kiss. I might only have one indescribably hot, sexy kiss – in front of a barman and a hoard of bored commuters – to remember him by.

The back of my neck is clammy, my armpits are clammy, the palms of my hands are practically dripping – I am one hot, soggy mess who is also suffering from palpitations and a weird kind of anticipation and excitement.

I spot him before he spots me, and I slow my pace for a

moment. It's a beautiful sunny spring day, very different to the wind and rain on the days I've seen him before, and for the first time I'm seeing him relaxed and not wrapped up against the weather.

He looks different. Even better.

His shirt is open at the neck, slightly rumpled. Even though he's wearing a jacket, and I'm not that close yet, I can see how the pale blue soft cotton clings to his chest, moulds to his body.

He's leaning against a building, one hand casually tucked into the pocket of tight jeans so that his shirt is slightly hitched up, the other holding his mobile phone.

The dark jacket is tailored; the way he wears it, it's a long way from too formal, but I can just imagine that in a suit he'd be totally to die for.

I slow to a complete halt, wanting to store this image of him in my head. Preserve this moment. Just in case.

The way his slightly too long hair flops forward, the broadness of his shoulders. The hint of shirt cuff showing. His long legs.

I want to take a photo, but if anybody sees me, they'll think I'm a weirdo. If he sees me he might do a runner.

'Hey!' My hand stops dead, halfway to my phone as he spots me and calls out. Yeah, I was tempted. I was going to do it.

He grins, his broad smile widening his face, his dimples giving him a cheeky, fun look, and my heart does a bunny hop. Then he waves as I thread my way between people to reach him, before dropping his own phone in his pocket and tucking the tips of his fingers into his jeans.

I wave back, cross my fingers behind my back and whisper a silent prayer.

I'm not ready for Joe to leave me. Not yet.

'Hey back atcha!' I reach him and smile, I can't help myself. It's infectious. Then he leans forward, and kisses my cheek, which sets my insides tingling indecently. It is far hotter than any smacker has ever been. I don't think I knew what the word 'anticipation' really meant until now.

'Shall we?' He holds the door of the café open for me, indicates a seat, insists on going to get the drinks. All I can do is stare moodily after him and let the nervousness rebuild inside me.

'Hey,' he says softly as he puts the coffee cups down on the table and sits down opposite me. Slightly formal, slightly reserved, not quite as comfortable and at ease as we normally are.

'Hey.' I smile back at him, pulling the cup towards me. I'm being daft, over-sensitive. Of course he's not relaxed. He's waiting to find out why I messaged, what the urgency was.

'Everything cool?' There's a nervous edge to his voice, hardly noticeable. But I notice everything about him. His normal tone is lodged inside me, the intonations in his voice as familiar as those of my family and close friends. I know him. He knows me.

I nod.

'So, are you heading home earlier this weekend for Easter?'

He's asking if this is why I'm here. If I wanted to meet so I could explain that I won't be seeing him on Thursday, to have a chance to see him now.

'No, I'm booked on Thursday as normal. You?'

'Same here, I'm pretty busy at work, they've offered me extra and so...' He shrugs. There's a pause. I need to tell him. Get this out in the open.

We're both hedging. This is not what we're about.

'But I'm not coming back here next week, I'm working from Mum's, I think.' This is not good, dodging the issue. I'm better than this.

'She'll be pleased.'

'Joe?'

'Millie?'

We say each other's names at the same time. But I have to do this, before I chicken out. I hold my hand up.

'I need to explain something.'

'O-kay.' His tone is soft, drawn out. He puts one warm hand over mine. It's reassuring, nice, gives me the confidence to spit this out.

'Can you hear me out, the full thing, before you say anything?'

'Sounds a bit scary.' I might be imagining it, but I'm sure there's the slightest of trembles in his fingers as they lie over mine.

'It's not. Well, it could be, but it sounds worse at the start, but when I explain...'

He nods. His gaze steady. I like this about Joe, his stillness. Well, I like a lot of things, but I really like his calmness, the way he seems to radiate a quiet confidence, the way it gives me courage, belief in myself and what I need to do.

'The column I write –' the air around us seems to hum with the silence '– it's not just been about random romances on trains. Well, I've been writing about us.' Phew, I've said it! He nods again, and something about the way he's looking at me makes me think he was expecting this.

'Okay, if it's cards on the table time, I've got an admission as well,' he says slowly, 'I read more after I saw you the other day. I got up to date, couldn't help myself.' His gaze meets mine. 'I read all of it.'

He already knows. He's read Episode 2, our first meeting, Episode 3, when I found his mobile, and Episode 4 when we shared the journey to Newcastle. He's waiting for Episode 5. The kiss.

'I'm sorry I didn't say so the other day, I should have. I should have warned you, but it's my job and well…. Well, I know you're a private person and you don't want everybody to know what you're doing. But I've not named you, and, I mean, you can't really tell it's you. Lots of guys go on that train, and wear red scarves and I guess now it's warmer you won't be wearing it anyway and…' My voice tails off. I'm making a rubbish job of this.

He slowly turns my hand over, his fingers trace over my palm, and my heart is pounding.

'Did you really feel like you had a schoolgirl crush?' he says softly, not looking up.

'Yes.' I breathe out, gazing at his forehead. Willing him to look up again, to realise that I do like him, more than like him, fancied him from the very first time I laid eyes on him.

'You minded that I got off at Newcastle?'

I nod vigorously, so vigorously the tremor goes down my arm into my hand and makes him glance up. My throat has gone dry, scratchy. He's read the column already, he knows I've not been upfront, he also knows how I feel about him. He has to know how I feel about him, that it's real.

My eyes search his face for a clue to how he really feels about this. 'Okay, so when we first met, I had no clue I'd ever see you again and it just started off as a bit of a one-off, it was fun.'

He nods. But now his gaze is locked on mine. 'I have to admit, I was jealous of the guy you fell on top of.'

The heat rushes to my cheeks. 'Er, that bit was made up, because I actually wanted to write about meeting you, but it was a bit—'

'Boring?'

'God no, the opposite! But I didn't think I'd ever see you again, so I was just taking the piss out of myself really. I kind of made up the tripping, but the feelings...' I stroke my thumb along the side of his, wanting to share, to make him understand how I feel. 'The feelings were real.'

Another nod.

'That's what I was trying to tell you, on the train last

week. It wasn't that guy I fell for. It was you. I wanted to touch you. I couldn't stop thinking about you, all weekend, I know it sounds silly but—'

'It doesn't sound silly. I couldn't stop thinking about you.' His words are soft, but unmistakeable. 'And I couldn't stop wondering why I hadn't asked for your number or something.'

'I looked for you. Every time I was there, I looked,' I say with total honesty. 'I wrote the truth in the second episode because I couldn't find you.' I shake my head.

'I can't believe that I was searching the station one day, and you were doing it the following day. I'm surprised I wasn't arrested for loitering.' His voice is soft, his hand is still holding mine, his finger on my palm, but his smile is slightly wistful, and it sends butterflies to my stomach.

What if he wishes he'd never met me? What if my writing about us really is a deal-breaker for him?

'Oh God, I know what you mean, I was so close to being thrown out! I was getting desperate.' I'm aware of the nervous edge to my voice, but I want him to know how I feel. 'I did actually go back on Thursday as well once or twice.' I admit, and my embarrassment is worth it when he grins back at me. 'But I guess I left before you got there.'

'You have to be kidding? Shit, I can't believe I actually worked late and missed you!'

It's my turn to grin, straight back at him. Our first meeting had been so random, the chances of us meeting again so slim. How could it not feel like this is meant to be? 'And people really loved the second episode and my boss wanted more.' I pause, I want to keep him completely on board, I desperately need to know he's okay about this. That he thinks we've got something. 'So, I looked even harder.'

'To keep your boss happy?'

'No, no! The more I thought about you, the more I knew I had to see you again. I even went early on Friday, in case Thursday had just been a one-off for you, but you were never there. It was like two or three weeks and then—' I take a deep breath '—and then I bumped into you again and it was pure chance, because I used to normally travel on a Friday, and I'd almost given up on going to the station on Thursday's as well.' A hint of a smile lifts the corner of his mouth and I go silent for a moment. 'But I did really want to see you again, just because I wanted to see you,' I say again softly, to make sure he understands that this isn't about my career. This is about me, and this time he squeezes my fingers lightly. 'I didn't realise that at first, until I actually did see you, and then it all kind of fell into place.' It did. Seeing him again had made me realise how much I'd wanted to.

'I knew I wanted to see you again.' he says, his deep voice soft but so certain it brings a lump to my throat.

'I want to be honest here, Joe.' I can't let myself get even deeper into this, share my feelings, fall harder – until I know he understands. Until I know he's happy with me being me.

I glance down at our hands, then back up so that our gazes lock. 'I could just drop this writing about us, but it is my job, and I think I can do it in a way that doesn't intrude on your privacy.'

'My sister has already guessed something is up.'

'Oh.'

'But she did catch me Googling you, so I suppose it was a giveaway.'

'Right.' Bummer. 'I've fucked things up before, really annoyed and upset people by writing about them. I don't want that to happen with us. That's why I guess I wasn't completely honest with you the other day, about what I write about.' He doesn't say anything. 'When I first wrote about us, I didn't quite know how to do it, and I guess –' the openness of his gaze makes it easier to be honest '– I didn't want to share my feelings. I wasn't ready. It felt too real, too intense, so I had to lighten it up before I could write it down. And I'm still doing that, but I think I've got it better worked out in my head. But I can't let you vet what I write before it goes out.' I pause. This is the truth. I've thought about it a lot. It totally screwed my productivity yesterday. 'But I promise it won't be too personal. I can't write stuff that's really personal, it's always been light-hearted and taking the mickey.'

'You're good at it.'

I glow slightly with the compliment. He's read my column; he thinks I'm okay at it.

'Look.' He pauses, and it's excruciating. 'My turn to be honest here. It did really rattle me when I realised it was about me.'

My heart pounds a bit faster. This is what I was afraid of.

'My family just don't—' he pauses, knits his fingers in between mine '—overshare. We don't even tell each other stuff, let alone the rest of the world!' Somebody comes and takes our empty cups, asks if we want more coffee, and we say 'no thanks' simultaneously then go silent for a moment until we're alone again. 'But I guess if this is about you, and how you feel, then I'm just a side player, aren't I?'

'I wouldn't exactly say that,' I say. 'You are pretty key.'

'But you're not describing me in too much detail.'

'Just the way you kiss.' I can't help but smile.

'That's pretty confidential info, not many people have experienced that,' he says in a conspiratorial whisper.

'But if you had really bad technique, and sucked my tonsils until they hurt or something, I might have to write about it. If it was funny.'

'If I sucked your something?' He raises an eyebrow, and to my shame I blush, my cheeks are burning. It makes him laugh, a deep, gorgeous vibration that makes it worse.

'You are getting a bit ahead of yourself, Mr Greenwood!'

'This could be a bit off-putting, not knowing what will make it into print, Miss Shaw.'

'I know,' I say softly. His tone is jokey, but there's an underlying truth. 'One guy ditched me after I wrote about the way he shrieked, "Screw me baby one more time" three strokes before his climax. I mean, the only people who would know it was him are the other girls he did it to! Then there was lovely Will who held doors open, carried my shopping and even carried me over a puddle,' I say wistfully. He was really lovely. 'His mates found out and he said he'd lost all his street cred and was a laughing-stock. I did miss him.'

'But doesn't it ever work the other way? People dating you just so they have a chance of getting a mention? I mean, there are loads of people who are desperate for their fifteen minutes, aren't there?'

'Oh yeah, there have been stalkers.' I try not to shudder. 'But they just don't get it, it's not about *my whole life*, it's about the funny bits, the highs, the lows, the stuff people wish they'd done or are massively relieved they haven't. They're edited highlights. It's about the things and people that make a good story.'

'Not every Tom, Dick or Harry?'

'Exactly.'

We look at each other in silence. Joe is not a Tom, Dick or Harry.

I squeeze his fingers and tell him. He smiles. The little crinkles at the corners of his eyes are so fresh, but so familiar all at once.

'You've read Episode 4? Yesterday's?'

'I have.' There's a hint of mischief in his eyes. 'I like the fact you picked up half a loo roll on the bottom of your shoe, and I have to say you have a great arse.' He chuckles.

'Unmissable.'

'It was a good job I was carrying coffee and didn't have a spare hand! Or bad, from my point of view.'

'Cheeky!' I think I'm going pink again, at the thought of

his hands on my posterior. I might well have ended up flat on my face and wriggling about asking for more. 'But you're okay with...?' I crack on to stop myself thinking about his warm palms on my bottom.

'I'm not sure. It probably sounds daft to you, being this sensitive—'

'It doesn't. I get it.' I can see the doubt in his eyes, the uncertainty.

'But –' he takes a deep breath, and there's a quiet determination in his gaze as it meets mine '– it was fine. When I got over the shock and read it again, it was fine. You're right, nobody but Soph would know it was me. But I guess Episode 5 involves the drink, the bar in Newcastle. The—' I might be being over-sensitive here, but I'm sure there's a hesitancy back in his tone, a note of doubt.

'Kiss,' I finish for him. 'But no names, and it was nice.' I stare into his eyes, willing him to understand, trying to ignore the flutter in the base of my stomach. I know he's not one hundred per cent happy. 'It was amazing, incredible, I'm not going to pretend it was anything else, or that it didn't make me want to see you even more. I'll write it as it was, but less.' Once I work out how. That is going to be a problem.

I want to grasp his hands, persuade him that I'm not going to overstep the mark, ruin things between us.

'I wish you'd warned me,' he says softly. 'Not left me to find out from Soph.'

Ouch. I look down at our hands, then back at him. 'I'm sorry.' I am. 'I got carried away, until I realised what I was doing, and that this was –' I take a deep breath, hoping my words are true '– not just some brief encounter, some quick fling.'

He pauses, his thumb stroking a steady rhythm. He's torn. I know he is.

'I do get that you're trying to do what works for both of us. Your job, my –' he shrugs '– inhibitions.'

I shake my head. 'Not inhibitions. It's normal. What I do is the abnormal bit!'

He smiles, a gentle, soft smile and my insides crumble a bit.

'I don't want to upset you with this, Joe. I don't want you to walk away.' That would hurt, really hurt, and leave a gap in my life.

'I'm not about to, unless you want me to? I get it, Millie.' He takes a deep steadying sigh. 'I do get it, and I can deal with it.' He nods almost imperceptibly. As though he's still trying to convince himself. 'I'd rather cope with having my feelings dumped on the public than lose the chance of whatever it is we might have.' He gazes straight into my eyes and it's like he's sending me a message, that he's trusting me. That he hopes I won't go too far and fuck up. 'I don't want to walk away.'

'I don't want you to,' I say back, softly. 'I really don't, but you are sure?' Relief washes over me even as I ask the question, but it's tinged with a feeling of responsibility. A feeling that this is teetering in the balance. That's he is saying it's fine, but he's not really convinced.

'Well, it's worth a try. We can at least do that, can't we.' It's a statement, not a question.

He squeezes my hand, then he smiles and my insides hum with pleasure. I imagine this is how a purring cat feels.

'We can.' My voice has a slight wobble. It is a true reflection of how I feel inside – I think it's relief.

'I mean, you might turn out to be some extrovert, kinky, attention-seeking lunatic who is nothing like the endearing, authentic, empathetic girl we all think you are.' His tone lightens, as though he's brushed his concerns to one side and the Joe that makes me laugh, that makes me feel happy, is back.

'This is true.'

'And I might be a welly-wearing pervert who comes into the city to befriend women and drag them back to my cabin in the wildest windswept part of the national park.'

'You might. I think we'd be well matched. Actually, have you copyrighted that, or can I use it?'

We grin at each other, then my mobile judders into life and I reluctantly look at the time. 'Oh hell.' The disappointment is real. 'I'm going to have to go. That's my fifteen-minute warning that I need to be back at my desk.'

'For sure. Me too. I'm trying to work two jobs at the moment.' He stands up, waiting for me to lead the way to the door.

We linger outside for a moment. The gentle warmth of the sun inviting us to stay out and play. I want to. I can't.

He breaks the silence. 'I'm glad we talked.'

'So am I.' I go up on tiptoes and kiss his cheek, its

roughness a sweet burnish against my skin. I want to ask him about his two jobs, about the interview he'd stopped off at Newcastle for, about his desire to be in London permanently.

That conversation on the train was cut off at the kneecaps by the bride-to-be. We'd been distracted by her dramatics, but now I'm not sure if he'd been dodging talking about his job situation. Or there's nothing he wanted to say.

But I guess now we've met up, then even if we lose our shared train journey, we can still see each other. Though I'd miss him like mad if that happened; I used to spend the time worrying about Mum or being bored to tears.

'See you Thursday then?'

'You can count on it.'

He puts one hand on my waist, pulls me in closer, and his dry, firm lips graze mine.

'Oh God, I wish I could stay longer.' He brushes his long fingers through his hair as he stares into my eyes, leaving me feeling almost tearful.

'So do I.' It comes out slightly breathlessly, as his other hand drops from my waist, leaving a cold gap. I want so much more. I don't want him to go. This is one of those moments that feels fragile. A turning point. Make or break.

He's decided to go against his basic instincts, to trust me. He's decided it's worth it to give us a chance.

If I mess this up, I'll never forgive myself.

'What have you done to me, woman?' He half smiles. Then blows me a kiss and winks. 'Thursday!'

I give him a double thumbs-up. 'Can't wait.'

'Two days feels like a lifetime!'

Then he backs away, takes one step, another, turning at the very last moment.

I rest my fingers over where his kiss landed, and smile to myself as I watch until he is swallowed up by the crowd.

This has to be the number one sexiest date I have ever had, and we've been fully clothed, alcohol-free and only had a chaste kiss. Does this mean I'm maturing?

Oh my God, I hope not. That is a word that should only be applied to cheese and alcohol.

Chapter Twenty-Five

MILLIE

'Can you calm down?' I know that saying this to somebody who is worked up can sometimes have the opposite effect, but it is the first thing that comes into my head. I am also talking to my sister, and she gets worked up whatever I say.

I am halfway back to my office; the sun is still shining, and my head is in the kind of space where birds are tweeting and any second now somebody is going to burst into song and dance around me in the street. Failing that, I was (until the phone interrupted me) quietly humming to myself and thinking about doing a little sidestep and shimmy. I am positively floating. Twittering, 'He loves me, he loves me not' and grinning.

I want to grab passers-by and yell, 'He's cool with everything; he still wants to see me again! He kissed me.' Instead – probably wiser – I say into the phone, 'I didn't get any of that apart from the word "Mum".'

I have missed three calls and four messages from my sister Lou while I have been drinking coffee with Joe.

'You need to get over to Mum's.' She huffs out. This is easy for Lou to say. She thinks that having a hands-on job, and hands-on family, means she has an opt-out. She therefore never has to come over when there is any kind of emergency – unless they are under a foot of snow (but not the kind that blocks roads or delays trains) and her in-laws have begged for some quality time with their grandchildren. And I do mean begged. Lou does not approve of any kind of parenting that is not one hundred per cent in line with her style. These grandparents are big on sweets, unsuitable movies and rollerblading in the house to hone fine motor skills. Yes, I know, I wish they'd been mine as well. I might adopt them.

Anyway, Lou considers looking after our mother to be my job, seeing as I have no pets or other dependants and 'the type of job you can do anywhere'. I can drop everything. And she can avoid facing up to her fears and loss.

'I will be going on Thursday,' I say in my most reasonable tone.

'You need to go today. Have you not heard a word I've been saying?' I can imagine she's tapping her foot and frowning.

'Not really. You were yelling and a bit garbled.' I can practically hear her bubbling up to a full head of steam. She is about to explode. 'Sorry, but it's noisy here, busy, not a good line. Tell me again.' It's not just the line and her high pitch, I have to admit that I am distracted. I am thinking about Joe and the way he touched my hand, and the way he said he wanted to try and make this work. Give us a chance to get to know each other.

'Millie, are you even bloody listening to me now?'

'Sorry, yes, I am listening now. I was distracted.' I'd love to be distracted more by Joe. A whole evening of distraction. Possibly longer. Those long, strong fingers…

'She fell off a ladder.'

I grind to a halt. 'What do you mean, fell off a ladder? Why didn't you say?' Lou can be melodramatic, everything is urgent, so I do tend to tune her out.

'I am saying! It was while she was trimming some shrub or other. She couldn't get hold of you so she rang me, and she thinks she's sprained or broken her ankle, she can't walk, she can't even get up, and the grass is damp. She'll freeze to death or something and it's your fault.'

'My fault!' I squeak.

'You told her not to sell the house. If she'd moved to a smaller place, she wouldn't be doing the bloody garden, would she?' Resentment tinges the words. She hates the fact that I might have influenced Mum's decisions, that I chat over stuff with her – but she wants me to take the responsibility and be there for her.

I can't win, can I?

'What do you mean, she can't get up? You didn't just leave her sitting in the garden?' As the panic seeps through my body, I up my pace again, dodging slow people with children or prams, and people dawdling because they're talking on their phones. The sunshine and song have faded out of my day. 'You didn't bloody expect me to drop everything and go and help her up? How long do you think it takes me to get there? I'm not just round the corner, you know, I'm in London! Did you ring for an ambulance, or at least her neighbour or something?' I think I may have forgotten about my reasonable tone and be shouting back at her.

She sighs dramatically.

'Well, I tried to get hold of you first because she didn't want to bother anybody, then when I called her back, she said her neighbour had spotted her from an upstairs window and gone round.'

'So is she okay? She's not still on the lawn?'

'She's gone to A&E for x-rays.'

'I'll give her a call.'

'You need to go, not just call her. Don't you care?'

'Of course I bloody care! You could go as well, you know.' I get on with my sister best when we are not talking about family responsibilities. When there is no crisis of any kind. When she has unexpectedly graced us with her presence for a few hours at a happy time like Christmas. Stress and sisters don't always go well together.

'You know I would if I could,' she says hotly.

'You can!' I mutter. 'When you say ladder, what do you mean?' I know my tone is laced with suspicion, but as far as I can remember, none of the shrubs are big enough to require a ladder for trimming. And I have never seen Mum up a ladder; standing on a chair is as high as she normally gets.

'I don't know. What does it matter?' Lou snaps. 'She still fell, and she still had to call me, because *you* were too busy to answer your phone.'

I count to ten under my breath. She's worried, that's why she's over-reacting. Don't respond. Do NOT rise to it, Millie. 'That's not fair, Lou! I talk to her loads; I go to see her most weekends. I'm busy as well. I do have a career, you know!'

'If you're going to get funny with me, I'm going. I was only trying to help.' My sister can do huffy with the best. 'You're just never happy, are you?' Luckily, she puts the phone down before I can respond, because I know we're heading into 'nothing I do is ever good enough for you' territory. I am also on the point of growling. My hackles are definitely up.

I jab at my contacts and take a calming deep breath.

Mum answers her phone on the second ring, just as I open the office door.

'Mum, are you okay? Lou just rang and…'

'I'm fine, darling, is everything okay with you?' Her tone is as even and calm as ever. If she's about to die an agonising death she's hiding it well.

'Lou said you fell.'

'Oh, I did have a bit of a tumble. I'm just waiting for a nice nurse to come and bandage me up. Nothing broken! If you ask me, a load of fuss over nothing. I did tell them I was all right. And I told Lou not to fuss, she can be such a drama queen. She shouldn't have been ringing you, I know how busy you are, darling.' I'm going to kill Lou.

'She was snappy,' I say, knowing I sound sulky.

'It's guilt because she isn't here,' Mum says simply. 'But I'm fine, honestly.'

I hadn't realised how tense I was, until the stress left my body. 'What were you doing up a ladder, Mum?' Okay, maybe I won't kill Lou. Maybe she was feeling bad, too far away, which is why she was so tetchy and demanding. And I would rather know if anything has happened. But it's just the way she does it. The way she popped my nice bubble with a sledgehammer instead of a pin.

'A ladder? I wasn't up a ladder. I was on that step that I use to reach my top cupboards because those little sticky-up bits had started to annoy me, and the gardener can't come for another week. I lost my balance and if I'd put my flat shoes on instead of doing it in the ones with heels, I'd have been fine.'

I have a vision in my head of my mother dressed up to the nines doing a 'spot of gardening'. I don't know about Lou blaming me, I blame her new fancy man. She didn't use to go in the garden in high heels. For a start, as she always told us, they leave marks on the lawn!

'Is that it, darling? Are you sure you're okay? You sound a bit stressed. I better be off, the nurse is coming with my cup of tea. Oh, a biscuit as well! Thank you, that's lovely.'

She's already distracted, more interested in the afternoon refreshments than in me. She can't be that bad. 'I'm fine. I'll come home today instead of Thursday.'

'There's no need.'

'Why, is your new man there to look after you?'

'No,' she says quite firmly, and there's a long pause. So maybe he's out of the picture. 'But I'll be fine. I don't need looking after, darling. I'm all grown up!'

'You won't be able to get around if your ankle's sprained.' I try and sound reasonable, not worried.

'They'll give me a stick or crutches, I'm sure.'

'You hate sticks. I'm coming. It's fine, I can work better at home.' The last time Mum had crutches she managed to take Dad's feet out from under him, and then nearly whacked a vase through the window. 'And Mum, please don't climb up steps, specially not in your best shoes.'

'Well, I can't now, can I? I'm going to have to wait for somebody else to do it.'

This is true. Out of the corner of my eye I see Carla gesturing.

'Sorry, Mum, I've got to go. I'll speak to you later when I've booked my train ticket and know what time I'll be there. Bye!'

Does Lou really feel guilty about the fact that she's staying away, that she can't face home? Is that why she can be such a cow at times? I tap out a text to tell her Mum is fine, that I'll go home, that I'll keep her updated, as I head over to Carla.

My phone pings with an incoming message before I even reach Carla. And it's pinged several times more before she's even told me what she wants. My fingers are twitching to look. What if Mum's changed her mind, what if the hospital gave her bad news with her cup of tea? Luckily, Carla only wants to confirm when I'm going, when I'll be back and when I'll have Episode 5 done and dusted, and I'm dismissed before I even get a chance to sit down.

I fish out my mobile the second I turn away from her.

Sorry. It's not Mum, it's from Lou. The first of several messages.

I over-reacted, but I just sometimes feel so far away. So helpless. I frown. That is all her own doing, am I supposed to start feeling guilty about shouting back at her? Because if that's what she's expecting, she's wrong. I read the next text.

*So guilty. I should be there for her. For you. I'm sorry. Really.
Lou x*

I'm sorry too. I type. *Sorry I talked her out of selling the house.* Maybe Mum was right, maybe Lou would find it easier to come back to see us if Mum was living in a new house, not her – her and Dad's – house. Maybe that's why my sister's instinct was to blame me for Mum falling off the step, why she was so upset, over-reacted. Maybe it hurts so much that she doesn't feel she can come back, and I've been stopping her in a way. Been selfish.

This doesn't just affect me; it affects all of us. I never thought. Mills x

You didn't talk her out of it, she'd never let either of us tell her what to do! It's not you, it's me. Lou x

I dial her number as I head into a meeting room and kick the door shut. We might hate each other sometimes, but she's my sister, and we love each other as well. I can sense she's close to tears.

'I miss him, Mill,' she blurts out, the second she answers my call.

'I know. I miss him too.' I sink down into one of the chairs and gaze, unseeing, out of the window.

'I don't mean to dump on you, but I feel so bloody guilty. I mean, we should be there for Mum, I know we should, and I plan to go, and I set off, then I realise he won't be there…' Her voice tails off. She sniffs. 'Seeing you and Mum, without him, it's just, it's not right, it makes it final. It makes it –' there's a long pause, I almost think we've lost the phone connection '– real.'

'I know,' I say softly. 'All the special times, all the times we should all be together, and he's not.'

'I thought it was easier not to go home, not to see you, but I miss you. I really miss you.' There's a louder sniff.

'Oh Lou, I miss you too. I get it, I really do, but we need you. I need you, Mum does too, and I do try my best to help her, I am trying my best—'

'I know. I know, I mean sometimes it's a bit shit.' She sniffs and it turns into a laugh, and I laugh back. A tiny glimmer of the old Lou. The one that used to take the piss out of me when we were younger. She was always better than me at cooking, at craft things, at all kinds of things, and when she'd laugh at my attempts to crimp pastry I'd yell out, 'I'm trying my best!' and she'd say, 'Well, it's a bit shit,' in a schoolteacher voice, 'must try harder, girl!' and more often than not I'd crush it up into a ball and chase her round the kitchen trying to stuff it down the back of her shirt – until we both collapsed in giggles.

I miss those times. I miss the young carefree Lou. 'A lot shit.'

'You're doing ace, Millie,' she says softly, the laughter gone from her voice. 'I'll try harder, I'll try and come more.'

'That would be nice.' I say simply. 'Mum is okay.'

'I know, I rang the hospital and talked to the consultant, and the nurse.'

'Talk to her, Lou. Doctors don't know everything.'

'I will.' I can sense her nod. 'I'd better go, the dog's just brought a chick in the kitchen.'

'Oven ready?'

'No, yellow and chirping. I think she wants to adopt them. I seem to spend half my life taking them back outside at the moment.' She sighs. 'I'll ring you back later though, and I will ring Mum.'

'Promise?'

'Promise. Both.'

'I'll call you when I get to Mum's tomorrow. We can Skype, you can show us the chicks and you can see her for yourself.'

'Deal.' There's another long pause. 'Are we ever going to feel less sad, Mills?'

'I don't know. Happier maybe, but I don't know about less sad.'

There's the faint sound of her finishing the call, then a message comes through.

Love you xx

Love you back xx I type and hit send.

Chapter Twenty-Six

MILLIE

Wednesday 13th April

Episode 5. *Confessions of… and then we kissed!*

The last real date I went on was around three months ago. I only realised this when I was working out how long it is since I first spoke to train-guy. I mean there is speed dating, and there is the slow boat to China. Or in this case, train. Can you believe that our first meeting was over a month ago, and we haven't even got to first base?

Anyway, this feels so different to hooking up through a dating app, or bumping hips at a late-night bar, or even a blind date. I've not felt so panicky about being stood up since I went to the school prom. Which was horrible. The whole school-dating thing, not school, or the prom.

I have been desperately worried that now we have had a proper conversation and arranged to meet, train-guy will stand me up. There are so many reasons for this; he might have departed at

Newcastle after he realised that I am an accident-prone kind of girl who can quite easily trail copious amount of toilet paper around in public, he could have discovered that I have been writing about him (and we all know how often that has ended in tears), or he could just not fancy me. I refuse to believe the latter, not because I am in denial or think I am irresistible but because I really felt that we connected. That you can't just fake that.

Anyway, I was wrong. He did not stand me up. And I was right – we do have a connection. It happened – we've had a date!

I am still tingling from the kiss, from the feel of his hand in mine.

Could this be the start of something wonderful?

I have scrubbed most of what I'd sweated over to write, because, let's face it, it did read like I was sweating. Laboured, and, well, frankly quite lumbering and boring. I had rambled because I didn't dare write about our first proper meeting, our first date, our first kiss. I think inside I'd been scared that if I said it out loud (or in my case typed it) then I was jeopardising everything.

Meeting up, and kissing again, has changed everything. The first kiss was not a never-to-be-repeated fluke. Putting everything into words was strangely easier, because the first kiss was less of a hurdle, it was still awesome, but I know now that there is more to come. I think before we met for coffee, I was worried that that could be it, and it was too precious to share.

I have also decided that even the title was wrong: *he* didn't kiss *me*, I wasn't some passive spectator waiting to see what we would happen. We both wanted this equally.

Carla will be proud of me. Well, no, that is not what this is about. I think that this is the first time I've gone into something with a guy and felt sure somewhere deep inside of me that there is equal want and hope on both sides.

The only thing that is causing a nervous flutter in my stomach and kept me awake last night was the thought that Joe could still walk away because he is rattled about being written about.

He said he was fine with me writing about us, he said he got it. But I could see that hint of doubt in his eyes. He's not as chilled about this as he says. He was holding back; he was upset that I hadn't warned him I was writing about us. I let him down. How could I be so stupid? I knew he was a private person and I just dived in and took a chance that either he wouldn't read the column and would never know, or he'd know and not mind.

Stupid, stupid me. I nearly messed everything up. From now on I've got to be more careful, more considerate, warn him what is coming next.

Because it's only going to get more personal from this point.

And I don't want to lose him, I don't want to upset him.

I fancy him SO much it's making me obsess over every single comment he's made – when he flatters and jokes it's like a hug that makes me grin when I relive it. I want to hold onto every word, capture every laugh. I've never, ever felt so many emotions when I've been with somebody – his smile makes me feel like I've been lit up inside, his slightest frown makes me worry that I'm cocking this up.

I've never ever spent so much time thinking about somebody.

Two days away from a guy has never felt like a lifetime before.

Which is why I'm not going to walk away because, well, because he's been brought up milking cows, and he is probably the most nerdish, smart, private, kind guy I've ever dated.

I don't have anything against cows, or milk, but I had come here imagining I'd find metro man and fall totally in love. Somebody who on the outside was a bit like dynamic Dale. The trouble with dating guys like this (and I have dated a few) is that they're quite like Dale on the inside as well. Shallow, self-centred and selfish. Be careful what you wish for, eh?

I am also sure that my writer's block was partly guilt. Guilt that I was sharing something private, something I was worried that Joe would not want the world knowing about.

And yeah, I was right. I knew it in my heart, I was just trying to ignore the niggling voice in my head. But now we've chatted it is like I have given myself permission, because he knows what I'm doing. I wish I knew he really is as cool with it as he insists he is.

He has doubts, I know he does. I have to show him, prove to him, that it'll be okay.

I can make it okay. I can make it work.

So, I am on a roll again, a tentative don't-mess-this-up roll, but even that is a massive relief.

For a moment there I was back to thinking I'd be investigating puppy poops, or something equally career-destroying.

'How's it going, Zoe? Are you still writing about doggy doo?'

'No. That story was buried, which if you ask me is the best place for it.' She peers over my shoulder. 'I've been promoted to "Easter Reads". I've got *Spring Gardening for Small Spaces*, some cookbook crafty thing and about a zillion kids' books to choose from, but I need some fiction. Murder's okay at Easter, isn't it?'

'Spot on.'

'Good that you got a snog in for your Easter edition. My chances of finding some romantic fiction to recommend are dwindling fast. All the ones I've been sent are summer beach reads.'

'That'll do, won't it? It's getting warmer, people are thinking about going away, sun, stuff like that.'

'Sex,' she says drily. 'How's your mum doing?'

I'm not sure if this is connected to the sun, stuff and sex, or she's changing the subject. 'She seems fine. Her neighbour Elaine kept an eye on her yesterday, and I'm heading home in a bit.' Mum had been quite adamant that it was silly me heading home immediately, as she didn't know how long she'd be at the hospital, and in the background Elaine from next door had been shouting that they were having a good catch-up and didn't need interference from their kids. 'Elaine did say if I could get back in time to buy a leg of lamb for lunch on Easter Sunday, and bake some hot cross buns, that would be super.'

'I can lend you the cookbook if you want?' Zoe waves the book in the air. 'Fifty recipes to make Easter memorable?'

'It will be memorable if I start baking.' I shake my head as she laughs. 'I booked a train for today and wrote a long list of everything we'd need from the supermarket including premium hot cross buns.'

'You can always take them out of the packet and say you baked them here? Just shove them in the microwave or something.'

'She'll know.' Baking is not one of my superpowers. A leg of lamb and a jar of mint sauce I can cope with. But mixing flour and stuff? Forget it.

'Couldn't she shop online?'

'Oh no! One Christmas they subbed Tampax with Twix, and she got Frazzles instead of streaky bacon. She's refused to do it again.'

'Interesting choice! But she is feeling okay?'

'She sent me a photo of this massive get-well bouquet that her man sent her.' I can't call him a boyfriend. That definitely doesn't sound right. I try not to roll my eyes, but I know there's a jealous edge to my voice. I honestly cannot remember the last time I was the recipient of a big romantic gesture like that. Well, never.

'Aww, sweet. Train-guy might turn up trumps with a maahoosive Easter egg for you tomorrow!'

'But I won't be there!' It never occurred to me that he might have planned to arrive bearing gifts; I'm not sure we're at that stage yet. Or that he's a big gestures guy. That's a bit flamboyant. He's more a thoughtful, small gestures guy. Coffee when I'm desperate. Asking about Mum. Caring.

My last words to him had been that he could count on me being there tomorrow, so it had made me feel double-bad when I had to text him to say I wouldn't be there. It worries me that we can't see each other like we arranged. I want to see him, be sure that he's happy with 'us'. What if he thinks I'm making excuses, that I don't want to see him? That I just want to go off and expose him to the world – go into print with everything we've shared?

Which is why I suggested we meet up over the holidays if we can.

And he said yes!

I try and stop the smile that is twitching behind my lips. Just thinking about seeing him again makes me want to grin. Even if it will be a bit delayed. He really wants to see me though, that is amazing! That means we're still good. That he meant it when he said he wanted to work things out.

'Oh yeah! Shame if he was planning on making Easter memorable with a combo of melted chocolate egg and body parts.'

'Zoe!' I try to look stern, and not laugh.

'This book's got a whole chapter on how to melt choco,' she says, looking innocent.

'To *make* eggs, I presume?'

'Maybe,' she says reluctantly. 'But who's got the time for that? Anyway, what are you going to write about for the next episode if you aren't going to be seeing him?'

I screw my mouth up, my thinking face. 'We did have a meet-up for coffee, not at the station, just a…'

'Date!' yells Zoe, announcing it to the whole office. Luckily most people don't seem to have noticed. 'You've had a proper date!'

'It was only a coffee,' I protest. 'At lunchtime.'

'But he kissed you again? He did, I knew it!'

'Just a tiny kiss.' When Zoe chuckles I suddenly realise I'm half-smiling and my fingers have moved to the spot where his lips brushed my skin.

'You really do fancy him, don't you?'

'He's very fanciable,' I say, sidestepping the question. But since when did a brushing of lips leave me weak at the knees? Well, actually, since when did a full-blown snog with anybody else leave me feeling like this? 'I need to text him, I said I'd let him know when I'd booked the train.' I need him to know that I'm really disappointed we won't see each other, that I really am desperate to get together.

'Text him! And the lady finally has his phone number! Way to go!'

I stick my tongue out at her in a very unladylike way and grab my mobile phone.

Episode 6 really will have to be 'where we had a coffee

date, no trains involved'. It is going to be so strange on the train on my own this afternoon, so strange not to see Joe until after Easter. Unless we can manage something over the weekend.

I'd already told Mum I'd work from home next week, rather than travel back down to London on Tuesday, then back up again two days later. I've always loved bank holidays – I'm not so sure I do anymore.

Unless it means I get to see Joe.

Chapter Twenty-Seven

JOE

Wednesday 13th April

Oh wow, I only saw Millie yesterday, and she's texted! My fingers have been itching to message her again, but I didn't want to come over too heavy. And, let's face it, I was shit-scared that I might have scared her off. She might have thought over what I said to her and decided that she's not interested in a guy like me.

She will have realised I'm not that outgoing metro man who is happy to share.

I lay in bed awake for hours last night, staring at the ceiling. Wondering if I'd chased away the most gorgeous girl I've ever met. If she'd realised that I'm not good enough. Not a man she wants to waste another moment on.

She's an independent city girl with a busy social life and I've also noticed that in her column she's mentioned more than once that she doesn't like to be hounded after a date. But I couldn't help myself. I'd had to text her.

I'd thought that my text yesterday evening saying it was great to see her was probably enough seeing as we're seeing each other tomorrow. Then she hadn't replied for at least a very long hour, and I'd gone into panic mode.

And when she did finally reply it was a pretty blunt 'was great to see you too' type of message, and even the kisses at the end didn't really convince me that everything was okay.

I'd talked through every scenario in my head, including the one where maybe she doesn't like texting. Some people just don't, do they? They prefer face to face.

But now she's texted me again.

Soz didn't reply until late yesterday, Mum had a fall and sprained her ankle. She's fine but fretting about how she'll get food for the long weekend so I'm heading home today. I'll miss you! The train just won't be the same on my own M x

Yesterday I was on a high – until the evening when I didn't hear from her. Today is turning out to be a total disaster. Bad news all the way. The email from my boss that I've still got open on my monitor is bad enough, and now I'm not going to be able to see Millie for ages, and I'm still not one hundred per cent sure that she's been straight with me. Is she really happy now she knows I'm not completely sold on the idea of our private lives being public? Or is she edging away from me? Does she need a few days to think about things? To be honest I feel totally deflated.

Although that is such a selfish reaction. What if her mum is really hurt? I should be thinking about her, and Millie.

Unless this is Millie's way of letting me down gently? Is this just an excuse not to see me? I couldn't blame her if it is. If, just like Lisa, she's realised I'm not the man she thought I was. That we don't have much in common. We're totally different people.

Or maybe she wants to put more personal stuff in her column, but doesn't know how to tell me?

I've cocked this up. I've put her off.

But why say she'll miss me?

Oh no, is she okay? J x

If she's not brushing me off, and is actually missing me, it still means it will be ages before I see her again. A lifetime.

She sounded fine on the phone. Nothing too serious from what she told me, but I'll find out when I get there! Sorry about tomorrow :(M x

Nothing too serious? Shit. She is avoiding me. *It's fine, as long as your mum's okay. See you in two weeks' time? J x* Bloody hell, two whole weeks. Two days had sounded bad enough, but two weeks? It sounds like for ever – it could be for ever.

You certainly will! Have a lovely Easter M x

I've started to type a reply, when another message comes through.

Or if we can work it out, we could meet sometime over the holiday? M xx

If you're not busy doing family stuff. Mx

Am I being too forward?! Mx

No probs if you are busy, I get it! M x

I can't help but smile as the messages land one after the other. She's not avoiding me. It's fine. I think.

Or if you don't want to see me. I get that too M x

Of course I want to see you!!! That sounds like a plan, then I can show you just how much I want to see you! I could call you tomorrow, after you've checked how your mum is? J x

Apart from Sunday lunch together as a family, we never do much over bank holiday weekends. Not even Easter. It's work as normal on the farm, milk production stops for no man, or religious celebration.

*Perfect!!! I really do need to check Mum is okay, she always says
she is, even if she isn't! Though I'm sure she is :) M xx*

I smile at the screen of my mobile phone for a moment –
waiting just in case there are any more messages – then
reluctantly put it down and look back at the email.

Apparently, my work here is nearly done. I knew it was
coming; there's always the pressure as we near
implementation date, the overtime, the emergency
meetings. But we're nearly there, it's about to go from full-
on to zero. The contract doesn't need renewing; my
company has new, more demanding projects in the pipeline.
The account manager is asking if I want to go to Bristol? Or
Birmingham?

Do I bugger. I don't want to go to either. A few months
ago, I would have gone with the flow, but things have
changed. I definitely want to stay in London, I want to give
me and Millie a chance.

If she still wants me. If I haven't screwed things up. But I
had to be honest, or it really would just be a repeat of Lisa.
I'd have only had myself to blame if I hadn't told her how I
felt.

Okay, a tiny bit of me is still worried (or slightly
petrified) about what she'll put in her column, but I need to
trust her. I can't just ditch things now, never know what
might have happened between us.

I try and push my worries about Millie to one side and
concentrate on my work situation. I knew this was coming –
which was why I'd been half-heartedly job searching. I did

think I had a bit more time though, but for once we're hitting the deadlines, we're in danger of actually making all the target dates and getting the final tweaks to the system in on time. Typical – the one time it would actually be good to run over, it's all going swimmingly.

It's now nearly two weeks since I met my mate in Newcastle, and he has not turned up anything worth applying for. Nor have the other recruitment agencies I contacted.

I read the messages from Millie again and know what I need to do. It's time to get my arse into gear and show a bit of the determination she does. I've got two choices. I either up my efforts in a general search, or I sound out Katherine.

'Hey, you got the email as well.' Talk of the devil! Katherine plonks herself down on a chair, wheels over closer. 'So?'

'So?'

'Looking forward to your next adventure, or?'

She leaves the question in the air. We've chatted, it's one advantage of living together. She knows I like it down here.

'Or?'

'You know I can't poach you? It's in the contract.'

'I know. I'll really miss the nacho and beer nights.'

She watches, assessing me through slightly narrowed eyes. 'You could take some time out, write your games, play your games and then… or take a short-term contract. I know somebody who's always on the lookout for sharp coders.' I nod. 'And then consider an offer here? I do need somebody to run this team, promotion? Bit of a boost to your salary.'

She says it as though she thinks I might say no.

Incredible.

Mum and Dad were proud before, they'll be even more chuffed to hear I've been offered a promotion.

'Have a think about it.' She nods towards the email. 'You've still got two weeks before they move you.'

'No.' She frowns. 'I don't need to think about it,' I add hastily. 'If you're sure you want a permanent lodger?'

She laughs, then claps me hard on the back. 'How can I say no, country boy. I'll talk to HR about getting something drafted out for you, then you can let me know if you're ready to hand your notice in. Yeah?'

'Yeah!' I grin at her.

And just like that the next stage of my future is set. Now all I have to do is get the girl.

I don't want to say anything to Millie until this is one hundred per cent certain, and I want to tell her in person. See her reaction. Maybe it's a good thing I'm not seeing her tomorrow, because I probably would find it hard not to share the news. This way is better, even though it would have been wonderful to see her.

Who knows, when we meet up in a few days' time, I might know for sure.

Chapter Twenty-Eight

MILLIE

Thursday 14th April

E *pisode 6. Confessions of… a proper date!*
       We had a date, no trains involved! This feels like a major step – this feels planned and the real deal. I cannot tell you how nervous I was. To be honest, getting to know train-guy has been a totally new experience for me. It has not involved alcohol, late nights or sex. It has also not involved romantic walks on windswept moors, or midnight star-gazing strolls. It has featured trains, draughty railway stations and crowded bars (one drink!) and now a café. But it has felt perfect.

He bought the coffee, and I spilled my deepest darkest secret, I unburdened my soul and confessed to my Confessions! As you know, this has been a deal-breaker in the past, and train-guy is the most private person I have dated for like e-ver. But he was cool. He got it, that this is my life, my career. He doesn't want me to change for him. Sounds like a keeper, eh? I am excited, and I am scared. Yes, I am frankly petrified because this feels like a bigger step than snogs, sex or staying over.

We held hands, and he traced his finger down the palm of my hand and it was the sexiest thing ever.

We have also planned to meet up again over the Easter holiday. I have realised that I don't want him to walk out of my life.

Is this the start of a proper grown-up relationship, where we share hopes and dreams as well as our lives? When it doesn't matter where we are, or what we have?

I'm not sure I even know what love is supposed to feel like – but maybe I am about to find out!

My finger hovers over the exclamation mark on the keyboard, and then my mobile bleeps.

Heading home for the weekend, train feels strange without you!
J x

I smile. He's texted! I've felt a bit uneasy coming home early and not being able to see him. I've been worrying about what it will be like when we do see each other again – if things will be the same, after our conversation. It was supposed to clear the air, but it's left an uncertainty, a need to see him as soon as possible again so I can be sure everything is okay. I know he isn't completely happy about my writing; I know he's unhappy that I wrote the first couple of episodes about us without telling him. He says it's okay, but he's holding back. And having to rush back to Mum early made things worse. I don't know why, but some tiny bit inside of me is saying that he thought I'd done it on purpose. That I'd made excuses rather than see him.

It almost feels like when we do meet up again it will be like we're starting over. Not quite sure about what the other person thinks.

But he's texted me, and a few of the butterflies in my stomach disperse.

I know what you mean! Work go okay? M x

I think I might have some news on the job front – looking promising! J x

In London? M xx

He sends back a thumbs-up and smiley face. I pause, let it sink in. *Wow, sounds good!* This is good! It's brilliant. Far better than him having the uncertainty. We will have our Thursday trips home together guaranteed; we can meet up in town in the week. Oh wow, we've barely had bodily contact and I'm planning our lives out! And I'm not panicking about it. Oooooh. I'm going to have to think about this. It's weird, it's strange. I'm grinning like a looney. I need to see him.

When are you going to tell me more about it in person?! M x

Thought you'd never ask!! How are you fixed for Saturday? Is your mum okay? J x

We're going to be okay. He wouldn't be pushing to meet up if we weren't. *She's good. Hobbling a bit, but out and about!! I'll double check and msg if there's a prob but sounds good. M xx*

Lunch? Hexham? J xx

You're on! Mx

Outside the abbey at 12? J x

Perfect! Can't wait!

I add a thumbs-up, and kisses. Panic briefly that 'can't wait' might be a bit too keen, then hit send anyway. I'm going to be brave, what's wrong with keen? I am. It's strange, but Joe seems to give me confidence, to be me, to push the self-doubts down. It's like I've stepped back to the younger me, the one that believed she could do anything. Before people started telling me I couldn't.

I flip back to my emails with a smile on my face. I've got to check Carla is happy with Episode 5, and I've got Episode 6 to finish – and then I'm going to sit back and enjoy a few days' break with Mum.

'Whatever it is you're frowning about, I think the answer is to keep it simple, and drink coffee!' Mum hobbles over to sit down beside me and hands over a steaming mug.

'And a biscuit?' One of the things I love about being home is that there is always a barrel full of biscuits, or a tray of homemade flapjacks, or cake. In an attempt to kid myself that I am capable of eating healthily, I try not to buy any of the above. This means that at the weekends, by 11 a.m. I am desperate for something sweet (even if I've had a sneaky croissant or pastry – it doesn't count because it is breakfast) and end up in the nearest shop stocking up on chocolate bars and crisps, then I binge in total relief. Mum's never-ending supply is probably healthier as there is no need to gorge. I can trickle feed.

I have tried buying 'healthy' snacks, like dried fruit and nuts, but they just don't do it for me. I still want sugar. This is why I will never be model-thin or even just the right weight. It is not my make-up, or my big bones, or some metabolism issue. No excuses. I just like food.

'I've not got any in at the moment. I need to keep trim for my salsa class.'

'Salsa class?' Mum is very good at making me forget whatever is bothering me. 'Since when did you go to salsa classes, and what about your ankle?'

'I've enrolled for a class that starts next week, but they've said they'll put me on hold if my ankle isn't up to it. Though it can't be that energetic when you first start, can it?'

'I don't know. Who are you going with?'

'John spotted it and we thought it would be fun.'

For heaven's sake, my mother is going to be in a hot clinch on a more regular basis than me! I really do need to up my game.

'So, what's bothering you, darling?'

The image of Joe's strong hand on my waist as one of my long legs slides between his and the other wraps itself round his firm thigh, as I throw my head back with complete abandon, is in full, vivid colour in my head. That is bothering me. For a start I'm not that supple, and I don't think he's that strong. Nobody has attempted to lift me up since I was fifteen. My heart is hammering harder than it should be at this time in the morning. I think I need more than a kiss. It was mind-bendingly hot, but I need more. I want to feel the warmth of his hand on my skin, I want to learn the feel of his, the smell of him. I need to touch his body and find out just how firm it is.

I need our bodies intertwined. I need to move with the rhythm.

'Millie?' Mum taps my hand. 'Trouble at work?'

The heat rushes to my cheeks, and I try and shake Joe out of my head. Boy, if I'd thought life was complicated before, trying to juggle work and my emotional need to be here, to support Mum, to be home, then I've just upped it by ten times. I never saw this coming. I never expected to feel like I want to see a guy so much, that if he messaged right now, I'd be very tempted to drop everything. And I do mean everything.

'Oh no, no, it's fine. Everything is great!' It is. Carla is happy that she has her Easter egg to present to our readers – she has the kiss. She has even made subtle comments about pay reviews and making the column more prominent. Giving it more space, a bigger headline. She loved that our plans changed, that we were derailed but found a romantic spot amongst the madding crowds (her words), that nothing could stand in the way of our growing desire for each other (I think she's been catching up on the classics or something), that he bought me prosecco (shall we up it to champagne? Or is prosecco more relatable?) and touched my hand, that we are one step away from SOMETHING BIG (her capitals).

Normally this level of intensity from my boss would scare me. I would start to wonder if I was up to this, if I could meet her expectations. But I am not scared. I have written this my way, I have worked to my own agenda, at my own speed, and it is good. People like it!

They are going to love our meet-up in the city for coffee, his mind-boggling gorgeousness as I spotted him through the crowds. The way he understands me and wants to support me. The searching looks he gives me that are as intimate as any touch.

Oh my God, am I finally getting my life together?

'And?' I glance up. My mother has one eyebrow raised and a half-smile on her face.

'Well…' There was another email. One I never saw coming, that dropped into my inbox a few minutes after I'd swapped messages with Joe. It's probably better that I think about this, not Joe.

'I've had this weird email from a publisher, and I don't really know what to make of it.' If I wasn't so wrapped up in my fluffy Joe-cloud, this would be taking up *all* my headspace. It is mega. 'They're saying they'd like to commission a book in the style of my Confessions, and would I be interested in entering into discussions?'

'A real book?'

'A real, proper book!'

'Wow! My daughter is going to be a famous author! Good heavens! Should I open the bubbly?'

'Well not quite.' I grin at her; I can't help it. 'It's a bit early, and I mean, I don't quite know if it's for real?'

'I'm sure it is!' Mum's smile drops slightly. 'But are you allowed to do that? Write what you have been doing, but for somebody else?'

'Well, according to this, I am. They don't want a copy of the column, it's just the kind of stuff I write about that they're after. It's *me* they say they're interested in, my style, the way I see life.' It is all a bit mind-boggling. Me. Who was ever interested in me? This is a full-blown proposal, not just a casual enquiry and just looking at it is making my heart race. I don't need prosecco, I'm already fizzy inside. This could be amazing! Like, really amazing!

I need to tell Joe! No, I can't tell Joe. That's silly, I need to calm down, check it out, be sure before I tell anybody. But, a book deal!

'Well, that is exciting! But have you got time? I think you'll have to stop coming home every weekend or you'll wear yourself out.'

'No way! I am not doing that, Mum.'

'I love seeing you, Millie, of course I do, but you know I can manage.'

'I like coming home!' I do, I really do. 'I wish I could be here more. I've missed you, I've missed the house, the place, I wish—' my throat tightens up '—I wish I'd been here more to see Dad.'

She squeezes my hand. Doesn't try and gloss over it.

'He would have liked that.' Her voice is soft. 'He was so proud of you, but he was especially proud of your independence, the way you went out and fought your battles, lived you own life. You know that, don't you? He knew it wasn't easy for you.'

I nod, biting back the tears that are threatening.

'You can't be in two places at one time, and we knew that.'

'But I do want to be here now, Mum.'

'I know, but this is so fantastic! You can't turn something like this down, and there are only so many hours in the day.'

'I know.' I bring the email up on my phone, read it for what has to be about the twentieth time. 'It is exciting, isn't it?' I take a gulp of coffee. I'm having palpitations, a flutter that's going all the way up to my ears.

It is. I really am excited, but it's a bit of a shock. Completely out of the blue. It's hit me and made my emotions bubble over. I've not been on the verge of tears over Dad for a while now, but I would have so liked him to be here to share this.

He'd be grabbing his jacket, sweeping us off to the pub to celebrate in style.

'Well, if you really want to do it, you could always ask for some time off, couldn't you? You could be away on a sabbatical or something, I mean it doesn't take that long to write a book, does it?'

'I don't know.' I stare at Mum. I have no idea how long it takes. I mean, I write every day, for sure, but that's like a sprint, and this is a marathon. Different tactics. Slower. More thinking involved.

She's right though. About the sabbatical, not the fact that you can write a book in a couple of weeks. I don't need to run myself ragged trying to keep up my column and all the rest, and do the book. I don't need to travel backwards and forwards between home and London, trying to keep all the balls in the air.

I can drop some temporarily. I could stay right here.

I could sort something with Carla.

But what about me and Joe? I'm pleased he's got his job in London, I am. Except he'll be there, and I'll be here if I do this. We can work it out; it's not for long. We can meet up in town in the week occasionally, and here at the weekends?

'You're frowning, Millie. You'll get lines!'

'Sorry, I was just trying to work things out.' I can talk to him when we meet. Okay, so exactly what shall I tell him? I do need to tell him something. I want to. This is big, exciting, momentous! I *want* to share it with him.

But I shouldn't. In case it all falls through.

'Oh, and I nearly forgot, have you planned anything for

Saturday? Is it okay if I pop out for lunch with a friend?' I do need to share this with Joe, in person, when I see him. He'll know what I should do.

'A friend?' She raises an eyebrow. 'Well actually, I was going to say you'd have to sort your own lunch out. I've got a date!'

Not again! I try not to groan. She's unstoppable.

'With Linda, so you can stop smirking! Honestly, what do you think I am?'

That question is hard to answer honestly, and not get my ears boxed.

'We're having afternoon tea, it's her birthday.'

'Ahh.'

'So you can meet your new man in peace!'

I don't bother objecting; I do heat up and make a funny squawky noise.

She tips her head on one side and watches me in silence for a moment or two. 'Oh, I see. So that's why this is so tricky. Well, whatever you decide, decide what's best for you, Millie. But remember to take care of your heart as well as your head. That's what your dad always used to say.' She kisses the top of my head. 'He was the best person I've ever known for getting the balance right, and that's why he was so happy with his lot. Right.' She switches to her brisk mode. 'I think it's time you learned how to make hot cross buns!'

Chapter Twenty-Nine

JOE

Saturday 16th April

I'm not a huge fan of scorching hot weather, but I love it when the sun is out. At the risk of sounding corny, it kind of lifts my soul. The world is a little bit more alive, people are happy and chilled, the grass looks greener, the spring flowers are bright and there's always that hint of a breeze that gently murmurs the bad things away. It's that kind of day.

Perfect for T-shirt and jeans, and a cool beer in a sunny spot.

Perfect for sitting chatting to a girl you fancy the pants off.

Oh my God, I'd been so nervous about seeing her today. So worried that things would be different between us. That it would be awkward. That she'd arrive with a script about how she'd realised how different we were, how it could only work if I was happy to have every aspect of our relationship documented, shared.

I'd lived through every scenario. Thought through every possible response.

And then I'd spotted her. There was a long, long moment when we'd looked at each other. My palms were sweating and my pulse racing, I'd been on the point of blurting out that we could make it work, that I'd try and push my fears to one side. All the things I knew in my heart shouldn't be said, wouldn't mend anything.

Then she smiled. And it was like the first time I saw her, but better.

How can I even think about letting her go?

I've got lager, and Millie has got ice-cold cider. She's got these big sunglasses on, which frame her face and bring out her delicate features. I can't keep my gaze off her lips, I'm a bit fixated on her gorgeous mouth, but I'm longing to see her eyes. As though she knows, she flips the shades on to her head and grins.

'Penny for them?' She smiles, her steady gaze never wavering.

'I was just thinking how lucky we are. Working the dream jobs in the big city but being able to escape to this.' I indicate the bustling square, the people sat around doing the same thing we are. The colourful pots of flowers.

Do I mention it, her job? Do I tell her I'm still having minor panic attacks and waking up in a cold sweat as I dream about the nightmare scenarios where total strangers analyse my sexual performance and my choice of boxer shorts?

'I know,' she says softly. 'It's beautiful.'

Am I kidding myself, or is it a bit stilted?

'I'm glad we could do this.'

'Me too. Joe—' she turns the glass on the table '– you are okay with my, er, dream job?' I open my mouth to answer, and she stops me. 'Look, I know you're not really, I know you said it's okay, but you're not and I get that, and I don't want to mess up, and—' She stops, takes a deep breath. 'I'm trying to say, I want us to be okay.'

I put my hand over hers, to still the movement. 'Me too.' And that's the truth, I know it is. I gaze into her eyes, and she's not Lisa. We're just two people with the normal differences that make us individual human beings, who both think we have something worth working for. I spend too much time analysing, thinking, letting things build up in my head. I need to tell her how I feel. 'I'm not going to lie, this is totally strange to me, alien, but it'll be fine.' It will be fine. 'More than fine. I'll fight the fear!'

'I'm sorry for not being more upfront. I was worried you'd hate me.'

'I could never hate you.' I couldn't. I could be upset, hurt, but never hate her.

'I was half-expecting you wouldn't want to see me again.'

'Well, I thought you'd come home early to avoid me.'

'Oh never!' She laughs then, and for the first time since we arrived looks completely relaxed. 'I couldn't believe it when Mum had her fall, talk about bad timing!'

'But she is okay?'

'She is.' She nods. 'She's raring to get back to her salsa classes!'

'Wow.'

'Enough about my mother!' She grins. 'What's this job news?'

'Well—' I finally feel myself relaxing properly '—I had bad news then good, you know how it goes? I got an email from my boss saying that my current contract was coming to an end and asking if I preferred Birmingham or Bristol.'

'Not Barbados then? I don't need to dig my bikini out?'

'Nope, not on the table, sorry. Though I wouldn't mind seeing the bikini!'

She laughs. 'But not quite London.'

'Exactly.' I smile at her. I can't imagine never seeing her again – and being sent to either of those places would make it tricky. I can't even see that I'd be making it home every week to see my family if I was in Bristol. A trickier commute. A commute without Millie. 'The manager in charge of the project I'm working on knew, of course, and she said she'd love to keep me on if she could. I've got anti-poaching clauses in my contract, of course, so I can't just start working for a client, but she reckons she can point me in the direction of some temporary contract work to bridge the gap.'

'Wow, we should be celebrating with fizz, not beer and cider!'

I don't need fizz if I've got Millie. I could be drinking water right now, and I'd be happy. 'It's not signed, sealed and delivered yet.' We grin at each other. 'But a good possibility. I wasn't going to tell you yet, in case it was tempting fate, but—' I shrug '—I think it's sounding good. And if Katherine, my boss, can't swing it, I think I'll just go for this work she mentioned while I look for something else.'

'Cool.' She runs the tips of her fingers up and down the glass, leaving trails in the condensation. There's the hint of a frown on her face, and a hesitation. It makes me feel jittery again. There's something she doesn't want to tell me. The bad news after the good. The bit where she tells me it doesn't matter if I'm in London, or the bit where she tells me her column has to be hotter. 'I've kinda got some news as well, but nothing definite.'

'Bad?'

'No, no, good. It's just, I'm a bit – well, I don't like telling people stuff unless I know it's going to happen. It feels like it will make it go wrong. And it isn't one hundred per cent yet. Hell, that makes me sound a bit of a weirdo.'

Phew. I laugh, I can't help it. It's relief that this is nothing personal, and also that it proves in some ways we are so similar. 'You're not a weirdo! Or you're saying I am as well. I do the same, I feel like you're kind of tempting fate if you tell people too early. A bit like telling everybody you're pregnant before you've even had the first scan, and it could all go wrong.'

She raises an eyebrow, her grin broadening.

'Well, that's what my sister told me! But—'

'I do know what you mean though!' She laughs.

'You don't have to tell me anything.' I shake my head, but I really would love to know. I want to know everything about her. 'I only shared because I know I'm going to make it happen. If Katherine can't sort it for me, I'll work out a way.' I'll work out a way to stay in the city, to stay on that train. To see you.

'But I do want to tell you! I've been offered this deal, I mean I can't quite say, but it's exciting.' Her eyes are gleaming. I can tell she is dying to say more. To share. 'It's like a dream come true, bigger than everything! But I need to work out if I can find time to do it, if maybe Carla can give me shorter hours for a bit, or something.'

'Oh shit, I'm sure she could! Your column is massive right now!' I can feel myself colour up. Despite hating being a part of it, being on public view, I haven't been able to stop myself reading what she writes. I'm obsessed. It brings me closer to her. She pours a part of herself into every word, and reading her stuff makes me feel part of her heartbeat, part of her life. I love it, but I hate it, because pouring herself in means she'll be doing the same to me. It gives me the jitters, but I can't help myself. 'I can only see the response online, but it's amazing!'

Her cheeks are pink-tinged. She's happy. I like making her feel happy. Even if it's not good for my blood pressure.

'I reckon right now, Carla needs you more than you need her. You can name your price, well, your hours! You're fab.' I lean in, let myself touch her hand that is resting on the table between us. Soften my voice. 'Honestly, Millie, go for it! You obviously want to, so make it happen. You can do it, and there's no way that your boss will want to risk losing you.'

Wow, I'm so pleased for her, and this could be great for us too. If she's working less hours in the office she could even come and work at my place some of the time, instead of in her own flat. We could have more time together. Our lives could move on together. A new chapter for both of us.

I might still have a niggle in my head saying I don't want my private life shared, but I do want Millie. And this just seems to be another sign. My job is coming together, and she's got a new opportunity.

She turns her hand over, wraps her fingers around mine and sends a shiver of need straight up my arm. 'Thank you.' Her words are soft, and so flaming sexy I want to grab her, wrap her in my arms, whisk her away.

Instead, I clear my throat. 'Do you think we should celebrate together when we get back to town, after Easter? I'm going back next Saturday, I think. But we could do Sunday, or in the week.' I gabble on, not wanting to stop and give her a chance to say no. Then run out of words, hold my breath.

'I'd like that. Sounds amazing!' She puts her empty glass down. 'I've not been down there on a Saturday night for months, since I started coming back here every weekend. It would be fun.'

She looks into my eyes; I look straight back. This feels like a step, a promise. Something we both want. A weekend together.

'Do you fancy a bit of a walk?' I croak out, aware of the rasp in my throat. 'If you don't have to rush back, that is?'

'I do, and I don't.' She stands up, still holding my hand. 'Mum is out having afternoon tea, they're probably comparing notes on salsa dancing and hot dates!'

'Your mum sounds fun!' I hesitate, not sure whether or not to add what I want to. But to hell with it. 'It would be nice to meet her one day.'

'You will! But be warned, she'll give you the third degree.'

'I'd expect nothing less. I'd do it if you were my daughter.'

'Joe?' She comes to a halt, looks up at me.

'Yes?'

'Thanks for being so supportive, it means a lot. Dad used to always encourage me to believe in myself, take the plunge. I feel like I've not had anybody in my corner like that for ages. I mean, Mum supports me, but mothers just do, don't they? It's different if somebody else does.'

'You're amazing, Millie. Resilient, brave, tough, clever, pretty… I think maybe I should shut up now.'

'No, no.' She laughs. 'Carry on, I'm liking this!'

I carry on. Churning out words as we walk, her laughter

sending shivers down my spine. I can't ever remember feeling this happy, this close to somebody.

'Are you happy?' The question comes out spontaneously.

She squeezes my hand. 'I am. Very.'

Chapter Thirty

MILLIE

Monday 18th April

I am not an early riser. I am the world's worst at mornings. But today I actually leapt out of bed and was humming as I brushed my teeth. Which is ridiculous as it was the kind of middle-of-the-night early that I normally only consider if I'm heading to the airport with the prospect of a fabulous holiday ahead.

Instead, I have the prospect of Joe. Which right now is even more exciting. Even if we are going to spend the best part of the day in a field.

He messaged yesterday, saying how great it had been to see me on Saturday and asking *Could you cope with seeing me again tomorrow? J x* With a fingers-crossed emoji.

Sounds great! M xx

There is a catch! It's a mystery date, it involves lemon curd, cheese and chutney J xx

Farmers market?? M xx

Got it in one! No flies on you! J x

And hopefully not on the cheese either!

Ha ha. Funny. It's a special Easter Bank Holiday Monday edition – I'd only invite you as my plus one to la crème de la crème of rural events! J x

When you say plus one, you mean you need a hand? M x

Two if possible. Man cannot live on bread alone, he needs our preserves – but I need somebody to pitch, while I package! I know my limitations J x

Sounds like it could be fun M

I add a smiley face.

If you find damson gin amusing!

You've got damson gin as well?! OMG Why didn't you say?! I'm in!!

I was saving it for my last pitch. So it's a yes?

It's a yes from me! I'll bring the lemonade and lime! And practise my sales techniques M x

You're a lifesaver! I love you!! J x

Market opens at 9.30 a.m. See you then? J x

No way, I'll help you set up. M x

I thought you didn't like early mornings? J x

Oh, I think I do if they involve you, Joe.

I'm up for it if you can provide bacon butties and coffee? From memory the ones at the market are to die for – Dad used to treat me! M x

Then it's a deal J xxx

Mum put in an order when I explained where I was going. She raised an eyebrow and grinned in a totally over the top way when I told her what time I was leaving the house, but gave me an extra big hug and kiss when we headed up to bed.

'Enjoy yourself tomorrow, Millie. You deserve some happy time.'

'I'm always happy.'

'I know, but this is different, isn't it?'

She's right, I think, as I park the car and head past the stalls on the lookout for Joe. This is a different kind of happy. I feel lighter, I feel like I want to sing, I want to smile.

To be honest, I was in a bit of a tizz when I met Joe in Hexham. It's weird but I felt like we were on a first date, and he was going to turn round and say he was backing out. That he couldn't cope with me, and my job. That he couldn't live his love-life in the public eye. That he'd only met up with me because he wanted to do it in person – Joe is not a dump-by-text kind of guy. But everything is going to be okay. Better than okay. And what is even more amazing is that I was worried sick that if I suggested I was thinking of asking Carla for a break, so I could work from home – here with Mum – then he'd really think I was dodging him. Us. But he didn't. He was so amazingly supportive.

'Ready to sell some chutney?' says a soft voice in my ear, the warmth of his breath sending a shiver down my spine.

I spin round, and we're practically nose-to-nose. His hands settle naturally on my waist. As though they belong there. 'Bring it on!' I grin back. Feeling alive, not the normal pre-coffee ghost of myself.

'But first—' he slips his hand into mine '—let me wine and dine you!'

I can smell the amazing aroma of warm bacon and the sharpness of coffee as he leads me towards the van set up at the end of the parking area. There's already a queue, but it's no hardship to stand next to him.

Our hips gently bumping each time the queue creeps forward. The gentle warmth of the early morning sun fighting the overnight chill that reminds us that it's still April. The friendly chatter surrounding us, but becoming a background hum each time he speaks.

'My treat.' He winks.

'Perfect.' I grin up at him, one hand warming on the coffee cup, the other clutching my bacon sandwich. I take a deep breath, gaze over the countryside, then glance back at Joe. Who needs fancy city eateries when they've got this?

He's so bloody handsome, I can't believe that 1. He's with me, and 2. He actually loves this place as much as I do.

He's not afraid of hard work. He's ambitious. He's kind. He loves his family, and yet he wants to use his skills, explore new places. Push himself out of his comfort zone.

How the hell was I ever lucky enough to find somebody like Joe?

'Penny for them?'

'You undervalue my thoughts! It'll cost you more than that!' I grin at him. Hiding my self-consciousness with jokes.

'One day,' he says, his voice lazy. No pressure. Then he wolfs down the rest of his sandwich, tosses the wrapper into a bin and slips his hand round my waist. 'Come on, we have jars to unpack.'

Working with Joe is fun. He's undersold himself – he's ace at drawing the crowds in and persuading them to buy.

He's so understated, they've parted with their cash before they've even had to time to wonder whether they really dare try chilli jam with their cheese.

It's his passion, his honesty that does it. His open face. His gorgeousness.

He's irresistible.

'Where are the other boxes?' I ask as he hands over the last bottle of damson gin with a flourish, and a free lime.

'That's it!' He brushes his palms against each other. 'We have the rest of the day to ourselves.'

'But...' I glance at the time. It's only 3 p.m. and a lot of the other stalls still have plenty to sell.

'Record sales! Mum will be offering you a full-time job.' He chuckles, his smile showing teeth that look whiter than ever against the tan he's picked up.

He's caught the sun. We both have. Although I don't think my glow is entirely down to the weather; I think a lot of it is down to the time we've spent behind this trestle table. The touch of his hand on my waist as he squeezes past to reach jars, or drop money into the box. The warmth of his breath as he whispers some funny comment in my ear.

'Come on, we'll pack up the covers and boxes and put them in the van and then I'll treat you to a special gin, I kept a bottle back!'

My back aches and I'm slightly breathless as we drop the last of the boxes and slide the tables into place.

'Okay?' He smiles, and I nod back hoping I don't look as hot and sweaty as I feel, then he locks the van and takes my hand.

He leads me beyond the last of the stalls, his stride long and confident, and waits to help me over a stile, catching my waist as I jump.

I want to capture this perfect moment, bottle this day as something I can look back on when things are not quite so good. It seems so long since I had free time like this. Time with somebody I like – a lot. No pressure, no work.

'Nearly there! This is one of my favourite spots.' He leads me down the bank. 'If I'm honest it was the real reason I asked you. I wanted to show you.'

I hold his hand a tiny bit tighter. I love that he wants to share with me.

And as he turns, takes one last step backwards and draws me to him, I love that he's brought me here.

'I can see why.' I sink down onto the blanket that he's just pulled out of his rucksack and look around properly. We're in a small hollow that protects us from the wind, but still allows us to see the amazing view. You can see for miles and miles. It feels like we're a world away from the farmers' market – even though it's just over the ridge, a short walk away.

Joe grins. He looks pleased with himself, and it makes me happy. 'Here you go.' He holds out two glasses, then fishes in his bag for the bottle of gin.

'Oh God, I was kidding about the lemonade and lime! I didn't bring anything!'

'Will this do instead?' His eyes twinkle, as he pulls out a bottle of prosecco.

'That bag is like a Tardis!'

'It's better. Cheese, chutney, pork pie.'

He's soon laid out a fantastic impromptu picnic.

'This is amazing, this.' I hold up my glass, then point at the picnic, and then to the wider view. 'It's all perfect.'

He smiles and I can't resist. I lean in, rest the tips of my fingers on the stubble on his chin, open my lips slightly and close my eyes as my lips meet his.

He tastes of damsons, of fresh air, of coffee, of need and I want him so much my entire body aches.

He sighs, pulls me in closer. His fingers tangling in my hair, his tongue dancing over my teeth as he shows me just how much he wants me. For a moment he pauses, his forehead resting against mine. 'I want to do better than Episode 5.'

'You've read it?' I'd almost forgotten that my latest post had been published today. The one where I told the world about our kiss at the station bar.

'I read everything,' he murmurs. 'I want as much of you as I can have.' His lips skim mine lightly.

'This is better. Every time I see you it gets better.' And the words might seem almost glib, like I could say them at any time. But I mean them. Each time I meet Joe, each time I touch him I learn a little bit more, I fall a little bit further, harder. It means a little bit more.

'I'd never stand you up,' he says. 'Don't ever think I could do that.'

'I don't now.'

I don't have a chance to say anything else as his mouth takes mine and I close my eyes, let myself sink against him, give a bit more of myself, learn a bit more about him.

We're both breathless, flushed when he finally pulls away. He brushes the hair off my forehead, tucks a strand behind my ear.

Then he smiles. Settles his back against the mound of grass and half turns me so that I sit between his legs. He lifts his knees, wraps his arms around me, pulls me as close as possible so that our warm bodies seep together and become one.

I rest my head back against his chest, look out over the fields and for the first time since Dad died, I feel like I belong. That this is enough. This is all I need to be happy.

Chapter Thirty-One

MILLIE

Saturday 23rd April

My body sways gently with the familiar motion of the train as it chugs along, and I ache for the feeling of his forearm bumping against mine, our shoulders rubbing as we meet and part in time with the rhythm of the train.

Joe. I can't stop thinking about him. I can hardly believe it's been a week since we met up for the drink. Five days since the market. It seems so much longer, especially with the way things ended when I saw him. Talk about anticipation. There was this undercurrent of 'we have to move on to second base'. Otherwise known as: I need to rip your clothes off, feel your naked skin, run my fingers along your muscles.

It was mutual. It was there in his eyes, and I'm sure it was in mine.

This must be the longest foreplay in the history of man, not just personally. It's been playing havoc with my concentration levels – it's a good job I've not been at work (well, just doing a few tweaks that Carla wanted for Monday's column), and that Mum has been fairly busy with her very active social life.

I had no idea she went out so much. I guess I'd preserved that picture in my head of how it was before Dad died. The two of them spending most of their time together. Pottering in the garden, going out for the occasional meal. And then when she was grieving, she had nobody to turn to and say, 'Well, what a load of tosh, isn't it?' when something stupid came up on the radio or television. She was just alone.

That was the hardest part for her. The times she'd turn her head to comment on a news item, or the weather, or anything really, to him – and there'd be an empty chair.

In my head, I'd not seen her move on. Emerge back into the world, but differently. They say nobody is the same, life isn't the same, after a loss, don't they? You don't move on, forget; you adjust. Find a new version of life that you can cope with.

Mum is working it out, she is coping fine.

I guess I knew this anyway. She doesn't need me here, although she does like to see me. She doesn't want to rely on me, I'm her daughter.

And deep down I know I've not been coming home every weekend because I have to for her, it's because I have had to for me. I want to be in Hexham. A little bit of my life isn't quite right. I thought I was happy with my job, my life, my flat – and I am. But I'm not content, as Dad would say.

I'm falling for Joe, I know I am. Meeting him has shown me that I'd lost confidence because I've surrounded myself with what and who I thought were the right things and people. When I've got the right things and the right people, I can ignore the niggles.

Joe is hellbent on making it in London, and that's good. It's his passion. My passion has shifted. It's still my work, but it's also getting the right balance. It's having what I know and love there in the background as well.

I'm happier now than I've ever been. And it's not just down to finding a gorgeous guy I want to get to know better, it's about the confidence inside me that has grown because I *know* I'm doing the right thing – not just hoping I am. I'm in the right place.

When I was little and worried about going into school, or talking to people, or going into the playground or party on my own, Mum would hold my hand. She'd squeeze it, and I'd know she was there, she'd got my back, she wouldn't let me do the wrong thing. And I feel like that now. Joe is holding my hand – even though he's hundreds of miles away.

And he was right about Carla. I know I'm half-smiling. I can't help it. I can imagine his reaction when I tell him about my phone conversation with her. He'll tell me that he told me so.

She was completely open to the idea of the book. She still wants the column, because it's doing so well, but she's happy for me to drop the rest and work from wherever I want.

I know it's not just that I'm irreplaceable, ha ha, it's that she thinks if the book takes off then it will draw more readers to my column. Which is fine.

She was so keen, she wanted to hint at the book as soon as we can 'get them drooling and checking in more often for news' in her words. The publishers were a bit more formal about it, but no way were they going to object. As long as there were no names mentioned until the contract was signed, they were thrilled at the idea of some teasers.

It's going to be amazing. I'll miss the Thursday journey with Joe, but we can meet up at the weekends, and I'll be popping down to London for meetings and stuff so I can stay over – and see him!

See him. Oh my God, if you'd have told me a few weeks ago that I'd be planning a man into my life I wouldn't have believed you.

And it's only going to be for a month. Four missed Thursdays. Then Carla and I will renegotiate.

To be honest, if you'd told me a few weeks ago that *any* of this would be happening to me, I would have laughed. My life is changing dramatically – and all for the better. I mean, my column has taken off and I'm back on track, I've got a guy in my life who is incredibly important, I've got a book deal and I'm heading back to Hexham – to the countryside! It's all a bit incredible. I don't know which bit is the biggest surprise.

I think I know which bit is the most amazing right now

though. Joe. How the hell did I bump into a guy so sweet, so supportive, but also so unbelievably sexy? I was scared shitless I'd frighten him off with my column, but he's cool about it. We've worked that one out. And the way he's supported me over the book, encouraged me to talk to Carla, giving me the courage to believe in myself and what I want to do, where I want to be – even though he doesn't want to move back to the countryside himself – makes him even hotter. How many guys would feel insecure if you talked about moving away for a while, would insist you stayed put and compromised? Every other guy I've dated, I reckon.

I am glowing inside.

Joe is special.

We've swapped lots of messages, but now I can't wait to fill him in on this. Tell him it's all been agreed. It's definite – I really am going to be an author, write a book! But even better – and I grin as the thought fills me – I'm going to see him. Soon! We've got the rest of today and as much of tomorrow together as we want.

Wow, what do I write about in my column? How much do I include? Monday is all about our coffee date, our first proper date, in London with a brief mention of our planned date in Hexham. Do I just write about that – which seems like ages ago – so much has happened! Do I include this weekend? Oh my God, this weekend. If it's a disaster, it will be easy to include. But if it's not, if it's as good as I want it to be, then I won't want to share it at all.

'*The train will shortly be arriving at…*'

Shit. We're here! I'm bubbling up inside. Is my hair okay? Do I really look the right amount of smart cas in my jeans and T-shirt, or have I gone too cas? What if he is planning on going somewhere nice? I've got my sneakers on, ready for walking, because that's what I always wear when I come back. But what if we're not walking?

Oh, oh, oh! This is killing me. I grab my stuff together, double check there's nothing left on the seat.

Have I got time to go to the loo? What if he's standing at the top of the platform waiting for me? I can't just rush off! What if I can't find him? If he's not here, if I wait in the wrong place?

I'm swept along by the rest of the crowd, keen to get out of the station, to enjoy their day shopping, their evening out at the theatre.

And he's there.

And nothing matters any longer.

His smile reaches his eyes, his hand reaches out for my waist, and his lips meet mine.

And I know I'm in the right place. I'm exactly where I need to be.

He breaks the contact, pulls back, but his hand is still on my jawbone. 'Want to go and grab a drink, unwind a bit?'

'Perfect.' My words come out all breathless. My heart is still pounding, and my lips are tender from his kiss, and I'd be quite happy to just stay here for a while and kiss him again. Just to make sure the first one wasn't a fluke, but I guess that isn't really an option.

And we've plenty of time.

He drops his arm to his side, takes my hand in his. Squeezes.

Take my hand, take my heart. The words jump into my head and lodge there. I glance up at him, and our gazes meet. I hardly know him. We've only met a handful of times. Can I really mean that? Has he really lodged himself in my heart?

I wish Dad was here to meet him, he'd like Joe.

'You look fantastic, have I said that yet?'

His words stop me dwelling on the thought. 'I think you might have done! You don't look bad yourself.'

He laughs.

'Apart from the hair!' I reach up, straighten his hair.

He pauses his step. Then runs his own hands through, a reflex action. 'I've been tearing it out! I was worried you'd get delayed.'

'Now don't blame me if you lose it all before you're forty!'

'I'll blame the trains.' He smiles, slips his arm around me so that his hand rests on my waist. 'Although I'm thankful for that particular train. If it hadn't been for that, I'd never have met you.'

'If it hadn't been for the rain and your umbrella, I'd never have been trying to hunt you down.'

'You hunted me down?' His grin is broad, his chuckle deep and sexy. 'I like that.'

'I like you,' I say simply.

He stops walking then, turns me in his arms.

'We're still in the station,' I say.

'I don't care, if you don't.' This time when his lips meet mine, they're gentle, teasing, soft against my skin as they travel along my jawbone, the touch of his teeth on my ear sending shivers through my body. He cups my face in his hands, concentrates on my lips, tugging at my bottom lip, skating his tongue over my teeth, exploring my mouth in a way that makes me groan. I move in closer, feel his body moulded against mine, slip my hands under his T-shirt so that I can feel the warmth of his skin.

He pulls back slightly, groans. 'I think this is the bit where somebody shouts, "Get a room",' he whispers into my ear. The heat of his breath makes me want to tip my head back, hold his tighter.

'I guess so.' My voice is husky. I clear my throat. 'Maybe we should get that drink.'

'I guess we can't go straight back to my place yet, can we? That would be...'

'Nice?' As I stare into his eyes they darken at my question.

'It would be nice.' His voice is rough-edged.

'We can do whatever we like, can't we?' We've got as far as the station entrance. 'We can get a drink any time.' These feelings inside me have been building up all week, I don't need to prolong things, build the anticipation. It's already there, about to burst out if we don't do something.

'Come on.' He makes a sudden decision, takes a firmer

grip on my hand and we dash out – his arm in the air to hail a taxi. I feel giddy as we bundle in, steal glances as we wend our way through the traffic, feel nervous as we stagger out onto the pavement.

'Okay?' he says softly.

I nod. Smile. Thread my fingers through his.

Chapter Thirty-Two

MILLIE

Sunday 24th April

Oh my, that was not sex. That was not a shag. That was almost like an out of body experience, except my body felt every bit of it. I am still throbbing – in places I didn't know I still had a healthy blood supply.

'Wow.' Joe says what I'm thinking. He shifts onto his side, so that his nose is inches from mine on the pillow. 'Good morning!'

'Good morning to you too.' I turn my head so that I can look into his eyes, study his face, and grin back at him. 'I better warn you, I'm not really a morning person.'

'Grumpy?'

'Definitely.'

'Would coffee help?'

I nod.

It's only when he leaves the room that I lever myself up and get a chance to look round.

His room is neat and tidy, like I guessed it would be. Though his desk in the corner is a jumble of stationery, gadgets and family photos that lure me over.

I love seeing other people's stuff. It's like a portal into their secret side, who they really are.

Joe is who he says he is. Hard-working, thorough, logical, family-loving. I pick up the family photo. He looks like his dad, the same studious air and slim physique. Joe's is overlaid with muscles, toned and strong; his dad looks more like he spends his time inside behind a desk. He looks studious, clever, but happy. They all look happy. His mum has one arm round Joe, the other round a girl who must be his sister. Mother and daughter share their eyes, the shape of their face, their hair. But their faces tell different stories. His sister shines out bubbliness, a love of life, something wild and free – the way she's standing, the way her head is tilted in laughter, her generous mouth (so like Joe's) open. I can imagine her talking ten to the dozen, chattering and making you laugh. I can imagine her teasing Joe, but throwing her arms round him. His mum has a quiet, serene smile, contained. A slight wariness in her eyes, though the way she's hugging her kids, the smile that reaches her eyes, says she's kind. I'd say she's the root of the family. The core. The strength that holds them all together. I can imagine her encouraging the son who is so like her in temperament, and shaking her head as she laughs in despair at her wayward daughter.

'Hey.' Joe makes me jump as he comes up behind me, the warmth of his body reaching mine before we actually touch. I love the husky edge to his voice. It's already lodged in my body as a signal that wonderful things are to come.

He puts the coffee cups down, leans his chin on my shoulder and wraps his arms around my body.

'Your family?'

'My family.' I can hear the smile in his voice. 'Mum, Dad and Sophie. And that,' he indicates with a tip of his head as I look up at him, 'is my little nephew, Ben. Cute eh?'

I can't help but smile at the warmth of his tone as I put the photo down, and lean back into his body.

'How did you put it in Episode 5?' His voice is as smooth as warm honey, which is even sexier than the husky side. His breath close to my ear sends shivers down my neck. 'You were still tingling after the kiss, wondered if it was the start of something wonderful?'

I twist round in his arms. Stare into his eyes, then rest my hands on his broad shoulders. 'I did. It was, wasn't it? It is. Wonderful.' Then I raise myself up and seek out his mouth. He tastes of coffee and sex.

His hands find their way under my top, his fingers tiptoeing their way down my spine and my entire body trembles in anticipation as he cups my bum, pulls me in tighter against him, so that I can feel every inch of him. One hand edges between my thighs, and oh my God I'm turning into a throbbing hot mess. Squirming and desperate for more.

He chuckles as he edges us back towards the bed, but

it's a chuckle that is deep, vibrating, sexy and turns me on even more than I already am. We topple, his thumb rubs gently as his fingers slips inside me, his mouth covers mine and the aching need tumbles into satisfaction before he's thought about his own needs.

'Oh my God, you are so sexy, have I told you that?' He pulls back from the kiss to gaze into my eyes, then his head dips as I reach out for him again, and his body covers mine.

The coffee has gone cold by the time we get to taste it.

But who needs caffeine, eh?

'I can make brunch for you, or we can go out? Your choice?' He smiles at me, his hair dishevelled, his T-shirt crumpled. I like it. I did that!

'I'm not fussed.' I could sit here all day, on this stool at the breakfast counter, dressed in one of his T-shirts, watching him.

'We should go out?'

'I guess.'

'I want to spoil you. Let me spoil you?' He's cute. So cute. What have I done to get a man like this?

'You are spoiling me, just being here.' Saying that should feel dangerous, but it doesn't.

He plucks a pink carnation from the vase and hands it to me. 'No red roses, I'm afraid.'

'You don't stretch to that?'

He grins. 'They're Katherine's! I'll tell her she needs to up her game.'

'Katherine, isn't she your—'

'Boss.' He finishes for me. 'She's my landlady as well. This is her place. Luckily, she's away this weekend, back tonight as far as I know.' He pauses. 'How long can you stay? How much time have we got?'

I laugh at his phrasing. I'm tempted to say, 'We've got the rest of our lives', but that sounds a bit much, doesn't it? Instead, I settle for 'Lots, I hope! Though I will need to get back later this afternoon, I suppose.' I pause. I've got a load of work to do. Tidying up Episode 7 for a start.

I'm liking Episode 7, it's about our date in Hexham, it's about springtime, hope, new starts. Maybe not as hilarious as some of the others, but I think people will like it. It also mentions that we arranged this weekend. I have no idea how I'm going to tackle Episode 8 – when we finally did it, and it was the most mind-blowing experience I have ever had. Not that I will use that as a title. I also need to draft book stuff so that I can send ideas, a rough outline, to the publisher. 'Hey, I spoke to Carla, and she was cool about me spending time on the book!'

'I told you so, you're indispensable!'

I grin back at him. 'I knew you'd say that.'

'Not cool?'

'Very cool. Thank you.' My features soften and I squeeze his hand. 'I get time off from most of my normal stuff so I can spend time on it for the next month or so, but still keep the column going. I can work from home! Win, win!'

'Amazing, it's amazing, you're amazing.' His voice is amazing. Chocolatey smooth. So deep it's doing indecent things to me. 'I told you, I knew you could do it! That is definitely worth celebrating. Come on, much as I'd like to spend the day ravishing you, I reckon the sun is out and I need to prove I'm not that cave dweller who just wants to keep you in his cave so he can fondle your gorgeous body –' he leans in, his eyes darkening '– kissing that luscious mouth, touching that silky skin…' He groans.

'Really?'

'Really! Stop it, you're making it harder to resist.'

'I hope I'm making it hard.' I hold his gaze, putting the emphasis on the last word with what I hope is a sexy growl. He doesn't laugh, like I thought he might. He cradles my face in his hands and kisses me. His tongue exploring my mouth so thoroughly it sets up a throb between my thighs.

He breaks the contact and I squeak an objection, but it's so he can move round to my side of the breakfast bar, so he can turn me round, move between my thighs.

'You're making it very hard.' His voice has that raspy edge that is *such* a turn-on. He cups my bum, pulls me in tighter against him – and I have all the evidence I need. 'Oh my God, to think we're going to have even more time together to do this, to do so much…' His words drift away as his mouth settles on my neck, as his tongue explores my skin. Scorching a track that sends a shiver through my body.

It's quite a bit later when we get out of his cave, and into the bright sunshine. At the moment I'm on a high, elated, as I hold his hand and practically skip alongside him.

Tomorrow morning, I reckon I'm going to be so knackered I won't want to get out of bed. But that is tomorrow, today I'm going to enjoy myself.

Enjoy him.

Chapter Thirty-Three

JOE

Monday 25th April

I can still smell Millie on my skin, still feel her lingering touch and hear her laughter as I wander to my desk.

Maybe I should be tired, but I am buzzing. I feel up there in the clouds, which is a feeling I can't ever remember having before. I also think I am grinning stupidly, but I can't help myself.

I feel kind of invincible.

It was too late to call Millie last night, after Katherine got back. But she'd told me that she's been in negotiations with my company. They're happy for me to work two months' notice here, and then accept a permanent job. A formal email with work conditions, new salary offer and all the rest is due today!

My life is all slotting together. It might seem keen, but I'm going to see if Millie's got time to meet for lunch and then I can tell her in person. I've got her, I've got my permanent job in London at last, and I've got more money. In my head I'm already moving out of Katherine's and into some amazing apartment that Millie will love to visit and stay over.

There'll be a desk by the window, so she can work if she wants. But only if she wants. I don't want to crowd her, I'm quite happy if she needs to work in her own flat and just spend time with me outside office hours. There's no rush. We've got plenty of time.

I guess really I should tell Mum and Dad first, but Millie is the person that I most want to share this with. Is that bad?

Mum will be planning a weekend celebration; Dad will dig out his best malt whisky – but first I want to crack the bubbly with Millie. A double celebration – her book deal is amazing! I grin as I open up my emails. Nothing on the work front yet; not surprising as it's only 7.30 a.m., but I couldn't sleep. I suppose I should wait for the full confirmation in writing, until I know it is really real, before I tell anybody. But it's so hard, I feel so fidgety!

The office is Monday-morning dead still, so I reckon another coffee and a sneaky read of the latest 'Confessions' column before I start work. Find out just how much Millie has told the world about us now. I guess what I really want to read is how she said it made her feel. We didn't get our standard train commute, so did she write about Easter? About our meet-up in Hexham. Did she mention we'd arranged a weekend together?

My fingers are trembling slightly as I bring up the

column on the screen. I can't help it, there's still that anticipation, that fear. I guess I can't change, I'm still a private person at heart, in my DNA. Seeing myself written about, laid bare, is never going to be comfortable, feel natural. But life isn't perfect, is it? You can't get one hundred per cent of anything, and everything else with Millie is good. This is a tiny sacrifice. And I trust her, I know she won't go too far. Push me completely out of my comfort zone.

Episode 6 – Confession of a proper date. The real deal.

I'm going to tell Mum and Dad, if Soph hasn't already. I decided last night, when I was lying in bed. Tired, but too wired to sleep.

I want them to know about her. I want them to meet her, because it just feels like she should be in my life.

Even the sex was perfect in its imperfection. Funny when we weren't quite in sync, when one of us did something the other didn't expect.

Will she write that, in her next episode?

It's scary. If I was a different person, if I was my sister, I'd probably think it's so cool that we've got the way we met, and everything, documented like this. Even if it's slightly changed, for public consumption.

Maybe, one day, it'll come more naturally. It will seem normal.

And it does kind of make me glow with some weird satisfaction to see people commenting, cheering us on.

Maybe it's addictive, this attention, this validation. Maybe one day I'll actually like it!

Oh my God, she's talking about this being a grown-up relationship, about wondering if it's long-term.

I grin. She's sneaked in a bit at the end about my job maybe changing, and about her book! About changes, about… I frown as I read the last paragraph. Re-read it to make sure.

What the hell does she mean? This isn't what she told me.

She says she's going to be working from home all the time. Home as in *Northumberland*. The place she's just realised she has left a huge chunk of herself in. Where she thinks she belongs. Belongs? That isn't what we talked about.

She'd agreed with her boss that she wouldn't have to go into the office, that she could work from home, from her flat.

I force myself to read on, even though the words are blurring before my eyes, and the pain is building in my throat, my stomach.

Her confessions are going to be about her returning to her roots. Seeing how she sees the place now she's been converted into a city girl.

She's asking if this will change us, when the anticipation of our romantic commute goes. No more King's Cross. Moorlands and a different kind of magic.

When she told me about the book, she just said her boss would be giving her more time to write it. Not that she wanted to move out of London. Okay, overreaction, not totally move out.

But this is what she's chosen.

She's not chosen me. *Us*.

I thought she loved London, like I do. That this was going to be her home.

Shit, I'm sounding stalkerish even to myself. Controlling, like I should have any say at all.

But we talked about this, the future. The future I thought we were going to share, our futures that slotted so perfectly together. We were on the same page, the same ideas.

But we've got seriously crossed wires here.

This *is* Lisa all over again.

I re-read her last few sentences.

I'm going home! Is that where I'm truly happy? Will writing this book bring me more than fame and fortune?! Fate has a funny way of bringing you what you need when you need it – but I've just met train-guy. The most exciting relationship of my life. We've planned to meet for a drink over the weekend. I just know it's going to be amazing (more news on that next time!!). But will it be the start or the end? Will we both return to the country?

The start or the end. My stomach has hollowed out. There's this strange feeling of dread filling my body.

If Hexham is really where she wants to be – which it must be, or she'd be staying here as normal to write – then she's right. Where does that leave us?

I click out of the article. I can't bear to have it on my monitor. I close my eyes for a moment.

I'm working permanently in London. She's working full time in Hexham.

My family are mega proud of me, of helping me get here. I'm proud.

I woke up on Sunday morning, beside her, feeling as though we were totally in tune. I felt like I knew her. Now I don't feel like I know her at all.

How can she tell *everybody* that she's moving out, before she's told me?

How can we share a weekend like that, and she leave me totally in the dark about what she's planning? What she really wants.

How can she drop a teaser in like that, saying she'll write about our time together?

It's like it's some kind of test. Or she's just throwing everything in the air for fate to decide. As though she doesn't have a say.

This isn't the Millie I thought I was getting to know.

This is just like Lisa all over again, but worse.

It's like she's been using me for her column – that this weekend was the climax. Ha ha. Not funny. Shit, if she's already said she'll be writing about our date in Hexham next time – what's she going to say about this weekend?

I bury my head in my hands. Have I got into something stupid? Fallen for a girl who isn't who I thought she was at all? No, no, I can't believe she's been using me. It was real.

I trusted her… I opened up to her – told her all kinds of stuff I've not shared, let her write about me. *Us*.

I need to talk to her; this is doing my head in. I need to know. I need to calm down and be rational about this. What she's written and the reality could be two different things.

I just cannot believe she'd be in my arms, congratulating me on my job, saying how happy she was to be with me, when she'd got no intention of hanging around.

Lisa had no intention of moving here. She lied. Pretended she was happy for me. She made out she would be willing to try city life, but she was just trying to keep me sweet. She didn't want to lose me, so she thought she could change me.

Then it all came out. Boom.

I know you can't change people. I don't want to. I didn't want Lisa to change, I just wanted her to be honest with me.

I thought Millie was being honest with me. And now this.

She made out she was happiest here, and now she is announcing to the world that her heart is somewhere else.

Not with mine.

I squeeze my eyes tight shut. Realise I'm clenching my fists and force myself to relax.

This can't be Lisa all over again. I went into this with my eyes wide open. We went into this as two adults, not two kids who weren't old enough to know what they wanted.

I thought it was different with Millie, but I guess I should have taken notice of that feeling of disappointment, of hurt, in my gut when I realised that she was writing about us. My instincts had been right, my head had been telling me not to get carried away following my heart.

Why did I persuade myself that it would all be okay? Why did I let myself fall deeper, get more involved?

If I pack in London now, I'll be guilty of misleading Lisa, I'll be letting my family down after they sacrificed so much to get me here.

I'm committed. I couldn't move if I wanted to. But I don't want to. I want to be here. Millie knows that.

I'm being ridiculous. This is not a deal-breaker. I'm a grown man, not some love-struck kid. We can work this out, whatever it is.

There will be an explanation.

I pick up my mobile phone and tap out a message.

Morning! Got time for lunch? Joe x

I'd been thinking about a lunch date so I could tell her my exciting job news, tell her it was now definite. Well, okay, I was thinking about a lunch date because I felt desperate to see her again, even though she'd only just gone.

Instead, I need to see her to find out if she means what she's written.

It's the fact she might not have been open, honest with me that is niggling me. I trust her. I trusted her.

Now the sense of disappointment is gnawing inside me, and I need to stop it taking root.

Would love to, but big reorg meeting at 12.30. … is everything ok? Mxx

Not really. I need to talk to you, soon if poss? J x

Chapter Thirty-Four

MILLIE

Monday 25th April

Oh wow, talk about the lull before the storm.

I wouldn't exactly call the weekend with Joe a lull (parts of my body that I didn't really know exist are now throbbing, aching or smarting in a disturbingly hot way that I am definitely not going to talk about in my column), but Monday morning has started with a bang in a totally different way.

Carla dragged me into the office before I'd even finished my first cup of coffee, to tell me that she was rethinking my column, since my book announcement. She was thinking more along the lines of 'Confessions of a long-distance love affair' seeing as everybody liked a bit of a crisis. They were all keen to know whether train-guy would survive my change of scene, whether he'd follow me to the sticks or stick it in the city, and whether sexting was all it was cracked up to be. She also said that when I mentioned at the end of Episode 6 that I'd met him at Easter, I had marked a shift that we could not step back from. The train had served its purpose.

We had disembarked.

We are obviously moving on. With this in mind she told me I was free to start working from home this week – after we'd had an all-staff meeting to explain my absence and assign new responsibilities.

I then phoned Mum, who squealed about how proud she was to have a nearly famous daughter, then said we probably needed some house rules if I was moving back (does this mean I have to be in bed by 10 p.m., and not drop biscuit crumbs on the sheets?). Then softened the blow by saying she had bubbly in the fridge, and what time would I be back? She'd booked theatre tickets for tonight, and her friend (no, I still can't call him a boyfriend), had let her down so if I could be there by late afternoon, we could have a girls' night out.

Why not?

I booked my train ticket.

I got the 'in an important meeting' message when I tried to call Joe, so I texted to tell him which train I was catching.

I'll call when I'm on it so we can work out when and where to meet next! I could meet you off the train at the other end for a change! This is so exciting – it's happening! Eeek! Can't wait to see you again, and make new plans M xxx

Then I went back to the flat, turned down the heating, watered the plants and packed.

Joe is standing at the entrance to the station. Where we first met. He's looking sexier than ever. Slightly rumpled because he's dashed over here to try and catch me before I go.

Nobody has ever made grand romantic gestures for me before. Nobody has been Joe.

I grin and run the last few yards to jump into his arms.

Luckily, I don't jump high because he didn't see me coming and doesn't exactly join in and try to catch me. I guess it's lucky I didn't flatten him.

'Oh my God! I didn't think I'd get a chance to see you before the weekend! I'm so glad you're here.' I wrap my arms round him, tilt my face up, half-close my eyes for the kiss.

Then open them again. I have not been kissed. His body is slightly stiff against mine, not warm and meltingly perfect.

'I didn't think you'd be in such a rush to leave London. I didn't realise when you said you'd work on your book from home, you meant you were going to your mum's and leaving immediately!'

'Nor did I! The immediate bit, it's just how it happened, and Carla said I might as well, and Mum had got these tickets...' I'm blabbering as fast as I can to get it all out, but my words tail off as his tone sinks in. If I didn't know him so well, I probably wouldn't notice. But he's detached, formal, not his normal self. He's not smiling. 'It's only for a while.' I half smile, as I rake his face for clues. I'm not quite sure what's going on, why it's such a big deal.

'I'm sorry I'm having to dash off, but we weren't going to see each other until Thursday anyway, were we?' We didn't arrange another date. I'm sure we didn't. No way would I have forgotten something that important.

'No. But I'll miss you, the train, everything.' His features have softened slightly, but he looks so unhappy.

Oh my God, he thinks I don't want to see him! He's hurt, not angry. 'Oh Joe, we'll see each other! I thought I could come down sometimes mid-week and we could go out? And we can meet at the weekends when you come to see your family. It's no big deal, is it? We talked about it, I thought you wanted me to do this book.'

'Millie—' his voice is soft '—you told the whole world you were leaving London before you told me.'

Did I? I frown. 'You knew, I told you. I said I was going to talk to Carla about time out of the office, you encouraged me! I told you she'd agreed that it was happening. I mean, I thought it would be in a week or two but…'

'I told you to persuade her to give you time to work on your book, I didn't realise you meant away from London.' There's a crack in his voice that it hurts me to hear.

'I said…' What did I say?

'No, you didn't. You said you were working out of office, from home. From your home *here*.'

This is getting silly. He's starting to worry me. My stomach has started to churn. I don't get how he misunderstood, how he assumed that I'd be working in London. My flat. I thought he understood, I thought it was clear. I know he doesn't want to go back to Northumberland, the countryside, but I thought he got that maybe I do. 'You're making a big deal of this, and it isn't!' I can't hide the tremble in my voice. 'It's for a month or so, and then...' This is fixable. We can work this out.

'And then what?' There's a deadness to his tone.

I shrug. 'I don't get what...'

'Millie, you aren't going back for your mum, you're going back for you.' He stares at me. Letting the words sink in. 'You want to be there, not here, don't you?'

I stare back at him.

He's right.

'I think so. But my job's here, I will come back after the book's done.'

'Unless you get offered another deal. What will you do then? Millie, this is what you really want, isn't it? Why didn't you tell me? Why couldn't you at least be honest with me?'

I can't speak. All I can do is look at him as the words bounce in the emptiness. There could be a million people pushing around us right now, but none of them count. This feels like... nothing.

He is right. This is what I want. It's more than writing a book. So much more.

'You made me think you were happy here, that this was where you wanted to be.'

The words he doesn't add, 'with me', hang in the silence between us.

'I thought...'

'I thought too, Joe. I didn't mislead you, honestly, I really didn't. I thought this was what I wanted, I thought I was going back for Mum, but I didn't understand myself.' I take his hand in mine, but he doesn't squeeze it back like he always does. 'I wasn't being dishonest with you, I didn't know.'

'But you do now.' His words are so quiet, but they carry loud and clear. He pauses, his eyes searching my face and getting the answer he is looking for. He looks so sad it brings a lump to my throat. 'It's not going to work for me. Millie, I can't go back. I work here, in London.'

'I know you do. I know that. But we can make it work, we can see each other...' He's shaking his head. I want to hug him; tell him we can make this right. But he shifts back as though he anticipates it. 'It's more than me going to Mum's to work that's bothering you, isn't it?'

'This new job of mine has more responsibility, I can't just waltz in and out, I'll have to be here on Fridays. I might not make it back at the weekends. I've just taken a full-time job here, and you've taken one miles away.' He waves a hand in desperation to illustrate. 'I've been here before with Lisa. I thought you got me, Millie.' This time, he puts his hands on my upper arms and the heat that sears through my body is fear, not lust. 'I'm not pining to go back; I go to see my family. Once Soph is back in a routine, I'll go back less. This isn't some happy ever after where you write us as two people who both ran off to the city, met, and then decided they had to go back. Don't you get that? It's not some fantasy, it's real people. *Us.* I don't want to go back. I didn't think you did.'

His hands drop to his sides as though he's exhausted. I swallow hard, as panic jitters inside me. 'Or you wouldn't have talked to me, the weekend wouldn't have happened?'

'Of course it would.' He runs his fingers through his hair. 'I didn't say that. But part of *us* is I thought we had the same aims, the same dreams. That's *us*, Millie.' There's a look of despair in his eyes. Almost pleading.

'Nobody has exactly the same dreams, Joe.' I can hear the slight stiffness, the self-justification in my voice.

'And you ended that column saying we were meeting for a drink over the holidays – and wondering whether it would be the start of for ever or the bloody end! And what's going to be after that? This weekend, wondering if it would be hot sex, or a sad goodbye? You can't write about what we did at the weekend, you just can't, that's...' He stutters but looks angry. I've never seen him looking angry. It's as though he's just realised what my writing really does mean for him. He thought it didn't matter, he knew it was my career, he seemed okay with it. He's not. I feel sick. 'That's private, Millie. That would be low, that would be attention-seeking, voyeurism. I don't want my fifteen minutes of fame in the sack.'

'I'm not going to write about our love-making, you know I'm not. Trust me, Joe.' I'm pleading.

He looks me straight in the eye. 'Trust you? I did bloody trust you, I shared stuff with you, but now I don't know what to think. You said fate brought you what you needed when you needed it. Was I just there at the right time to boost your career? The guy who couldn't say no, who couldn't resist you?' He's shutting down on me. He's standing still but drifting farther and farther away. Harder to reach.

'That isn't fair! Joe, it's never been about boosting my career with you. When I first bumped into you, it was something funny to write about, but then I got to know you. This weekend meant something.' I'm trembling. The words pouring out of me. Oblivious to any looks we might be getting.

He shakes his head. 'None of this is fucking fair, Millie. I don't want to share my love life with the nation, I don't want to share you.' He's getting more flustered with every word, and I want to hug him, but I know he's not going to let me. 'I don't want you to tell other people about your massive life decisions before you tell me. That is so out of line. I don't know what is and isn't fair anymore. But I do know we're chasing different dreams now. Aren't we? Your bloody fate has given me what I want here, and it's given you the chance to go back.'

'I never thought this would happen. I didn't know, I still don't know.'

'We're totally different people, aren't we? They're calling your train. You'll miss it.'

'Joe.'

'Go. You need to do your thing, I need to do mine. I've never wanted to change you, I just thought you were somebody different. My mistake.'

'But—'

'Please just go. Chase your dreams, be famous. Share your life, go back to the countryside. But I can't come with you. It's not my journey, Millie. It's yours.'

I can't believe him. I put my hand out to stop him, but he's already backing off. His face is shuttered. Stiff.

Mine feels like it's about to crumple.

'I can't pretend to be somebody I'm not, Millie. I can't do it with you, but I'll read about it. I won't be able to stop myself.' His smile is twisted, his words soft. Then he takes a final backwards step, then turns around.

And just like that, he's gone. Pushing through the crowds.

I dither, caught between my need to run after him and try and explain, and my need to run in the opposite direction and catch my train.

I catch the train.

Stare out of the window at the scenery whizzing by. My eyes smarting and my throat choked up.

What just happened?

Is it over, just like that?

My phone vibrates. Carla asking when I'll have Episode 7 drafted.

How the fuck am I going to finish writing about hope, new starts and spring? How am I going to write Episode 8, our mind-blowingly incredible weekend, when I now know it ends in goodbye?

I start to type, but to Joe, not Carla. *Can we talk this through? I can't just walk away from us. Please. M x*

The silence is deafening. The background hum of people, the clatter of the train barely noticeable.

We're out of the city, the landscape opens up and I clutch my phone. I'm just about to put it down and give up when the screen lights up.

Sorry, not ignoring you. I just can't see our future now. I could, and it's shattered. Sorry. I'm not trying to be dramatic, but I can't have you, knowing you'll never be mine really. I'm not a maybe kind of guy. Joe.

There's a dampness on my face that I try to ignore, then a tear drops onto my mobile. I put a hand to my face to brush the next one away. Close my eyes to try and stop them. Bite back the wail and clench my teeth. My face hurts, I hurt.

How can it be this painful?

Chapter Thirty-Five

JOE

Friday 6th May

It was odd at Easter going home on the train without Millie. But the journey last Thursday was a million times worse. It was bad enough getting to the station and knowing she'd left on Monday.

But to buy a coffee for one while I waited for the delayed train. To look for a seat for one. To know we weren't going to share the journey ever again left me empty inside.

I miss her like hell. I miss her more than I ever missed my family when I left for London, I miss her more than I've ever missed anybody or anything. Every time I see somebody that looks vaguely like her in London my heart skips a beat. I'm looking out for her everywhere without even knowing I'm doing it.

I've even thought about skipping the trip, staying in town for the weekend. Breaking the expectation.

I've got enough to keep me busy, with the handover of my contract work and figuring out my new extra responsibilities. And I've got a launch date pencilled in for the game I'm writing. Full-on work. It should be helping. I'm not sure drowning myself in computer code is a big enough distraction though. It's my heart, my body, that hurts – not my brain.

She's left London, she isn't coming back. All I have is her column to read. A regurgitation of the happy times.

Episode 7 on Monday was bittersweet. I read it over and over. Searching for a hint that she missed me. That her heart ached at least a little bit.

It had its funny bits, but her description of her anticipation as she travelled to meet me that day in Hexham, the way she felt when she saw me... the laughter, the hope... the promise was like a love letter that was never posted, and it left my stomach lurching with dread when it mentioned that Episode 8 would report back on the weekend we'd arranged.

I stopped reading. I put my headphones in, played music, and stared at the ever-changing scenery whizzing past the window. Without really seeing it.

And then I decided I couldn't do it. I couldn't travel on *our* train without her. I'd only be looking for her, hoping something had changed. I'd be searching for her. But if I caught the Friday train it would be different.

So, I spent yesterday evening trying to distract myself by designing the next level of a game I've been working on.

It just frustrated the hell out of me. How can I

concentrate on my PC monitor when all I can see is her? Her hazel eyes, with flecks of green, her silky hair that tumbled onto the pillows framing her face, begging me to reach out and run my fingers through it.

Now, I'm sitting in my parents' lounge, with my nephew on my knee, and even his funny I'm-about-to-fart smile isn't cheering me up.

'God, Joe, you look like a real wet weekend.' Sophie plonks herself down next to me and slips her finger into her son's hand. His tiny, perfect fingers remind me of Millie. Everything reminds me of Millie. Sophie leans into me. 'Okay, let me guess what's up, don't tell me!'

'I wasn't about to.'

'It's about a girl. Am I warm? Okay, that scowl says it all.' She makes gurgling noises at Ben. 'Oh Joe, you've not had a fall-out with Millie? I just knew you'd really fallen for her. It'll be fine though, just—'

'It won't be fine,' I say stiffly.

'Oh shit, I'm sorry, she's not...?' She pauses, studying my face. 'Uh-oh, no, oh Joe! *You've* dumped *her*?' There's shock on her face. 'Oh my God, why? I've been reading her stuff, nobody would know it was you! I mean, she goes on about fancying the pants off a *gorgeous* guy!' She pokes me in the ribs and laughs. She's trying to snap me out of it, make me smile. I can't. My face feels solid. 'Somebody who's fun.' She shifts round a bit in her seat, so she can stare at me better. It's uncomfortable.

'I don't want to be rude, little sis, but can you P off?'

'Leave you to wallow in your... oh Joe, you really are

miserable.' Her tone softens. 'You've fallen hard, haven't you? You—' she moves in closer so that she can lower her voice '—you went back the other weekend so you could be together!'

I nod.

See her. Touch her. Taste her.

Shit.

'What happened?' When I don't answer, she pulls her mobile phone out of her pocket and starts to tap. To read. She frowns, then drops her hands into her lap. 'She said she was coming back up here, moving out of London?' I can almost see the pieces drop into place, as it clicks what it all means to me. 'Oh Joe, Joe, Joe. You silly twat.'

'Oh, thanks for that. Great, I feel much better now.'

'Millie isn't Lisa!' She cuts to the chase, as normal.

'I do know that,' I say stiffly.

'She was a stupid, selfish cow with her own agenda who didn't think your opinion mattered at all.'

'I feel even better now.'

'Come on, is Millie like that at all? Honestly?'

I look her direct in the eye. 'She didn't even talk to me about it. First I knew was when I read that.' I point at her phone.

'Really? Are you sure?'

'Well, maybe we had crossed wires.' I say grudgingly. 'But it doesn't alter anything. She wants to be in Hexham. It *is* like Lisa, all over again.'

'Oh Joe-bro. Don't you know anything?' She leans her head on my shoulder, looking at the baby not me, her voice soft. 'It's about the person not the place. It doesn't matter where she wants to be.'

'Yes it—'

'Shh, let me finish. Millie isn't Lisa, she's just a girl exploring her options, discovering who she is. That's what she says in her column. She's not got some agenda to trap you and drag you back here, has she?'

I shake my head. I can't accuse her of any of that. Using me to spice up her column maybe. But trap me?

'Did she congratulate you on your new job, or look pissed off?'

'She was pleased for me.' I sigh. 'Maybe because I never have really featured in her life in the future, her real life.'

'So she looked over the moon when you dumped her, eh? She said fan-fucking-tastic, I can write about breaking up now!'

'Well no, but…'

'And she's blocked your calls?'

'I haven't called her.' Sophie glares at me. 'She texted, I thought we should give ourselves time to settle into our new jobs.'

'God, you can be pompous at times. Nobody needs time! Look, read what she writes—'

'I do!'

She ignores me. 'She makes mistakes, changes direction. She's human, like us, and that's why we love her, isn't it?' I try not to sigh. It is. And I do. Love her. 'It's not the end of the world if she's just realised that her heart is still up here, is it? She's nice about you.' She sneaks me an upwards glance. 'Far too nice. If you ask me, she actually fancies you! But hey, ignoring the slushy stuff, it is about who she really is inside, whether you like that person. Everything else is just excuses, not reasons. What you tell yourself, not what you believe. Now ask yourself this, bro – why did you and Lisa split?'

She holds a hand up before I can open my mouth. Soph likes to talk, and she's got her audience here cornered. I can't exactly tip the baby off my knee. 'It's simple. Okay, you were racked off with her lying and trying to run your life, but that wasn't why you ended it. You did it because you realised you weren't in love! It was nothing to do with not letting Mum and Dad down.'

'Hang on, I—'

'Shush with squeaking, we all know that half the reason you're a workaholic is cos you want them to be proud, the other half is cos you're a weirdo. Now, where was I?'

'Way over the line.'

'You never loved Lisa; she was just the first girl who agreed to date you at school. Face up to the facts, kiddo, you're scared! You fancy the pants off Millie, and you're scared of it going tits up. You're shitting yourself that she'll tell the world about your dodgy sexual prowess—'

'Hey—'

'And—' she looks me full on, her tone softens '—you know why I really think you're sitting in here hiding? You're not scared of a woman who knows her own mind, has her own career, treads her own path – are you? That's not you.

Oh no, you are rattled because it's crossed your mind that you might be prepared to do it. Follow her back. You're torturing yourself cos you don't want to let anybody down. … am I right, or am I right?' She doesn't give me a chance to answer, just snuggles back in and carries on talking. 'Dad gave me *the talk* when I had a meltdown the day before my wedding.' This is news to me, the meltdown and the talk. 'He said that life is about making goals and going after them, but not at any cost. That changing your mind isn't failure, it's a choice. That sometimes you have to admit doing something else might be better. He said he nearly missed out with Mum because for him it had always been about Oxford.' This is even more news – the missing-out bit, not Oxford. 'He'd been set on being an academic, not a farmer, but then he found her, and he fell in love. He said all the rest is just dreams, it's about trying to work out your place in the world, but what he had with Mum was the reality, it was his heart. Though—' she sits up straight '—he could have gone all slushy and romantic on me because he thought it was time I moved out and was somebody else's problem!'

'Probably.' I can't help but smile at Sophie. 'He'd also already paid the hire for his wedding suit.'

'Cheeky bugger! Anyway, that's enough of the philosophical crap, I've got nappies to change, haven't I, cherub? And you need to sort your shit out, before you miss the boat, or train or whatever!'

The cherub smiles in a slightly suspect way, so I pass him over quickly and the two of them leave me in peace again. Well, apart from the loud rendition of 'The Wheels on the Bus'.

I sit back and stare blankly at the wall. My sister does have verbal diarrhoea at times, but I think in all that there might have been some truth.

Is Sophie right? I really do like Millie. I always have. I guess if I didn't feel in my heart that she really was the one for me, then I wouldn't be feeling totally rubbish like I do.

And I wouldn't be worrying about how my parents would feel if I said I might be thinking that one day I could move out of London, and date a girl from down the road, if I had absolutely no intention of actually doing it. Would I?

Chapter Thirty-Six

MILLIE

Friday 6th May

I reluctantly hit send on the email and let go of Episode 8. Let it whizz its way over to Carla.

Writing it totally drained me because every sentence took me back to my weekend with Joe. I felt his every touch, saw his every smile as I tried to write something that was authentic, but didn't overstep the mark and stray into private territory.

The problem is that emotions are private, aren't they? I didn't want to overshare, to show what it felt like with my words, I just wanted to keep it light, funny, real in the way an observer would tell it. Because the way I feel it is far too raw at the moment.

I also couldn't include our goodbye, because to write it is to admit it's real. It happened. I'm not ready for that yet.

On Monday I will have to start Episode 9, and I haven't got a clue how I'm going to do it. What I'm going to say.

I've parted company with London for a brief time, and I've parted company with Joe. For ever, it seems.

I switched my phone off after he'd replied to my message, and when I put it back on, he had texted again – but only to apologise, to say that maybe in a couple of weeks when we'd both moved on a bit we could maybe talk. He could explain.

There was no underlying 'we could try again' vibe.

I don't think Carla is going to get the 'long-distance love affair' she was hoping for.

I guess in Episode 9 I'll have to say we've left the door ajar, but I don't know if we'll reopen it. I don't know if we can.

I blink back the tears that are threatening. It's been nearly two weeks since I last spoke to him.

Burying myself in planning the book has taken my mind off him for a bit. But the moment I've stopped work he's been there. In my head.

It's Friday though, and the sun is shining. I need to get my act together, think positive. I've got a book deal, I've stopped letting Carla walk all over me, and I've ditched Dale. They say people come into your life for a reason. Maybe Joe came into mine to give me confidence, help me believe that I am good enough as I am. That I don't have to put up with toxic relationships – there are good people about, like him.

I stifle the sigh. For a brief moment there I thought my

and Joe's paths had crossed because we were more than just good for each other, we were good together. But I guess life is telling me I was right about one thing, there's no room for a relationship. I should be concentrating on my career. My family.

A robin flits past the window and settles on the tree and although I'm sad I can't help but smile. For quite a while after Dad died, if a robin came to watch Mum in the garden, she'd say it was Dad keeping an eye on her. Checking she was okay.

This one is flitting about, coming nearer then drifting further. If it is Dad, I think he's telling me to stop moping, get off my butt and enjoy the day.

I close the lid of my laptop and dig out my old walking boots from the bottom of the wardrobe.

It always seems to be windy in this particular spot, but the views are spectacular. We scattered Dad's ashes out here, because it was his favourite place to be when he needed to sort out a knotty problem, or just – as he used to say – breathe easy.

He'd joked that if we scattered him here, we'd each always carry a part of him with us because the wind would make sure that a portion of whatever we threw would always swirl back.

I settle down and smile to myself. It's impossible not to carry Dad with me – even if we'd scattered him a million miles away, he's wrapped so firmly round my heart that even though I barely hear his voice these days, he's here. He's listening.

'Well, Dad, you always laughed when I came to you for advice and said that all you did was listen and I worked it out myself. So here I am, hoping it works. Because I really don't know what to do. I've never met anybody quite like Joe before. I wish you'd met him, Dad. You'd like him. He's a bit like you, he doesn't say too much – he just makes the right noises and listens, and the magic happens – I work it out.

Joe told me I was strong, resilient, I could succeed at anything I set my mind to. You used to do that. I would never have made it to London without you. You used to smile when I told you I was going to be some city hotshot and say, 'Well, do it then.' And I did, Dad, and I still want to be that girl, but I also want to be me. I'm good enough. I don't need to talk the talk, wear the right clothes, live in the right place. Joe showed me that. But I think I've just realised that I took what I've got here for granted, I didn't see it properly because I wasn't looking.

I was thinking about you this morning. Well, I think about you a lot. You were happy with what you had. Loved your life and us and I don't think you had any regrets, did you? I think I would have. I love my life, Dad, but not my lifestyle. That's why I jumped at the chance of coming back here to write my book. I didn't have to, Joe was right, I could have stayed in London to do it. But it feels like it was meant to happen, I was meant to get the chance to make this decision. I'd gone chasing my 'best life', but what you get isn't always real, is it? Sometimes it's touched up beyond reality, anybody's. Some bits are amazing, but I guess I need to find the right balance for me.

Mum's doing well, you know? She's getting happy again and I know you wanted that for her. I realised the other day that she doesn't need me, she doesn't rely on me, she just likes to see me. I know I shouldn't feel guilty, and I get now why she wants to move. It's a bit like me needing to move out of a permanent place in London. It's just time to make the next step. I was trying to stop her because I was scared, but she's taking you with her, like I do.

I remember when Lou was scared about moving away, you said to her that it's about the people, not the place. That a house becomes a home because of who is in it.

Lou misses you so much, Dad. She's kind of clammed up and is storing it all up inside, pretending she's too busy to deal with it. I guess she's a bit like Joe though, she doesn't want everything public. She doesn't handle things the same way I do. Maybe that's why Joe felt so familiar from the start? I guess I've taken both of them for granted, not stopped and taken the time to explain how I feel, not asked them how they see it.

Joe was proud of me, Dad, and I'm proud of him. I don't want him to give up what he's doing, but I do want him to understand what's going on in my head too.

How do I do that?'

_____

A robin suddenly appears. I never see robins out here. It's not their territory. But he's here, brave, far from home. He's here because I need him.

I can't help it. I find myself smiling as I stand up, rub my slightly dead bum and dust the bits off.

'*Thanks, Dad!*'

I can imagine him smiling. Ruffling my hair and saying, 'Well, I'm glad I sorted that one out for you!'

I know what I need to do. I need to stop writing about Joe, prove to him that he's not just a prop in my life. I know he's a private person, and I've taken him for granted and not looked at it from his point of view. And I'm going to talk to him. I'm going to show him that I don't have to be here all the time, that isn't what I ever wanted. I just need to be here some of the time. But it's not the same without him.

I don't know quite what I want, if he's not going to be a part of it.

But I do know that just as I wouldn't have got to London without Dad's support, I wouldn't have made the decision to come back here without Joe's. It's ironic really, but Joe has opened my eyes, he's shown me that I don't need to be in London all the time to achieve my dreams.

'I know what I'm going to do, Dad!' I shout at the sky, as I march down the hill, my phone in my hand.

I pull up the last email from my publisher and all of a sudden, I love the sound of those two words 'my' and 'publisher' in the same sentence again. Some of the joy had gone out of it since I lost Joe, but now I have a plan. I can make this work!

The commissioning editor had suggested we have a Skype meeting next week, but I need to be there. I want to go down to London, next Thursday. I want to be at King's Cross station in the evening to catch *our* train back. I am going to find Joe, talk to him, persuade him that we can make this work. Together. I'm going to somehow show Joe that I am the girl he thought I was. The girl he fell for.

———————

'You look happy.' Mum smiles at me as I walk through the back door and tug my boots off. 'Does this mean you've got a plan?'

I grin back at her.

'You always were happy when you had a plan! Coffee and cake?' I nod. 'Well, I've got a plan as well. I've been doing some thinking, and if part of your plan involves being here then we should chat, don't you think?'

I nod again and take a giant bite out of the slice of carrot cake. I've worked up an appetite with my walk, and the decision. 'Great! I've just had a chat to Dad.'

She sits down opposite me and smiles gently. 'I know how much you miss him, but it's getting easier, isn't it?' I nod again, my mouth full. 'You two were so close, I felt like I was playing raspberry sometimes!'

'You didn't!' I stop mid-chew.

'I did, but I didn't mind. I liked seeing you both happy. And I know he loved me. What did you chat to him about?'

'This place, coming back, Joe.' I shrug.

'Ahh, Joe. And did he help?'

'Yep! I still want to have it all, but my all has different criteria.' I smile at her.

'You do know you don't have to be here for me? I don't need you to feel responsible for me, and I really don't want it to cause any issues for you.'

'I know, but—' She squeezes my hand to stop me talking.

'I think I've been staying here for you, not me. It's time I moved, Millie. I didn't want to upset you by selling the house, but I do think I should. At first, I talked to Sam and thought about doing it because I didn't want to be a burden, relying on you – your dad would never have wanted that. But now I just know it's the right decision for me.'

She looks worried.

'I know,' I say softly. 'I do, I understand. And you're right, I think Lou would like it. But I'm going to be here anyway now, so there's no hurry.'

'I know, love, but Sam rang and said somebody is interested. I think I should talk to them, don't you?'

'I do.' I smile at her. 'Yes, I do, Mum. I haven't really got a clue where I want to be, but I know if I do decide to move back then I need my own place.' I had been worrying how to break this news to her, it was something that had been bothering me. But the look of relief on her face is almost comical! 'I'd hate to cramp your style!' Eurgh, the thought of having to hide in my room to give her some privacy, the thought of bedroom, er, noises. No thank you!

'You do! And you might have Joe?' She pauses. 'I take it Joe is train-guy?'

'He is.'

'And did you leave him on Platform 3, or might you want to bring him back here?'

'It's complicated.'

'It always is, Millie. It always is.'

'He thinks I've broken his trust, but I didn't, I really didn't. And he thinks I only want to be here, and never wanted to be there, and that's what he wants.' I stop twittering, because talking fast isn't stopping my eyes from stinging. I take a deep breath. 'I'm going down for a meeting, and I'm going to try and talk to him. But what if he doesn't want to, Mum?'

'The bravest things to do are the ones you're scared of, Millie. We're all scared of failure, of being rebuffed, of not being wanted, but if you don't try, you'll never know, will you?'

'No.' I swallow hard. 'I'm going to make more time to see Lou too, go and see her.'

'Good. She'll like that.' She squeezes my hand. 'She told me yesterday how much she misses you. I'm glad you've been talking to each other more. I want you both to be happy, your dad would have wanted you to stick together.' I nod. 'Right, hang on. I want to give you something and I'm pretty sure your dad would say now is the time!'

I listen as she goes up the stairs, then she comes back clutching a chain.

'This was your dad's St Christopher, Millie.' She presses

it onto my hand. 'I gave it to him not long before he proposed. He was a real adventurer was Finn, when he was younger.' She smiles, a soft smile that reaches her eyes. 'I didn't want him to feel that being with me meant he was being tied down, I wanted him to know that he had my blessing if he wanted to go off into the wilds, but I wanted him to come back safe.'

'And did he? Go off?' I've never thought of Dad as an adventurer. I've never really thought about the fact that he must have had dreams of his own, I just knew he was happy, that he told me he was content, he'd made the right choices, and had everything he could want.

'He did for a while. He went all over the world.' She closes my fingers over the pendant. 'And then he chose to come back and settle down. Because he wanted to. I was scared, my best friend said I was stupid, I should have been planning the wedding and getting pregnant, not sending him off. But it wasn't up to her, was it? You've always been brave, Millie. So, if it matters to you, you'll do it. Go after him, tell him how you feel. Take a risk and know you can live with whatever the outcome is. It's true, you know; you do only get one chance.' She kisses my cheek. 'Take it. Right, I better get these dishes done and then we can decide what we're going to tell Sam. Isn't it exciting?'

Chapter Thirty-Seven

MILLIE

Friday 13th May

'It was so lovely to meet you, Millie. I'm such a fan!'

'Oh wow, thank you! I'm so glad I got to meet you as well. It's been amazing to see the office and put faces to names. We'll have to meet up again soon.' My book editor Jenny is the loveliest person imaginable. She's tiny, pretty, bubbly and so enthusiastic it makes me feel a bit old and jaded. Well, it did, now I am fired up.

She leans in and gives me a big hug, then looks a bit shocked at what she's done. I laugh, hug her back and wave goodbye as I leave her and head through the revolving door.

It's good to be back in London as well. I've missed the hustle and bustle. The best of both worlds rings true right now. Well, not quite the best. One important part is missing.

The downside of our meeting today was that it is a day

late. Jenny rang me on Wednesday, apologising profusely and asking if we could reschedule for Friday, as she couldn't make Thursday.

I was gutted. The disappointment hit me so hard I had to sit down. I felt like somebody had popped my inner bubble.

My whole plan destroyed, just like that. And Mum is right, I need a plan. Having a plan makes me feel positive, optimistic. Rip it up, and you sweep the ground from under my feet.

And Friday the thirteenth? I ask you!

Mum had been pretty philosophical about it and said it obviously wasn't the right time and place. She didn't say Joe obviously wasn't the right man for me, but I'm beginning to wonder.

I can't even go to his place and surprise him, because he won't be there. He'll be back in Northumberland.

Though that could be a good thing. He might have been shocked, upset, angry – or with somebody else. Are surprise visits ever a good idea in reality?

The station is busy. Friday isn't the best day to commute, because far too many other people are doing it. If Joe was here now, I wouldn't mind the crowds, the noise, but he's not. And it feels different. It feels lonely.

I check the board; my train is running on time.

I've got time to go and grab a coffee, but I'm not really bothered.

Instead, I fish my mobile out on impulse. Bring his messages up. Hesitate.

I came to London because I wanted to see him. Messaging isn't the same, but it has to be better than nothing. I can't just leave this, not even one second longer.

We deserve one last try.

I start to type. I'll just tell him I'm down here, that I'd hoped I'd be here yesterday. Hoped I'd see him. But it obviously wasn't meant to be.

No expectations. No pressure.

Chapter Thirty-Eight

JOE

It has been one helluva week. I was very tempted to stay down here for the weekend, but then Katherine dropped hints about entertaining her new guy and it didn't seem fair to be here. It is her place after all. I think once my job is all sorted, it might be time to sort a place of my own.

I shoulder my rucksack and start to weave through the slow-moving crowd at the entrance to the station. Automatically slowing to check out a girl with russet brown hair who catches my eye.

It isn't Millie.

It wouldn't be. She's not here anymore. And it's a Friday. My new commuting day. And it's a later train than she used to get on a Thursday.

Sophie keeps bugging me, sending me snippets of Millie's column. She thinks our meet-up in Hexham sounded dreamy. She is definitely team-Millie. The more she bugs me though, the more I think she might be right.

Millie definitely isn't Lisa. She would never try and stop me living out my dreams.

I wished I'd met Millie on the moors, not in the town. It would have been nice to see her where she seems to be happiest.

I guess if in her heart she wants to live in the wilds, where wellies and a jacket with a hood aren't optional extras – then wouldn't a guy who really cares about her want to help? Be willing to compromise for the girl he loved?

I lean against the wall, check my phone for any last-minute important messages from work, and my stomach lurches.

Millie.

She's messaged me. Today.

I flick it open, my heart hammering.

She's here! I glance round wildly, half expecting to see her standing in front of me.

Then I realise. She messaged a while ago – while I was chatting to Katherine, having 'one for the road'.

Shit. I've missed her. She was actually here. Why the hell haven't I looked at my phone since I left work?

The let-down is real. I feel totally deflated.

But she wants to talk to me. She's been in touch. Maybe, maybe she'll agree to a meet up over the weekend?

My fingers feel too big, too awkward as I fumble with my mobile, trying to reply to her message. Tell her I'm still in London. That we've just missed each other.

I finally hit the send button. My palms clammy, my

pulse pounding. Then glance up to check the departure board.

And then I see her. Too far away to shout. But it's her. I swear it's her. The way she walks, the lift in her step, the bounce of her hair.

Chapter Thirty-Nine

MILLIE

I must be bonkers. He didn't answer my text, but for some reason I just felt he was here. So I didn't get on the train. I waited. I stood on the bloody platform and watched the trains come and go. Joe didn't show, of course he didn't.

I really don't know what I was thinking. Now I just feel a bit silly. I've been waiting for some romantic moment when the train comes in and he's there. On the platform.

He never is. No big surprise there then. My instincts when it comes to Joe seem to have deserted me.

I sigh. Suddenly tired and deflated. The next train goes in ten minutes, which gives me time to visit the ladies – and face up to reality.

He doesn't want to see me, or he'd at least have replied to my message.

There's a queue in the Ladies, and the train is announced as I'm washing my hands. Typical! If I miss this one, after hanging about for so long, it's going to be the perfect end to the day. I hoist my bag over my shoulder, dash out of the toilets and start to power walk towards the platform.

My phone rings just as I get there, I'm tempted to ignore it, but then the tannoy booms to say there's a slight delay. It'll be Mum, wondering where I am, what time I'll be back.

I reach for it, half turn as I lift it to my ear and press the answer call button. And I see him.

Joe.

'It's me,' he whispers into the phone. His voice slightly hoarse. Totally Joe.

'Oh,' I say back. Before he rings off, pockets his phone. Picks two coffee cups off the bench he is standing next to.

He holds them up as he slowly walks closer. Turns them so I can see the writing.

Jilly and Mo.

I stare at him. Drink him in.

I'd gone to London looking for metro man, for a Dale. Instead, I found Joe.

Joe is more like the guys I'd left behind. Familiar. Solid. Which I guess could be why he felt so familiar, why I felt like I knew him from day one. But he still loves London, like I do. He's still exciting and a bit unknown.

I guess sometimes you don't really know what you want until you find it.

'Come here often?' His chocolatey deep tone wraps itself around me like the hug I've missed so much.

'Not often enough.' He's close enough to touch. He holds out the cup. 'You're a life saver,' I say softly, and I can hear the tremor in my voice. Is this real? Is this happening?

'There are times when nothing beats a coffee.' One corner of his mouth quirks up in the hint of a smile as he repeats those words he said so long ago to me.

'There are, but I don't think this is one of them.' My voice is husky. I take a step closer to him, take both cups from his hands and stoop to put them on the ground. Then I put my hands on his shoulders. And I kiss him.

My lips meet his, and he doesn't hesitate, he doesn't falter. He wraps his arms around me to pull me closer, then deepens the kiss. I slip my hands under his shirt, desperate to feel the heat of his skin. I play my fingers along his spine, and he groans. Lifts his mouth from mine.

'I don't think you should do that.' He leans his forehead against mine. Gazes into my eyes. 'I've missed you.'

'I've missed you too.'

'I never meant to upset you, Joe. I never used you. I never intended to go back.' All the words I had planned out, all the explanations, have flown clear out of my head. I just want him to understand. Words teeter on the tip of my tongue, now's the time to say them. 'I never expected to fall in love actually.' That was the surprise. That was the part I haven't acknowledged until now. Until I was back on our platform, on my own.

'You fell in love?' His voice is soft.

'I fell in love with a guy wearing a red scarf and I can't live without him.'

'Even without the red scarf?'

'Even without the red scarf.'

'I fell in love with a girl who is funny, clever, smart and sets my heart pounding every time I see her.' He cups my face in his hands. Rubs his thumb along my jaw, sending a shiver through my body. I cover one of his hands with mine.

'I still love the city,' I say slightly breathlessly.

'I still love you,' he says and kisses me again.

The people disappear, the platform disappears, the whole world melts into nothingness.

There's just me, my train-guy and this kiss.

His firm lips pressing against mine, teasing me, asking for more. His tongue running over the tips of my teeth making me groan. His tongue exploring my mouth. The taste of him, the smell of him, surrounding me.

There's nobody here but Joe. His firm body the perfect fit against mine. His fingers tightening slightly in my hair, his warm mouth against my neck.

It's a gentle kiss, but it's a kiss that says, 'I know you'. That says, 'I care'. That says this is right, this is perfect, this is how it should be.

We pull the slightest distance apart as we're jostled by the crowds, surging forward as the train appears.

I'm panting, quivering, but I feel more alive than I have for what seems a long time. Since I last saw Joe. 'Wow.' I meet his gaze, smile. But he doesn't smile back.

'I can hardly breathe,' he whispers against my mouth. 'But I'd give you the last breath in my body if it meant you were here for just another second with me.'

I can't move. All I can do is look into his eyes. Barely registering the slamming of doors, the sound of the train as I cling onto him.

'I'm here for as many seconds as you want,' I finally reply.

There's an announcement that the doors are closing, that the train is about to leave Platform 3.

'We're going to miss it.' His eyes never leave mine; he doesn't move.

'There'll be others.' But we only get one chance exactly like this. This moment.

'I realised when I was sitting on that train the other week, that you're more important to me than anything else. Being in the city doesn't matter.' His arms tighten around my waist. 'I'd give it up to be with you.'

'I don't want you to give anything up,' I say softly, reaching up to kiss him lightly. 'We can do anything we want. Everything we want! The world is our oyster.' I grin and throw my arms wide open, and he laughs.

'You're amazing! Slightly mad, but amazing.' Then he stoops down, picks up the coffee cups as the train pulls out. Without us. 'Let's ditch the coffee and go for a proper drink! Crap idea, coffee! What was I thinking?'

Chapter Forty

JOE

Saturday 21st May

'What do you think of this one?'

I look at the photo of the cosy lounge, and I feel happy. Happy for Millie, and not at all scared about what this means for us.

It's a huge relief, because despite all the talk and being sure we can work this out, I honestly didn't know how I'd feel when we started looking at places she could rent.

'Really?' Her eyes search my face intently, and I know that what she's really asking is if I can see myself there. With her.

'Really. Though those beams might be a bit low.' My hand instinctively goes to my head. 'You could book a viewing, then we can try it out for size?'

'I'll add it to the list!' She smiles. 'Fancy a walk? I'm going boggle-eyed looking through these.'

'Does it include a pub and a pint?'

'It could!' She laughs. 'But I want you to meet somebody first.'

An hour later I'm wheezing as we stagger hand in hand up the last few feet to the summit.

'I thought you were fit!' She giggles.

'Farm fit!' I raise one arm and flex my muscles, which makes her laugh even more. I love the sound of her laughter. I love the smile on her face. I love seeing her this happy. Millie has definitely done the right thing for her, which means it's the right thing for us. 'No hills, just lifting bales.'

I take a deep breath and look around. We fall silent as we stand side by side. It's breath-taking. Not another person in sight. Just blue skies with swooping birds, and fantastic scenery.

'I come here to talk to Dad,' she says softly. 'I would have loved it if you two could have met, but…' She shrugs, and I squeeze her hand. 'I always feel he's here though.'

'He's always with you.'

'He would have liked you,' she says, certainty in her tone. 'I get now why he loved it out here so much. It's funny, isn't it, how you can know your parents in one way, but know nothing about them in another? Well, not nothing, but…'

'I guess parents just don't tell their kids everything.

They'd traumatise us!' I say, smiling at her. Thinking about my own dad, and his pep talk to Sophie.

Thinking about the million and one adventures our parents probably had when they were our age, younger, before they fell in love and settled down. Before they poured everything into their children.

'Mum said he loved to travel before they got married, explore.'

'A bit like you? And he came back to his roots in the end.'

'Maybe.' She lets go of my hand and searches through her pockets. Then turns to face me properly. The wind catches her hair. She really is beautiful. Beautiful and slightly wild. This place suits her. 'Mum gave me this.' She runs her fingers over a chain, then holds the pendant up before letting it drop back into her palm. 'It's a St Christopher. Mum gave it to Dad before they got married.' She holds her hand out towards me. 'She said to me that you give because you love, not because you want a return on the investment. That it has to be unconditional, or it doesn't mean anything. I guess I want you to have this for the same reason she gave it to him, I want you to be safe, I want you to go wherever you want and I want you to do what makes you happy.' There's a glint of a tear in her eye as she stares into mine. 'I want you to have something that means a lot to me, but I don't want anything back. I'd never try to change you, Joe.'

'I know.' I'm all choked as I close my hand over hers. 'I was a dick; I shouldn't have run away from you.'

'You weren't. I should have been clearer. I just took you for granted, but I didn't mean to. I'm going to give up the column, I know you hate that type of thing.'

'Oh no, you're not! That column is you, Millie. No way are you doing that. I can live with it, honest. I love you for being you, I wouldn't want you any other way.'

She smiles. Threads her fingers through mine and stares out over the moorland.

'I'll just have to leave the country if it gets too much!'

I guess at the end of the day Millie is more important than everything else. My parents will still be proud I went to uni and got a degree, wherever I end up. Home can be anywhere if you're with the person you love. Where they are is where you're meant to be.

Chapter Forty-One

MILLIE

Sunday 24th July

I bury my nose in the sweater and breathe in Joe. He's only been gone a few hours, and I'm already looking forward to going down to London on Thursday so I can see him again.

We don't know where we'll end up, but it's working out well so far.

I've finished the first draft of my book and am waiting for edits – and we're already talking about what comes next. Working with my editor, Jenny, is as wonderful as I'd thought it would be. She's lovely, funny, sparky and she gets me so much it's frightening. She's the perfect person to work with. It's almost a relief though sometimes to switch off from the book and work on my column for Carla, so there's no way I'd want to give that up.

Joe's been fab at getting me to stick to my guns and negotiate hours with her. I feel like I've got an army behind me – Joe, Mum, Mum's lovely but slightly eccentric friend John, and Jenny. Millie's army!

I finally said goodbye to Dale. I'd hung on to my tenancy for a while, not wanting to let go of London, but then realised that I have got Joe for keeps. We're looking for a new flat for him in the city – well, for both of us. His boss and landlady Katherine insisted on meeting me, so that she could 'make sure she's not going to kidnap my best coder', she'd said to Joe.

And we've got this place.

This cottage is perfect. Not too far from Mum and her new place, handy for the train station, and a short drive away from the moorlands and Dad.

I lightly smooth my hand over the indent of Joe's head on the pillow. I've got the scent of him on the clothes he's left. He's got his side of the bed, his spot on the sofa, his chair at the table.

Exactly as it should be.

I fold his sweater up and lay it gently onto the bedside chair, and then spot the note.

Love you loads, missus! See you on Thursday, meet me on Platform 3! ;)

I smile and turn the ring on the third finger of my left hand.

I'm not quite his missus yet. We've had a whirlwind romance, but I reckon it could be a long engagement. We're both so busy.

But it doesn't matter, does it?

We're living our best lives. Our way.

Acknowledgments

Big thanks to my fabulous agent Amanda Preston, and my wonderful publisher Charlotte Ledger – I love working with both of you. You make my life, and my books, so much better! Thanks also to the rest of the wonderful team at One More Chapter, HarperCollins, for all your support and hard work.

Thanks to my family and friends who put up with my brain-fog, accept my hermit-like behaviour when I'm on a deadline, and help me celebrate the victories big and small.

And thank *you* for picking up this book, for chatting to me on social media, for sharing your stories and taking the time to get in touch.

Zara x